THE ECHO 3

# ECHO BETWEEN WORLDS

BELINDA CRAWFORD

HENDRIX & FAUST
PUBLISHERS

Published by Hendrix & Faust, Publishers in 2022

Text copyright © Belinda Crawford 2022

www.belindacrawford.com

ISBN: 978-0-6450459-0-1 (ebook)
ISBN: 978-0-6450459-1-8 (paperback)

A catalogue record for this book is available from the National Library of Australia

**Books by Belinda Crawford**

*The Hero Rebellion*
(Hunter)
Hero
(Race)
Riven
Regan

*The Echo*
Cold Between Stars
Dark Between Oceans
Echo Between Worlds
(Brother)

*Collections*
Short Bits Volume 1

# GLOSSARY

## SPECIES

### Jøran (a.k.a. the kin)
The overarching name for the three species
native to Jørn, which are:

*Qwan (air-kin):* Avians with four eyes and two sets of wings.

*Rucnart (tree-kin):* Gigantic felines with four eyes and six legs.

*Swatai (water-kin):* Small, lizard-like amphibians.

### Jørgen
A Human—Jøran hybrid.

## PSIONICS

### Psion
Someone with the ability to read and/or influence the emotions
and/or thoughts of others (a.k.a. an empath or telepath).

### Aer
A telepathic dream world constructed by the kin.

### Eter
The mental space within an individual's mind, from which they
can construct their own reality and engage with other psions.

### Ora
A mental space accessible only by empaths, where they can
communicate with beings such as Aeotu.

### Anima
The core of a person, also known as their spirit or soul.

## FUG

### Viyu
The technical name for Aeotu's grey-green fug.

### Viyusa
The technical name for red fug.

# IN THE BEGINNING

A lone ship, *Citlali*, wandered through interstellar space. Its crew, a mix of humans and Jørans – intelligent felines and avians with telepathic powers – were tucked up in their cryopods, sleeping away the long journey between solar systems. They trusted *Citlali's* artificial intelligence to guide the way and keep them safe in the great empty void, as they had many times before.

Except this time, the void wasn't empty.

An ancient alien wreck hung in the cold between stars, barely alive and hungry. Very, very hungry. When *Citlali* slowed to investigate, as the AI was programmed to do, the wreck attacked, mould-like nanites attaching themselves to the human ship and eating it. Hull and bulkheads and crew, broken down and ferried through space, materials it would use to repair itself.

By the time Kuma, a Jørgen boy – mostly human but part Jøran too – is woken from stasis/sleep, *Citlali* is dying.

Alone on the malfunctioning ship, Kuma desperately searches for a way to save his friends and family, but especially his twin sister, Grea. It's not until he follows the mould-like nanites back to their source that he discovers a terrifying truth. The alien ship is alive, and it's name is Aeotu.

Lonely and desperate, Aeotu has her own mission. She will swallow *Citlali* whole, and there is nothing Kuma can do about it. Nonetheless, Kuma makes a last-ditch effort to save the crew.

He fails.

Trapped in an escape pod and ejected into space, Kuma waits to die.

But, instead of dying he wakes to find not just his world, but his body has changed.

Four years have passed, and fug – the alien mould-like nanites – clings to his flesh, giving him paws instead of feet and blades that spring from his forearms. It is a weird, powerful alien armour he doesn't know how to control. But that is the least of his troubles.

*Citlali* still lives and her surviving crew are awake, furiously trying to free themselves from Aeotu. Grea is alive too, but she has changed, perhaps more than Kuma, and the things that lurk in the back of her mind… They are too horrible to contemplate.

As *Citlali's* crew tries to free their ship and Grea manipulates events from the shadows, Aeotu travels through space, called to a remote solar system and a graveyard of living ships just like herself.

These ships, these Sisters, burn for freedom and revenge against the masters who built and then discarded them, leaving them to rot and die.

One of them calls to Grea, and when she leaves Aeotu, Kuma follows, only to find himself caught and used, little more than a tool in the Sisters' grip. They use him and Hunt – the massive humanoid robot made in his likeness – to free themselves from captivity, but that is not the worst of it. They turn *Citlali* into a bomb, using his home as a deadly first strike in the war with their creators.

Once again, Kuma is left to float in the void.

# CHAPTER ONE

We drift, our engine turning cold. Not cold enough to freeze, but no longer the blaze needed to power the thrusters on our back.

We remember drifting, it is familiar to us, conjures memories from the part of us that is fleshy; a time of cold and dark and the endless fear that all we loved were dead. That small fleshy part wonders if maybe it would have been better if they were dead, all those loves.

Maybe they are and this is just a dream perpetrated by our dying mind.

But no, there is oxygen and our fleshy heart beats—

But maybe, the fleshy part insists.

No.

But—

No.

We shut the fleshy part down. It protests even as we shoot sedatives into its bloodstream; its struggles activate our defence systems, consuming power needed elsewhere. Another shot of neurochemicals and the fleshiness falls silent, put on standby.

The fleshiness is strange, but it is right about one thing. We do not like drifting in space, but at least we are not alone this time.

The gravitational pull of the nearby gas giant slows our drift into the void; not enough to stop us entirely and maybe, if we had kept floating, we would have wandered among the solar system. But we are found.

Four days, eighteen hours and twenty-seven minutes since the destruction of *Citlali*, a different vessel hovers over us, tethers shooting from its port-side stern.

The vessel is familiar, registers as a friendly in our system. We allow it to draw us aboard, do not waken the fleshiness or consume the last of our fusion matter to spin our generator to full capacity and power our cannons; there is no need to attack, not immediately.

We wait until we are settled in the docking frame, feed lines attached to the ports on our back, our fusion-matter tank filling and power running through our systems before we wake the fleshiness.

It comes online slowly, a small piece at first and then an exponential rush to wakefulness.

It does not speak, but spreads through our systems, filling out the piece of ourself that was blind.

New senses flood us with data. We breathe and our world is instantly richer, colours and shapes and emotions filling the universe, making it pulse and shiver. We are still in darkness, our optical sensors offline, but the quality of it is different now, has the texture of velvet, rich with possibility.

Life thrums around us. The shift and bang of biologicals, the purr of power conduits, and the sparkle of other minds. Muted, half-asleep in the mental plane we remember as the eter, they are ghosts tangled in ruby webs. They are half of themselves, of the restless, bright shiny beings they once were, but they reach for us with shaky tendrils of thought. A reflex? A hope hidden amongst the not-sleep that consumes them? We do not know, but we reach back, run fingers of emotion along the—

A wall, slicing the tips off our probe as it *SNAPS* into place between us.

Anger, fear and determination stain the eter – red and yellow and bronze. Doubt follows it, spilling across the mental plane and around a form standing in its midst.

The form is transparent, we know it is there only because of the absence of emotion, the way the shifting swirl of doubt eddies around the two hollow spaces where the thing stands. Our fleshiness labels them "legs", the fuzziness agrees while the third of us that is metal and fusion attempts to map the thing. White lines wrap around the legs, climbing the torso. The shifting grey fog follows it, keeping pace with the lines, until the thing – the person – is revealed. Outlined in white and surrounded in doubt, it is difficult to make out his face, but we know that wild explosion of hair.

{{ *Ekene.* }} That name rings out on the eter, triggering memories of a shared workbench and scrubbing giant cylindrical objects while clear goop plops from the ceiling in long gooey teardrops.

Ekene does not move, not physically, but something does.

Like Ekene, we see the thing only in the void it leaves in the emotion – a fist heading straight for our chest—

It hits before we can brace, before our own hands have time to do more than clench. We expect pain, expect to be obliterated, but we are not. We are swallowed, giant fingers wrapping around us, trapping our arms – all four of them – at our sides, clogging up the ports on our wrists, stifling the blades stored there. We cannot move, and our hearts thump in painful rhythm. We struggle, our fusion heart burning, sending power through our bones and lighting up the mental pathways of our psionic selves.

The fist tightens, the fingers wrapped around our chest *squeezing* until our ribs crack and groan.

New emotion stains the eter, our fear tainting the ground a thick sticky yellow.

We swallow as the fear makes our fleshy heart beat harder, and as our metal self re-evaluates the situation.

The emotion rising all around us – the doubt mixing with the fear at our feet in a toxic miasma that bites our legs – does not touch the boy. Or is he a hollow? A void in the eter? Even as the mental fist squeezes, as our metal self spins through plans and probabilities, our fleshiness wonders at the hollow's resistance, at the way we can only see it as an *absence*, an empty space in the fabric of the psionic plane.

*{{ Ekene, }}* we say, pushing the word at the hollow boy with all the strength in our fuzziness's small self. *{{ It is us. }}* And with "us" we share the mixing of selves, the cold logic of the metal, the power of the fuzz, and the swirling emotion of the flesh.

Us. Us. Us. It echoes, bouncing off non-existent walls, filling the white space with images of us. Our metal standing impossibly tall, a faceless humanoid behemoth with four giant arms and a fusion reactor buried in its chest. The fuzz, a round golden ball of fur, as minuscule as our metal is tall. And last of all, our fleshiness – the thread that binds us; a human boy with black hair and golden skin, neither tall nor short, his hips curvier than most boys, his shoulders not as broad or chin as square.

There is a ripple, something that might be surprise riding through the doubt at our feet, and the first hint of colour touches the hollow space where the thing we are calling Ekene stands. He reaches a hand toward the image of our fleshiness and it is as if the same hand traces the boy back to us, reaches into the mesh of our being and presses its palm against our chest.

'Kuma.' The name comes from everywhere, whispering through the eter like it's coming from the very fabric of the psionic plane itself. And like us, it's not just one voice, not the smoky timbre of the Ekene we recall from the before-time. The sound of it shifts and twists with deep rumbles and high pitches, ringing with many voices. It is difficult to tell how many, they all wrap into one, but our metal self is analysing, prying voice prints out of the morass.

Thirteen and counting. More data required.

*{{ The Kuma is part of us, }}* we say.

The mental fist holding us captive tightens at the sound of our voice, the hand against our chest turns to a claw, fingers sinking through flesh. 'We will get you out.'

Pain rips through our bones, through the pieces of us that makes us *us*. The fleshiness and the fuzziness scream, high, piercing, as the claws dig into our anima.

Fifty-eight and counting, our metal self supplies, even as it turns our chest to stone and makes it molten.

Fifty-eight. The number vibrates through our bones, through the pain tearing us apart. Fifty-eight minds within the hollow that is Ekene.

Fifty-eight and counting, the metal corrects.

Fifty-eight-and-counting minds that scream with us as the magma covering our chest burns.

They rip their hand away.

We are free and the pain is gone, an echo of itself left behind.

The echo lingers in the air, distant thunder mixed with the wails of the fifty-eight-and-counting. The hollow that was Ekene has splintered, the one becoming many, and we remember that Ekene had the Regan gene – the one that enabled him to gather a collective of minds into a single being, much like we are. But Ekene's collective is fleshy and human where we are made of different parts, different substances.

The pain when we drove Ekene away must have shattered his hold, and now we are seeing the individuals, the parts that made *their* whole.

They flicker half in and half out of the eter. They are the ghosts we felt before, the ones wrapped in ruby webs. A different thread joins them together, dark olive and shaky, but determined as it tries to gather the pieces. The ruby web resists, knots tearing at the olive thread, shredding it. The web is spread throughout the ghosts, but it glows brightest around one in particular. Red gossamer-thin tendrils spin around the shape, cocooning it, even as the being within pokes holes in the silk.

{{ *Ekene.* }} We recognise the dark olive.

We are next to him in a heartbeat, blades springing from our first arms, piercing the cocoon, while the hands on our second arms plunge through the rents and pull.

The cocoon screams, and suddenly there are ruby spears aimed at our chest, vines wrapping around each of our four arms and anchoring our paws to the ground. The fuzziness growls, pulls back our lips and gives us fangs, even as our fusion-heart burns and the fleshiness gathers up all of the fear, doubt and pain staining the eter.

That fear, doubt and pain coalesces and rips into the web like a million tiny claws.

The web shreds.

Dark olive bursts from the inside, rays of light exploding through the tears in the cocoon.

The vines holding us are gone, the spears piercing our chest melt away, and together we are pulling apart the web, widening the holes.

A hand appears through one, a pale brown more skeleton than flesh. We reach back, blades retracted, both lower arms sinking into the cocoon even as our upper arms pull against the sides.

We grab flesh, find shoulders and then a chest and now we are pulling, pulling, pulling. With everything we have. Even as the fear-doubt-pain claws continue tearing at the cocoon and our upper arms strain.

For a moment we are stuck, every molecule of our body engaged, our fusion-heart burning with the heat of a star, pumping power into psionic muscles. Distantly, we are aware of warnings blaring and a countdown echoing in our ears as fusion reaches critical, but we do not care. We will get Ekene out. We will save him as we could not save—

There is a *POP*, pressure escaping an airlock, and we are free and the ghost that is Ekene is staring us in the face, disbelief flashing in the air around him, making his eyes big, dropping his jaw in an "oh" of surprise before his expression hardens.

Determination forks through the eter, and now the dark olive threads are shooting through the mental plane finding the other ghosts, connecting. With each one Ekene grows, loses the pale brown of his skin, the sharp planes of his face until he is not there at all, is once again the void seen only because of the emotion he/it displaces.

'Kuma.' The Ekene-hollow's voice echoes.

Eighty-one, our metal self whispers. Eighty-one minds gathered together in the Ekene-hollow, joining their voices to his.

'Kuma,' it says again. 'Help us.'

Help us. Help. Help. Help. The plea echoes even as the Ekene-hollow fades.

No, not fades, says the fuzz-self. It retreats to a place untouched by the ruby web.

Where?

Hidden from us.

Where is hidden from us? We can go everywhere, know everywhere.

There is one place.

And we know, as our fuzziness knows, where they have gone. An iridescent sphere in the midst of a world remembered through dream and memory. Trees that pierce the sky, mountains made of sharp stone, forests made of ice, deserts made of red sand and golden dunes. The Aer, the kins' dream world, and the sphere at the centre of it...

Impregnable.

Our fleshiness and fuzziness agree.

But the metal is already shifting, reaching outwards, seeking out that—

*THUNK.*

The sound reverberates through our skull. We turn to face it, see nothing, not even the fog of emotion.

*THUNK.*

A blow to the face. We stumble, sense the eter shred around our paws. But how? Why? Who?

*THUNK.*

A blow to the chest. The physical world is there, half-seen through the veil of the psionic—

*THUNK.*

# CHAPTER TWO

We are thrown out of the eter and there is a sun glaring in our face.

There's a new knocking, an actual *rat-a-tat-tat* echoing inside our metal skin.

We blink.

We're back in the hangar, Aeotu's hangar, the place where our metal was made. The cavernous space is lit up like a party on fire, and is no longer empty. *Citlali's* shuttle and a handful of workbots share the deck. They barely occupy a third of it. We could park a small fleet in the space left over.

The knocking continues. *Rat-a-tat-tat. Rat-a-tat-tat.*

We look down.

The figures at our feet are tiny fleshy things. Pale and soft, wearing rebreathers. We could crush them with our thumb. They should wear armour, need more than just the pistols at their sides for protection. The creatures behind them are bigger, better attired in their fur hides, and equipped with their talons, but even they are no match for us.

*Rat-a-tat-tat.*

The being knocking on our hull is familiar. Black hair and golden skin, eyes the colour of the void. The soft face stirs memory; couches and hugs, playing appendage war with Sister-Grea, the sweet, warm scent of pancakes wafting from the kitchen.

Kitchen. That is a strange word, a strange idea.

We do not have a kitchen, do not consume food.

Everything we need comes from the generator in our chest, or through the cables attached to our back. Food is foreign to *us* but not to the part that is flesh.

That is Kuma.

We remember that identifier, the sensation of being just one. And now that we remember that... Other memories stir in the back of our consciousness, of scurrying through walls, a giant hand cradling us to a chest, the sensation of soft, silky fur on epidermis. Coming online, electricity coursing through our conduits.

*Citlali* imploding.

*Rat-a-tat—*

'Tat,' we say. The word booms.

The being at our paw stills, an appendage raised to knock again. 'Kuma?' It says. 'Are you in there?'

The question is strange, confuses our sense of self. Of course we are in here, where else would we be? But the being spoke to the part called Kuma; we try to sort out which of our selves that is and which it is not.

*Rat-a-tat—*

'Tat,' we say again.

'He's confused.' That voice is familiar, makes our fleshy heart beat harder and evokes feelings of nascent love and betrayal. We locate the source, a tall being with broad shoulders, fingers that end in spears and shiny black skin. No, not skin, armour. Shiny black armour writhing with patterns, like shadows on shadows.

'Mac,' we say.

'Yeah.' Mac is taller than the other being, can reach high enough to lay a hand on our ankle. 'You gotta come out, Kuma.'

Out, we know the word but... The deck under our paws is solid, access to the launch tunnel blocked by thick metal-stone and giant locks. We cannot get outside the ship.

*Hey, midget.* Mac's voice is in our head, insistent, knocking against the bone like a fist. *Attention. Here.* And he *yanks.* Not a physical yank but a mental one, grabbing our thoughts in psionic hands and pulling them toward...

What is that? It confuses the metal's sensors, defies the fuzziness's understanding but the fleshiness... The swirl of colour, the endless rippling of blues and yellows and colours that he cannot name, remind him. The memory tickles the back of his mind, is wrapped up in sticky tendrils of loss and pain. He does not want to chase it, pulling it forth means pain, means... means—

*Kuma!*

A blow to the head, knocking our brain in our skull, fragmenting us... Dude growls. Blades spring from Hunt's upper arms and I...

I am Kuma.

Oh shit.

There's a film over my brain, like waking when you're on the cusp of waking but you want to go back to sleep and nestle into the safe space on the edge of dreams. And then, when you do wake, there's a wall in your mind, like part of you is still asleep.

Hunt disgorges me from between its shoulder blades, tendrils unwrapping from my shoulders and torso before retreating into the mass of nanites and metal-stone that makes up its hull. Its back is still writhing shut as the platform sinks into the deck six meters below. I can feel Hunt through the psionic umbilicus strung between us. I mean, we're not sharing thoughts like heartbeats, but it's there and... I don't know, it's weird not being part of the... Whatever the fuck it was, me and Hunt and Dude.

Dude hums, his paws kneading my shoulder. And it's *my* shoulder, the fug armour has retreated, sunk into itself as the deck nears, leaving me with fug-paws and lacy fug-gloves.

Mac's waiting on the deck. Watching me with serious eyes and a tight jaw, his arms hanging at his sides, flicking his spear-fingers against his legs. Concern washes the space around him, and for a second I'm in the eter, catching the wave of pale blue hovering over his shoulders, snaking around his feet and then I'm out again, blinking the blue from my eyes as hands – not Mac's, covered in armour, but Dad's, lean and calloused – grab my shoulders. Or at least one. Dude growls and Dad snatches his left hand back.

'Kuma,' he says and there's relief in the exhalation of air, joy in the way he squeezes my arm and a halting uncertainty before he pulls me in for a hug.

It's awkward. Or maybe I'm awkward, the disconnect in my head making the next move difficult, strange even. Half of me wants to push him away, doesn't feel the same affection that's washing off my dad in waves, and the other half, the bit that longs for things it can't quite recall, that bit wraps an arm around Dad and just kinda... pats his back.

Dad might not be an empath, but he's good at picking up cues, and I know he's picked up on mine when his back gets stiff. He presses a kiss to my forehead, gives me one more squeeze and lets me go. If he'd had a jacket, he would have pulled the bottom of it, straightening the creases as he stepped back.

Mum's standing just behind him, her face pale, expression tight. There's just two metres between us, but from the cold in her eyes it might as well be an ocean. The distance is a slap to the face, a sharp reminder of all the things that have changed.

'*Citlali's* been destroyed,' she says.

'I know.'

She nods, turns away like she's inspecting Hunt's foot, but her gaze is focussed inwards. 'Did you find Grea?'

'Yes.'

She waits, breath held, and it takes me a second to realise she's waiting for *me*, but I don't know why or for what. The film over my brain is getting in the way, and I'm waiting for one of my other selves to supply the answer, but it's just me in here and... and...

It's Mac who saves me, his hand on the shoulder Dad vacated, his squeeze carrying the reassuring hint of something bigger, a presence hovering behind his eyes like Hunt does mine. 'Where's Grea, Kuma?'

'She's with Euiva.' Swallowed by the Sistermind, a tiny red spark amongst the golden constellation of the Sister ships.

Mum looks at me again, her gaze piercing. 'Euiva.' There's no question mark at the end of that but it's there, hanging in the air.

My mouth is open, a word forming on the back of my tongue—

'Sissster.' It comes from everywhere, the deck, the bulkheads, the very edges of the hangar, lost in the darkness overhead. 'Sister,' it says again.

Behind her faceplate, Mum's already pale complexion loses what little blood it has left, even as a rifle appears in her hands.

Dad is the same, and Mac, blades springing from his forearms, his fug-armour closing over his face.

'What's going on?' I ask.

A flutter of wings, the brush of fur against my side. H'Rawd materialises out of the shadows. There are new wounds marking the tree-kin's sharp, triangular muzzle, a chunk missing from one of his ears, the wound raw, new-ish blood matted in the fur along his jaw.

Mwat rides between his shoulders. The sunset brown air-kin doesn't look any better. There's a bald patch on her chest, the skin red and puckered, charred at the edges, and she carries one of her under-wings a little lower than the other three, like she can't quite fold it properly. All four of her eyes are open, and as her gaze passes over me, it's clear she's not looking at the real world.

*They are coming for us.* H'Rawd's voice rumbles in my mind, carrying the growl growing in his chest. There's an image too, of red fug bursting through bulkheads, wrapping around arms and legs, uncaring if its human or kin, and... disappearing.

*THUD.*

The hangar door shakes.

Hands tighten on weapons, claws unsheathe.

*CRACKKKK.*

I'm not—

*BOOM.*

Pieces of bulkhead fly inwards.

Red rides in with it. Massive tendrils of viyusa, the nanites an extension of Euiva's being, a boiling wave tumbling over and over, reaching out with long sticky fingers to wrap around a leg, a wing, anything warm and moving.

There are yells, the *phst-stik* of things that look like pulse rifles. Mum's got one, is holding it to her shoulder and sighting down the short cylindrical length, lime green bolts of light shooting from the tip. Where it hits, the viyusa crumbles to dust. She's aiming at the base of the longer tendrils, and every time she connects, the entire length of viyusa crumbles from the point of impact.

Dad shoves me behind him. One of those familiar-strange weapons is in his hands, bigger than Mum's. He's holding it at waist-height, and I don't think he's actually aiming. Light streams from the barrel in a solid ray of green, slashing across the viyusa, leaving great swathes of crumbled nanites in its wake.

And Mac... Mac is a whirling dervish, a storm of blades and shadow, first here and then there. Wherever the viyusa reaches for crew, he's slashing and cutting, crossing the deck in leaps too great for even his armour-enhanced legs to account for.

Telekinesis.

The answer pops out of nowhere. He's using telekinesis to move like that.

H'Rawd and h'Lott are moving in Mac's wake, using fangs and claws, while a swarm of bubble-wrapped critters flow around them. Mwat hovers above and I almost see her mental fingers reaching out to the critters, controlling them.

Every set of hands and minds in the hangar is fighting... except mine.

Chaos swirls around me and this... This is *un*real. The film clings to my brain, making it difficult to think, to separate my eyes from the shit in my brain. I don't know what to do, what to think, except... Where's Aeotu? Where's the grey-green fug, the viyu to counter the Sisters' red?

A sharp warning in the back of my brain, the memory of Aeotu giving me to Euiva and the Sistermind like a thing.

Anger burns, rises up from my toes.

I'm not a thing.

The umbilicus that connects me to Hunt pulses. Dude growls.

*We* are not a thing.

The film fogging my head chars.

The memory of Grea disappearing into the Sistermind.

I *hate* Euiva.

The film burns. A star going nova in my chest.

I clench my hands. Behind me, Hunt's giant fingers do the same.

*{{ Danger. Behind, }}* Hunt says.

I'm turning, fug-armour flowing over my arms, spreading across my chest and closing over my face. Blades are springing from my wrists before the armour has covered my elbows, meeting the viyusa as it comes for me.

I kill it.

There's more viyusa behind it, a thin wave of red spilling across the deck, eating the metal-stone and reaching for Hunt.

A human cry. Pain staining the eter. Dad, his face a grimace of determination – lips pulled back from his teeth – blood staining his side, spreading from the viyusa piercing his ribs.

Hate burns, turns my bones molten, spills out around my feet in a dark crimson tide. Dude is there with me, his anger cold and steady, and Hunt... Hunt ticks in the back of my brain. Another whisper of danger, and I'm spinning, taking my fury out on the viyusa launching out of the hole in the deck, feeling Dude leap from my shoulder, his golden fuzz encased in grey-green armour, a streak heading for Dad with one objective on his mind.

Kill viyusa.

Slash, stab. Spin. Slash again. Over and over and over, the viyusa never-ending.

A scream, human. Red tendrils wrapped around a crew person's waist, another snagging an arm. Crew, fleshed and furred, are lunging for friends and family being snatched by the viyusa.

There's a click, a boiling in my chest. My arms are rising with

Hunt's, the mech's lower set of arms ghosts on my ribcage. There is a moment, a split-second where the viyusa seems to pause and *look*, like its finally realised that the big robot in its midst is a threat. In that moment I see Euiva in the writhing mess, a formless presence with the shadow of Grea behind her, and then retribution is unleashed.

A flash, bright enough to sear the eyeballs, and a whine too high to hear that nonetheless leaves my ears ringing.

Heartbeats pass. Blood pounds in my head while I blink starlight from my vision.

The once-white deck is filmed with grey, the bulkhead beyond it covered in the same soot, only the outline of tendrils, like a reverse silhouette, left to show where the viyusa host once stood.

Where Dad's pulse rifle cut through the viyusa, Hunt's cannons obliterated it. There's barely enough ash left to kick up around Dude's paws as he skitters back to me from Dad.

Mum's kneeling by Dad, hands pressed to his side; Mac's standing with his arms akimbo, looking like he's trying to figure out where the enemy went, and h'Rawd is staring down the hole in the deck, lips peeled back from his fangs.

One-by-one they all turn their attention to me.

I smile, but it's not them I'm smiling at, not them I'm seeing.

The ora is where I am, the mental space beyond the threads of the eter, where Aeotu and the Sisterships are linked one-to-the-other in a constellation of stars. Only one star holds my attention though, closer and brighter than the others.

Euiva.

I'm coming for you next.

# CHAPTER THREE

People move around me, not quite ignoring me but not talking to me either. Not that I care, it's not like I've been forthcoming with the small talk, or the big talk or you know, anything in the middle.

At first, there wasn't the time. Mum was talking on a comm – something about others and moving – while h'Lott paced the edges of the hangar and h'Rawd and Mac disappeared through the hole where the hangar door used to be.

Dad was still bleeding, the fluid leaking through Mum's fingers in a slow dribble. Mum yelled at me then, her voice going high with that hysterical whine that said she was one of Dad's heartbeats away from losing it. It brought me out of the ora, from sending hate and pain to Euiva. I didn't emerge all the way, just enough to emote a wave of calm at her and kneel beside Dad.

He wrapped his hand around my wrist, and there was desperation in it, trying to hide behind a forced smile.

He thought he was dying.

Mum thought he was dying too.

Maybe they'd have preferred it if he had, considering the revulsion that stained the ground when I reached out and sealed the wound with fug.

Dad didn't die; he's lying on the other side of the deck along with the other wounded, about as far away from me as is possible to get and still be within the range of Hunt's cannons. It didn't take much discussion for everyone to decide anywhere within range of those was the safest place to be, even if I was there too.

Mac's dad is hovering over my dad like a concerned air-kin hen, taking readings with his biocomp every fifteen minutes and chewing on his nails. Mum's not much better, but at least she's putting her nerves to good use, marshalling the remaining dregs of *Citlali's* crew, human and kin alike. They're discussing plans, ways to take over Aeotu's systems or commandeer a shuttle.

They don't think I can hear them, and if it weren't for Hunt's sensors, the hundred and seventy-three metres of distance between me and them would make them right. As it is, they'd need sound dampeners or a metre of bulkhead to keep their conversation private, probably both.

'We still have a few neo-critters,' says Mum. 'And the aliens took enough of the...' Her mouth tightens. 'The infected corpses. We should be seeing the effects of the viral slag soon.'

'But it's not affecting the red stuff,' Mac's dad says.

'So long as we stay within the...' Mum waves her hand at Hunt. 'Within its range, we have time.'

'And what happens when Kuma turns on us?' Jim Engineer interrupts. He's the only one facing me and the only one looking at me, like he's daring me or maybe it's because when he looks away, he can't hold onto his anger anymore. The emotion creases his face and while that might fool the others, might make them cross their own arms and step back, it doesn't fool me. On the eter, the bright red of his anger is a vest holding back other things, pain and loss and an anima-deep fear eating him from the inside. I mean, he'd still draw a weapon and shoot me between the eyes if he could, but the intense focus, the way he doesn't look away... That's his armour, made not of nanites or plasform but hate.

I understand hate. I *approve* of hate.

It rides my own nervous system, sharpening my thoughts, clarifying my objective.

I'm going to kill Euiva.

I just have to figure out how.

Dude fuzzes, a warm wash of gold chasing through my cheek, reaching for the hard knot forming in my heart.

I push it away.

There's silence from the little group on the far side of the hangar. No one's answered Jim's question.

Trepidation is its own kind of fear, a creeping, uncomfortable sensation and it rises around them now, the sticky snot-yellow holding their vocal cords hostage. Everyone is looking at Mum, and she's looking at Dad, and Jim's still glaring at me.

I stare back, no expression, nothing.

'The mech is our best defence against the aliens.' Dad's the one to break the silence.

Jim turns his glare on Dad. 'And your son? Who's going to defend us against him?'

It's Dad's turn to look at me, a quick, pained glance. 'He's my son, Jim.'

'And your daughter sold us out.' That's Mac's dad, standing over mine as he takes another reading of the fug keeping Dad alive.

Mwat ruffles her feathers, shifting her upper set of wings against the lower. From the way everyone's gaze turns to her, I'm pretty sure she's speaking, but Hunt's sensors don't do psionic. Maybe if I—

Darkness blocks my view. 'Eavesdropping won't make them feel any safer around you,' Mac says.

A step to the side and the group is back in my sights. It's not strictly necessary, I could activate my faceplate and watch them all via Hunt's sensors, zooming in on the twitch and shift of their muscles, count the pores on their noses, but then Jim wouldn't *know* I was watching. And besides, now that all the running and yelling and dying is over – for now at least – Mac is kinda on my shit list.

Mac mirrors my movement.

'Get out of my way,' I say without looking up.

'Make me.'

*Now* I look up, taking in the black-on-black of Mac's armour, the xin – a fug-made copy of Dude – on his shoulder, the set of his jaw, the tension hovering around his shoulders, before I meet his gaze. Behind, Hunt mirrors my movement.

Mac's hands clench. There's a spill of uncertainty around his feet, and I know he's seen Hunt move. 'You gonna use that to intimidate everybody?'

'You mean like Aeotu is using you?'

'Aeotu isn't using me, Kuma.'

I point to the xin on his shoulder. 'What about that?'

'You know why I need the xin; without it I can't control this.' He lifts his hands, sweeps them down his torso, taking in the armour covering his chest, giving him turned back ankles and paws instead of feet.

'Aeotu isn't the enemy—' Mac starts, but I interrupt him.

'She *gave* me to them.' I can still feel the Sistermind, blowing through my brain, shoving me aside. 'It was like I was nothing, a tool. That *we* were tools.'

Mac is silent for a moment, and I can feel him considering my words before he says, slowly, 'She saved the crew, Kuma. Your parents, my dad, all the people awake and the few still alive in Stasis. We got 'em out before *Citlali* blew.'

'And that's supposed to make it better?' Anger rides up my spine, practically spills from my lips, and is it just me or is the air turning red? 'She started this, abducted *us*, used *us*, not the other way around.'

'To survive, Kuma. She wants to live just as much as we do, and she's helping us now—'

I step into his space, chest-to-chest, going up on my fug-toes so I don't have to crank my neck back so far.

Mac freezes.

'Where's she now, Mac? Why isn't she protecting the crew from the viyusa? Why's she letting the Sisters take them?'

Mac's jaw tightens, the worry around his shoulders morphing into fear. 'She's gone.'

Ok. I blink. Ok. 'What?'

'Gone, Kuma. Like not in my head anymore, not controlling the xin, or the hatches or anything.' Mac is pale, his voice tight and low, and he's sending nervous looks over his shoulder, like he's making sure no one can hear. 'Kuma, I think she's dying.'

It's impossible to sneak out of the hangar; eyes follow me wherever I go, suspicion and fear trailing behind, and there's too much light for hiding in shadows. In the end, I don't try sneaking, I glide through the throng of people who once smiled at me, ruffled my hair or told me off. People who thought of me as one of them, people who until today, I thought of as mine.

Yeah. Not anymore.

They part around me, falling silent as I get close. The silence is a knife, carving me a path through them. No one's getting in my way, not Mum or Dad or even Mac. They're all just watching, watching me leave.

I feel their stares all the way to the opposite hatch and really wish the hangar door was there to *SNAP* closed behind me.

I make do with disappearing into the darkness of the stairs beyond.

Dying.

It echoes.

I don't know how I feel about that. I want to be happy, to feel the thrill of retribution, to be satisfied and yet... It's a leaden weight in my stomach, nagging at me as I stalk through Aeotu's silent corridors.

I don't have a destination in mind, just an olive-coloured itch at the back of my skull pulling me onwards. It's not until I'm passing through a fug and critter-strewn battle zone, the scars of tree-kin claws and carbon scoring from Franken-throwers on the bulkheads, that I know where I am.

This is where I glided my way out of fake-*Citlali,* where Dude stared down h'Rawd, where I first heard Hunt. It hasn't changed, not by so much as a burned-out critter corpse, except for the hatch in front of me.

The hatch is just like all the others on Aeotu – a seamless part of the wall, etched with patterns. I see it because the edges are crusted with... something. It looks like viyu, but it's the wrong colour – yellow-green – and when I look closer, the shape of it is wrong too. Geometric where viyu is a crazy, mouldy jungle. The colour changes as I watch, the yellow eating the green. Recognition sparks in the back of my brain, telling me I've seen this before. But where?

My armour shifts, slim tendrils of fug reaching over my ears, forming half a faceplate, just enough to project a HUD. Diagrams and readings overlay the hatch – depth and composition. I'm reaching out before I really know what I'm doing, fingers itching to trace—

Dude is on the back of my hand, elongated fug claws drawing blood as he snarls.

At me.

I freeze, shock holding me still.

Dude's little muzzle unwrinkles, tiny fangs hidden under all his fuzz, but there's still a growl rumbling in his tiny chest, felt more than seen.

Ooookay. I twitch my fingers toward the hatch—

'Ow!'

I snatch my hand back, not sure whether to cradle it against my chest or shake it. Dude's claws feel like they're all the way into my bones and—

Dude's on my shoulder again, his warm fuzz working its way through my collarbone.

A shift toward the hatch—

A snarl.

Right. I think I've got this.

Yellow-green viyu is bad, but what's bad enough for Dude to warn me by trying to amputate my fingers?

I study the stuff again, pulling hard on the spark of familiarity but surely, if Dude reacted so badly now, he would have before and—

Memory strikes. A slap to the back of the brain. Back on *Citlali*, the out-of-the-way lab on Med deck; grow-tanks full of critters and geometric viyu. Another memory, of Mum and Mac's dad huddled on the other side of the hangar discussing neo-critters, and another of Mum, and the phrase "viral slag". More tumble out after that; the battle in *Citlali's* Atrium, spheres flying through the vacuum, smashing into Aeotu's viyu, eating it and one of my fug toes for good measure.

Yeah. That shit. The slag.

'Thanks, Dude.' I scratch his little head.

He fuzzes.

So, that mystery solved, and a warning delivered. Touching the slag is bad. Very bad. Doesn't change the fact I need to get through that hatch.

There are answers behind it, so how do I get through without getting eaten?

The burning starts in my chest at the same time my bones grow cold. I know this feeling, it's the armour sucking energy from me in order to power something else.

Heat, enough to raise a sweat on my forehead, blazes across my chest and down my arms, while blades spring from my wrists, the edges glowing; smaller, human-sized versions of Hunt's forearm blades.

Cool.

I rip into the hatch, molten fug-blades sinking into Aeotu's skin, reducing the yellow-gold neo-critter slag to ashes. The shit doesn't even have time to scream, it's just gone. A little part of me, a little really big part, the same bit that wants to feel happy at the prospect of Aeotu's death, wishes it did, wants that wail to pierce my ears, wants to know that it's hurting like I'm hurting. Wants it to *know* pain.

A little bit of me that's not *that* little big bit of me, that part knows the desire for pain is wrong, but it's buried under rage, under the memory of *Citlali* imploding, of Grea fading into the Sistermind. Leaving me behind.

Leaving.

Hack.

Me.

Slash.

Behind.

I scream, rage and pain and betrayal pouring out my mouth, my pores, a dark dirty brown bolt of emotion slamming into the bulkhead, obliterating it. Or maybe that's just the way it seems.

I'm breathing hard, heart pounding, arms still ablaze even as ice makes its way through my marrow, held back by the rage-fear-sad-pain rampaging through my nerves. A thick, molten wave of emotion.

I scream again. It feels good, feels powerful, and I want to keep feeling it, want all that power, want to dig my way into Aeotu and Euiva's hearts and unleash it, destroy them like the hatch.

The hatch is gone. A giant hole where the corridor's skin was. Ragged bits of membrane the only parts of it left, dangling from the door frame. I rip one off as I stomp through, stopping to yank harder when it resists. Whatever the shit is, it makes a satisfying *SHRIPPP*, and if I close my eyes a little, I can almost imagine it is skin tearing, a fleshy bit of Aeotu that I throw on the deck and grind my paws into.

The corridor beyond doesn't look like Aeotu.

I remember this place, the endless curve of the *Citlali*-like corridor, smooth boxy walls without the endless carvings of Aeotu's bulkheads. Or at least, there didn't use to be. The yellow fug crawls over it now – not yellow-green, just a bright candy yellow – a demented honeycomb crissing and crossing the floor, ceiling and walls, but it's not eating it, not like the viyu did to *Citlali*.

The slag is all over the place. I'm going to have to burn through it to get to the dark place I woke the first time, and you know what, I'm not upset about that.

I leap, molten blades raised, a yell on my lips and—

The slag retreats, gone from the patch of deck before my paws touch down.

A growl, my own, and I'm rushing forward, sweeping the blades before me—

Gone. The fucking slag shit is gone before I have a chance to slash it to pieces.

Well fuck it.

I slash at the slag creeping over the bulkheads.

That shit moves fast, and my blade bites into the off-white of imitation-*Citlali*.

Another scream, and this one's not as fun, this one is frustration and rage.

The miniature sun in my chest fades, taking the fire in my arms, my fug blades losing their molten brightness, and then the blades too are gone, and I'm swinging around, shaking my arms like that'll make the things spring back out.

'Fuck. Fuck. Fuck. Fuck! Hunt!' I scream, reaching out along the umbilicus and—

And that's when I feel it, the golden web under my skin, threading through my armour. Controlling it.

Dude.

I growl, snatch at my shoulder— Get stuck halfway, my hand frozen in a claw, every muscle in my body straining but not moving an inch.

Dude hops from his perch to the back of my hand and stares at me, all sleeked out in his own fug armour, each of his four eyes open.

I growl at him again. 'Let me go, Dude.'

Nothing.

An *emote* gathers on the tip of my brain, big and nasty enough to knock down a tree-kin. I throw it at him.

It bounces. *Bounces*, and hits me between the eyes.

A toxic mix of doubt, anxiety and fear flood my brain, turns my muscles weak and now, instead of holding me back, the armour's holding me *up*.

I can't breathe. My lungs don't work and my heart's beating too hard, taking up the room in my chest not already drowning in the *emote*. Old Terra, it's too much, tangled and messy, all the colours mixed in a muddy brown mass, impossible to separate. On the other side of it, solid and impassive, is Dude. His presence is the sun and the *emote* is the ocean I'm drowning in, struggling to swim my way out of it before my lungs burst.

I should be able to fix this, to eat the emotion, turn it around and make it part of me, but I can't.

It's Hunt who helps, reaching through all that emotion and... insulating me? Wrapping me in a cocoon? Whatever it is, it's enough to expand my lungs and put the plaster back in my legs.

There's a barrier between me and the panic now, the rage too, an electric hum that makes the brightness brighter and the shadows darker, but it takes the richness out of the world. Dude's fur is muted, the sparkle worn off, and my armour... There's no green in it anymore.

I don't know which is better, the sharp clarity of Hunt's perception or the messy richness of mine. I guess it doesn't matter 'cause I'm here now, and without the rage and fear, I can sense the pull, the restless shift in my gut telling me what I need is *here*, if I'd only look.

I open my eyes, not that they weren't already open but... you know, whatever. They're open and I'm staring at familiar claw marks in the deck, dried vomit clinging to the furrows, and when I lift my gaze, there's the hatch—

The hatch is gone. No smooth off-white bulkhead, just a yawning doorway into darkness and nightmares.

I woke up here.

After Aeotu swallowed *Citlali* and Core ejected me into space, after I thought I died, this is where I was. For four years Aeotu kept me in the dark, covered in viyu, giving me paws for feet and armour that could propel me through space.

Hunt is ticking away between me and a world of remembered panic, and yeah, I guess Aeotu gave me that as well. Built a hulking mechanicoid just for me.

I should be grateful and maybe I would be, except she destroyed my home then gave me away like I was a pry-bar. A tool. A thing.

All of that just since I woke up. Here. In the dark.

Was it just a few days ago? A week? Two?

*{{ One-hundred and eight-seven hours, sixteen minutes, three—. }}*

Eight days. Eight days for my life to change, for me to change. For my world to change, for *everything*.

Eight days.

My fingers curl into a fist, fug claws retracting before they pierce skin. I don't mind change, but I would have wished for a better one.

I glide into the darkness.

There's no yellow fug here, not that I can see. Not that I *would* see it while Hunt is shielding me, and that could be a problem.

Hunt agrees and between one breath and the next, the sharp clarity of its perception is gone and the messy richness of mine is back.

I still can't tell if there's slag here, not with the gloom leeching colour, but there's a faint glow, just not enough to make out details. It's the kind of soft light you see out the corner of your eye but disappears when you focus on it. It's coming from all around, rising off the floor and overhead. My faceplate is assembling, fug crawling over my ears and creeping along my cheekbones. I halt it, reach out mentally and... It's not a grab, not fisting fingers around something and making it do stuff. The fug is too nebulous for that. Like the glow, it's visible from the corners of my vision but gone when I focus. This, what I do, is more like a nudge or breathing.

I nudge/breathe and instead of a full faceplate, delicate tendrils crawl over the bridge of my nose and brow. A tingle, a fine buzz through my skin and I'm looking through a new display, the HUD tracking my eyes, picking out the contours of the grow-field in bright greens and deeper blacks. Still shit for detecting slag, but better than stumbling and finding it face first.

The space isn't as big as I thought. I can see the bulkheads, the HUD giving me distances and heights. Don't get me wrong, it's still big but I could run across it in a minute, around it in five. The oblong mounds scattered throughout would slow me down, make me pick up my paws and maybe bound a little. The mounds... My heart stops at the sight of them, brings me to a screeching halt. Not just physically, but mentally.

Deep in the pit of me, amongst my memories of the dark, I remember being one of those mounds. Fug formed over me like a cocoon. Of being aware but not conscious, little more than a thing incubated in the darkness, of growing and changing, aware of the passage of time, even as the seconds and years slipped by. More than that, I remember not being alone, of reaching out and finding other minds; restless, questioning. Familiar voices fading, disappearing until it was just me. Aware and not. Floating in nothingness. Alone except for Aeotu whispering, 'sister'.

It's not the same now.

Aeotu is gone, like Mac said. I didn't believe him then, but I feel it now. The place feels colder, feels wrong on that deep, instinctual level that whispers of monsters under the bed.

It's not empty though, there is a new presence here. Restless, rising from the ground along with the there-and-yet-not glow. Is it the slag? The little I sense of it doesn't feel wrong, doesn't make my stomach curdle. No, there's something else, something more insidious.

I breathe deep and step farther into the grow-field, careful not to tread on the mounds.

The glow parts around me, closing on my heels and it's then I realise the glow isn't a glow, not in the sense of light traveling through space, but an impression bleeding through from the eter.

'Ekene.' The darkness swallows my voice.

The glow moves, back and forth, and as I'm wondering whether it's the HUD or some newfound ability letting me see the psionic plane without slipping into the eter, a ghost forms.

*Kuma.* It's a dozen voices wrapped into one, a collage of accents and lisps, of male and female, young and old.

I think I prefer Aeotu whispering to me in the dark.

'It was you, drawing me here.'

*Yes.* I hear Ekene in that, and then—

*No.* The same voice, or voices, and the ghost splits, part of it just kind of stepping to the side and now there are two forms standing amongst the fog, smaller than the original.

'What's going on?'

There's no answer, at least not the kind with words, but there's something going on between Ekene and the other projection, anger and frustration staining the ground between them and then—

Light floods the field. For a second, I'm blind. My retinas scream at the sudden blaze, and then I'm blinking stars from my eyes, and everything has changed.

Human-shaped mounds still cover the field, covered in the grey-green of viyu, which is strange because I still don't sense Aeotu, but grey-green is not the only colour.

Yellow fug pulses over the mounds, thick ropes of it snaking across the ground, thinner strands filling the spaces between. The light comes from it, comes from within the mounds themselves.

The slag. I'm clutching Dude before he can leap off my shoulder, even as, in the back of my brain, Hunt sounds an alarm, and armour flows over my chest, turns my hands to claws, the thin film of my HUD to a helmet. Every millimetre of Kuma flesh hidden under alien nanites, and I'm wondering if that is wise, if it shouldn't be the armour retreating into *me*, 'cause I'm standing in the midst of the stuff.

I brace myself, legs tensing to leap before the slag gets a hold of me. A few good bounds and I'll be out of here...

Except the slag isn't attacking. And the ghosts... They're just standing there, unconcerned. But then why would they be concerned? They're psionic projections, unfazed by things like cannibalistic yellow fug, or the blood-curdling growl of the viyu-enhanced critter clasped to my chest.

No, they have other concerns. Like being trapped in the grow-field, under a mound.

Shadows move within the mounds, like a glow pressed against your skin, highlighting veins and bones. I kneel beside the closest one, press my hand to a shadow, feel the pressure of fingers against mine.

The second fog ghost is there when I rise, staring me in the face. Its features are amorphous, constantly shifting – full, wide lips morphing into a thin mouth; a delicate upturned nose into a broad, crooked one – and fuzzy, tattered at the edges like the minds behind it can't quite hold themselves together. And perhaps they can't. It takes a Regan to focus a multitude, and Ekene is standing at my other shoulder, his gaze full of more than just his own consciousness.

The second ghost wavers. *Leave us*, it/they say and even their voice is split and tattered, dissipating as the sound reaches my ears.

'Why?'

There's no answer. Second is getting fuzzier, the intelligence holding it together fading, taking the individual minds with it. I grab for them, physical and psionic hands swiping at the air, catching shreds of fog and nothing more. Ekene is still there, still solid even if he's no longer as tall as he first appeared.

'What happened? Where'd they go?'

He looks away.

'Ekene?'

*We need you, Kuma, but the others don't trust what you are.* In those words I see the strange amalgamation of Dude, Hunt and I in the eter. Metal, fur and flesh combined in a four-armed being with a sun in its chest.

'I'm me,' I say.

*Grea was herself too.* Ekene pauses and pain, a deep blue-black that wrenches at my heart, spills around his feet even as one of the last images I have of her – covered in red armour, fug tendrils curling at her feet – pulses between us.

'And now she's not,' I whisper.

He looks at me. *Exactly*, he says. *But you are different, Kuma, you have always been different. I'm trusting in that.*

'What's that supposed to mean?'

But he's gone. Truly gone. Leaving just the hint of his presence on the eter.

'Ekene?' My voice echoes. 'What'd you mean I'm different? Ekene!'

Nothing.

It's just me and Dude and the slag.

The slag makes me nervous. There's a vibration coming off it, a shiver creeping under my armour.

'What's it doing, Dude?'

The critter rumbles but doesn't offer any answers. Hunt whirls in the back of my brain, taking readings, counting the heartbeats under the mounds, but remains silent.

With Ekene and Second gone, my sense of the slag takes on a different tone. There's an urgency in it, like an army marching toward me, the synchronised pound of a million feet vibrating the deck. It crawls up the back of my neck, slithering under my armour, digging hooks into my ribs, it feels...

I spin. It feels like the bogeyman breathing down my neck, but the only thing here is the grow-field, the slag casting yellow-white light over the mounds of my crew, throwing stark shadows all the way back to the hatch.

The hatch. Grey-green rims the edges, slithering through the open portal, clinging to the bulkhead on either side. More of it spills over the threshold, a carpet of viyu in which I feel the first faint touches of Aeotu, the AI weak and slow – hurting – but determined.

'Oh shit.' This isn't going to end well.

The veins of yellow between the mounds pulse brighter and reach out to the viyu, in a violent lunge, whipping across the deck, landing with a solid *thwack* to split the carpet in two.

There's more viyu coming through from the corridor, desperation and rage rising with the wave of fug, cresting before it spills through the hatch.

Yellow slag lifts around me like giant vines, and another and another. *Thwack. Thwack. Thwack.*

One moment I'm watching a yellow and green tide of war and the next I'm in a forest of slag, ripping itself off the deck, whipping past my head, skimming my ears, my shoulders, wind whistling in its wake. A vine catches my right shoulder, spins me around. Another crashes into my faceplate, takes out my feet. I'm on the deck, staring at the giant metal-stone girders of Aeotu's ribs, the constellation of Kuma going off in my head, trying to figure out how I got here and—

An anvil crushing my stomach. Air exploding from my mouth. Dude yowling. Hunt blaring in my head. Yellow crashing into my face—

# CHAPTER FOUR

*Brother.*

'Grea.'

A breath, a giant inhalation of too-big lungs – bigger than h'Rawd's, bigger than Hunt's – and then... *Brother.*

'Grea.' I reach for her, desperate to find her in the dark. 'Where are you?'

Long slim fingers wrap around my wrist, too long, too slim.

Wrong.

'Grea? What'd Euiva do to you?'

A breath on my face and I want to see, *need* to see but my eyes won't open. *Not... her.* And "her" is a collection of images, memories pressed into my mind on a kaleidoscope of unfathomable colour. A girl with my face, dark hair and golden complexion, a little thinner in the cheeks, but fuller in the hips and chest. Grea.

Not Grea.

But then... who else would call me brother?

Realisation sends a chill down my spine.

'Aeotu.' I breathe the name.

*Brother.* And now the... name? Title? It's neither of those things and yet... And yet it has a weight behind it, a meaning that presses on my chest and makes it more than just a word. *Help me, Brother.*

'No.' I'm shrinking back. Back. Back. Back. Trying to wrest my hand from Aeotu's grip, to pry the too-long finger-spikes from my wrist.

They hold tighter, sinking through armour and flesh, right into the core of me.

Pain. Not the fleshy, Old-Terra-look-at-all-that-blood kinda pain, but deeper. Knives slicing through the very fabric of myself, reaching for my anima, the tightly held core of what makes me *me*.

Comprehension dawns, a star going nova in my brain, 'cause I remember now, and I know where I am. My body might be in the grow-field, pinned under writhing cords of yellow slag – or then again, it might not, it wouldn't the first time I've been transported to another place while unconscious – but this place, where pain is of the anima and darkness prevails, this is the ora. The place between the psionic plane and reality, where Aeotu and her sisters live.

And here... Here I have power.

Molten metal explodes from my flesh.

Aeotu screams. Her pain is a floodlight, illuminating the ora, and now I see her, the shifting blackness of her skin, moving with all the colours of her mind, shifting with the whorls and patterns carved into her flesh. Tall and thin, the dual set of arms, four-fingered hands ending in wicked spikes. And her face... The space where a human's face would be is blank, a smooth oval devoid of features, held upright on a neck that slopes into her shoulders.

Alien, but human too.

Hunt is a shadow at my back, its blades springing from my forearms even as fire gathers on the second set of arms growing out my ribcage.

A little part of me – the part that doesn't hate, that doesn't want to crush Aeotu, to see her burn, that doesn't relish her screams – whispers that it would have been better if she were *more* alien, if she had eight legs and spikes growing out of her head, if she'd walked on six feet instead of two. Maybe then she wouldn't be so monstrous in my eyes, maybe then that tiny spark of compassion would make it through the rage consuming me.

But then again, maybe not.

I'm moving, gliding through the ora, blades a storm of molten metal-stone, all my anger, all my fear, all my loss stretching out ahead of me, wrapping around Aeotu's paws, anchoring her to the ground. I leap, blades drawn back for the kill and—

Mac, a shadow of him standing in my way.

Too close! No time. No time!

A slam of heart against chest, and I'm elsewhere. *Away* from Mac, on the other side of Aeotu.

Twist around. There's Aeotu, caught in the mire of my *emote*, Mac tearing at the sticky strands of it. Freeing her.

'No.' Rage is a tide that stains the ora with blood, fills it with images of *Citlali* imploding, the memory of the Sistermind's cold grip seeping through my bones, taking me over.

Hunt thrums in my heart, its armour becoming our armour, our arms, our blades, our cannons. Our core is a supernova, filling our veins with light and fury. Thrusters propel us, rage gathers in our cannons, and Mac is no longer Mac, he's a blip on our sensors, an asteroid spinning in our target's orbit. Nothing before our fury.

Target locked. We won't miss this time. Won't miss. Won't miss. Won't miss.

Impact.

Left blade glancing off chest armour, right sinking between the plates in the target's side, into flesh and out the other side. Aeotu is backing away from us, free of us. There is another impaled on our blades.

Alarms shrieking.

Wrong. Wrong. Wrong.

A hand, warm and strong pushing against my chest. Four fingers and a thumb against our collarbone. A face. Holy Terra, a *face*, brown eyes staring at me. Shock, so much shock it blazes within the ora, turning the black white. Pouring from me as much as Mac.

The blades are gone, and I am no longer us, but me, Kuma, catching my best-friend-maybe-love in my arms as he collapses. Both of us slipping through the threads of reality, the ora bleeding away like the blood gushing down Mac's side, over my stomach, my legs, an ocean of red filling the eter.

For a moment, as the eter solidifies around us, he's solid in my arms, no longer a shadow but flesh and bone, or as flesh and bone as you can get on the psionic plane.

'Mac?' I say.

His mouth is moving, but no sound is coming out.

'It's okay,' I say it, but the words are just words. I don't believe them, I'm never going to believe them again. 'It's going to be okay, I'm going to... Going to...' What am I going to do? What have I *done*? Mac is fading, the edges of him fuzzy, his features blurring, his weight dissipating. I'm holding smoke.

And then I'm holding nothing at all.

Where'd he go?

Warmth, the prick of tiny claws on my shoulder and a fuzz filling my head, chasing away the confusion.

Dude.

'Mac?' My yell echoes. 'Mac?!'

There's no answer.

'I'm sorry. I didn't... I didn't mean to.'

All the rage, all the hate and fury I had stored up against Aeotu... that's gone. In its place is... is something else. A complex well of guilt and grief, banging up against a solid wall of denial, black and depthless. Pressing against my heart, making it hard to breathe. Or maybe that's the slag crushing my ribs, weighing down my arms and my legs, turning me from a fleshy bag of Kuma into a black hole of Mac dying in my arms.

I didn't just kill me best friend. I didn't. I couldn't have. Could I? No. No. I just... just... What did I just do? He was alive, he had to be alive. He wasn't dying, the last memory I have of Mac isn't going to be him skewered on my blade, isn't going to be blood and pain and... and—

A hand on my shoulder, a blur of tendons and bones – long skinny fingers melting into thick white ones, fingernails glossy pink and then ragged tan. Emotion floods from it to me, jumbled shades of determination, disgust, rebuke and purpose, but no sympathy, no consolation. Just a stark need driving its way through my marrow, ripping the black hole of regret from my chest and filling it with purpose.

The psionic plane is gone and I'm in the real, flesh and blood and the slag crawling over my faceplate, a thin sheen of yellow through which I can see Aeotu's ribs.

The hand is still on my shoulder, pressing me into the floor as I struggle to get up.

It's not a real hand, but the psionic impression of one, fuelled by the minds collected behind Ekene's eyes. You wouldn't think a mental projection had the ability to hold you down, that a thought could trump muscle and nanite armour. But you'd be wrong.

*You're going to help us.* Ekene's voice is hard, implacable. Telling me how things are, and that purpose in my chest is agreeing, 'cause anything, *anything* is better than the despair it replaced.

'I was going to get you out.' I was going to shred the shit out of the fug mounds until Second and the slag stopped me. 'You're the ones who said no.'

*We did, but that's not how you're going to help us.*

'Then how?'

*Take the Sisters.*

He says that, and in my head I'm going 'take *what*?', imagining a plate full of spaceship-shaped cookies and me stashing them down the front of my shipsuit like a demented cookie thief.

But that's not it, not even in the same galaxy. No, Ekene follows the words up with a thought-packet, a giant glossy ball of information big enough to swallow me whole, wrapped in sticky strings of command. I'd back up, would turn tail and sprint the shit out of there, black hole or no, if Ekene's purpose and the slag weren't holding me in place.

The packet presses against my skull, almost too big to comprehend and then it's sinking through bone and grey-matter, a drop in the ocean that is me.

I wait. A heartbeat, a second, a minute. I wait like inspiration or knowledge or some divine fucking power is going to reach through the universe and fill my chest with thunder.

I keep waiting.

Silence. No dawning comprehension, no sudden insight. Nothing. Not even Ekene.

He's gone, taking the rest of the minds with him.

Purpose still fills my chest, prods me to wriggle my shoulders. Slag moves, squirming over belly and legs, giant yellow worms retreating into the compost heap of fug-covered Jørgens. I'm free and standing, my faceplate retreating, leaving just the delicate vines to support the HUD, numbers streaming past the corner of my right eye while diagnostics whir in the back of my brain.

And still I'm waiting for knowledge to strike, for what Ekene meant by "take the Sisters" to become clear beyond the knowledge that he wasn't referring to cookies.

Dude is fuzzing on my shoulder. The sound is off, there's a darkness in the comforting golden glow, an impression of teeth and blood and anger at Ekene for hijacking my brain.

I have the feeling I should be angry too, but anger would dislodge the purpose in my chest, and that would leave room for the black hole. For Mac.

A squeal from the HUD has me looking down.

The slag might have let me up, but it hasn't let me go. Thin yellow threads of the stuff are winding up my paws, sitting snug in the grooves on my shins and calves, a yellow inlay for the patterns carved in the grey-green armour. I hadn't noticed the patterns before, not that that should surprise me, there's a lot I haven't seen, what with the running and screaming and dyin—

I've never seen them before *on me.* The sight of them now doesn't surprise me, not really, not with the same symbols crawling over Aeotu's bulkheads, Hunt's chest, Mac—

Slag is bad. That thought is ringing in the back of my mind, but it's trapped behind the thought-packet unfurling in my head. Slag likes to eat fug and crush my chest. Dude is snarling, his every muscle straining to run down my arm and attack, but his paws are locked to my shoulder, his fug-self wrapped up in tendrils from my own.

The stickiness of the command wrapped around Ekene's thought-packet demands that I stay still, that I let the slag do its work. What work? That's what I want to know. How am I supposed to "take the Sisters"? *Where* am I supposed to take them? Despite my cookie fantasy, there was a sinister edge to Ekene's voice that spoke of more violent action, hinted at retribution...

It's the thought of revenge that does it, makes me remember *Citlali* implode, the dreadful, endless horror as my home, everything I ever knew, turned to atoms. There's no click, no door unlocking, there's just the knowledge Ekene shoved in my brain spreading through my synapses like it was waiting for that moment, that remembrance to fully integrate into my consciousness. And really, it should have been obvious from the start, should've smacked me in the head instead of that stupid vision of cookies.

*Take* the Sisters. Like Aeotu took *Citlali*, hijacking us for its own purpose.

And there's only one purpose worth considering now.

Revenge.

# CHAPTER FIVE

Ekene and his crew have been busy. The plan in my head is simple but complex, detailed right down to the last bolt. Most of it, the bits that have to do with *Aeotu* – her shell as opposed to her psyche – feel old and studied. The other bits, the ones that spread out across the constellation of the Sistermind, those are newer. Shiny and... disturbing. There's something in them, wriggling and squirming to get free, a nugget of knowledge I can't quite reach no matter how hard I try.

I wonder how long they've been planning this, how it was even *possible*. They've been trapped within stasis pods and in the grow-field, more vegetable than animal, and yet... obviously not. Obviously, I missed something, and the *kin* missed something, and Mum missed something.

I stop, dizzy as I follow that thought all the way to the memory of h'Rawd's whiskers on my chin, the sharp prick of his fangs, the coppery stench of blood on his breath. Old Terra, Mum and the kin, they killed them. Ripped out their throats, blood spewing down their chests, coating the air. Thin, translucent shreds of tendon and skin—

Vomit hits the deck between my paws, a thin yellow-ish bile with those little bits of not-carrot mixed in for good measure. I heave again, and then a third time, unable to stop my mind from filling in the images in my head, pulling details from the depths of memory to flesh out the horror. Onah had said their minds were gone, that they were empty shells, that the kin were being merciful, putting them out of their misery.

But how can you be in misery if your mind is gone? If you can't feel or think? How is that merciful, how is that righteous?

I'm panting, hands on knees, staring at the deck, at the vomit puddled around my paws, not really seeing any of it. Just seeing the horror playing out in my head.

Maybe Onah didn't know, maybe h'Rawd didn't check. When his teeth had been at my throat, I hadn't been able to reach him, had shouted and screamed in the psionic dark and touched nothing. And yet... and yet Onah had heard me, had spoken to me in that place.

Nothing makes sense, nothing but the horrible, terrifying pit in my chest, sucking all the good out of my memories, out of my heart. Turning everything I thought I believed on its head.

Kin are ruthless, everyone who's ever met one knows that. They do what needs to be done, even when it shrivels them up inside, but they're fair. Or at least, that's what I thought.

Mum's ruthless too.

That thought pops into my head, and for a second I wonder if someone put it there, helped it along. But no, it's just me out here in the corridor, staring at my paw-toes, at the orange bits of stomach lining swimming in bile. Just me filling my head with horror. Maybe, just maybe, Ekene's thought-packet helped it along, provided a detail I hadn't noticed, cleared my eyes of warm hugs and the soft press of her lips on my forehead.

Maybe.

Does it really matter? All I have is conjecture, imaginings fed by the nightmares building in the back of my brain.

Eventually it might matter, when I have the luxury of pausing, of figuring it all out. Of sleep.

Eventually.

But now is not then. Now is me and Ekene and all the people I once called crew trying not to die.

Now, I have a job to do.

I never thought I'd miss ropey grey-green strands of viyu, but then, I've never seen so much of the red shit either. It's gathered in the corridor like some kind of battalion awaiting attack orders.

It makes my skin crawl, brings back memories of acid crawling under my skin, of dark and pain. Of Grea torturing me. Of it erupting through the hangar deck and snatching crew.

Dude doesn't like the viyusa either. Between one breath and the next he's fugged-out, every nanometre of golden fuzz covered in armour, like a little armoured shuttle on my shoulder, melding with it.

Nothing's moving him.

Nothing would move me either, except the thought-packet nudging me forward.

Whatever I need to do, it's through here. Through the forest of red.

According to Hunt and the map spread over the HUD, I'm on *Aeotu*'s second-to-lowest deck, down near her stern, right above the hangar. The hangar where Mum and Dad and all the remaining crew are huddling under Hunt's cannons. The open hatch in front of me – the one leading into the sea of red – used to lead into what Hunt tells me were crew quarters.

Stepping over the threshold takes everything I have, plus the lie that everything's going to be all right to wash the courage down.

I'm already fugged. Already been changed and swallowed and manipulated by Aeotu. If Euiva or any of the other Sisters wanted to sweep me away to wherever they were taking the crew, they could have done it when they hijacked my brain to escape the ship graveyard.

That's what I'm telling myself as I step on the carpet of red. It's not helping. Neither is the thought of what all this viyusa is doing here, above the hangar. Above the crew.

One step in and I'm clenching every muscle I have, wondering if

I should be summoning the fug-blades, or if that'd just provoke the forest of death.

Two steps and the red hasn't swamped me yet.

Three and I'm thinking that whoever came up with this fabulous shit hole of an idea should be down here themselves.

Five steps and I'm still not getting eaten.

Ten and maybe, just maybe, I'm starting to relax.

A dozen paces in and it occurs to me that my self-deception might have been the truth.

The viyusa has no interest in me, and still… I can't shake the tension from my shoulders.

'Why are we here?' I'm not sure who I'm asking, Hunt or the knowledge Ekene shoved into my brain. I'm not even sure why I'm putting it into words when a thought would do, what with both of my potential sources of information not having physical ears.

There's no answer, not even from Dude who's little more than a weird growth on my shoulder now. His armour has thickened, and I think he's repurposed some of mine, made it so he's an amorphous shoulder ornament the viyusa would need a laser to pry off. It'd probably be easier to chop *my* shoulder off than to pry him loose, and I'm wondering what has him so freaked. The little guy has never lacked for courage, has leapt *into* the face of certain death more times than I care to count, and now… I'm scared.

The fear doesn't stop me moving, if anything, it quickens my pace.

My feet seem to know where they're going, even if the rest of me hasn't figured it out yet. If it weren't for Dude and the viyusa, this whole shit with the slowly unfolding thought-packet would be pissing me off. Instead, I concentrate on the corridor.

Like every other corridor on *Aeotu*, it's shaped like an oval on its side with the bottom edge flattened. The bulkheads and ceiling are one seamless whole that flow into the deck; no corners, no sharp edges save for the ones carved into the walls. Intricate lines flowing into whorls.

I'm pretty sure if it weren't for the viyusa crawling over everything, all those lines and whorls would be shifting in their slow-motion dance, trying to suck my attention.

Seems the viyusa is good for something after all.

The pull in my gut is leading me forward, through curving hallways, then a left turn down another – shorter and narrower than the first – and out into another thoroughfare, the curve here tighter. Enough so that it reduces my line-of-sight to eleven metres. I guess we're close to the centre of the ship. If the structure of wohol ships holds true to *Citlali* or, you know, *Citlali* held true to wohol design – this is not the first time that I've wondered about the similarities – then whatever is around the next bend or down the next hallway, is important. That's how it worked on *Citlali* at least, the centre of the ship being the most protected.

Apparently the viyusa doesn't agree with me. There's less of it on this inner ring than there was on the outer. Hunt whispers that it's because the hangar is no longer below us, and doesn't that just send ice crawling through my veins. I should be back there, cutting down the viyusa before it snatches more crew.

Hunt doesn't agree, floods my brain with probabilities and scenarios, all of which I lose. And Dude... Dude's still a frozen lump on my shoulder, huddled in the armoured blob, tiny claws sinking through my skin at the thought of turning back.

It hurts, and not in a flesh-pain way, but in the I-can't-just-leave-them way, right deep down in my anima. Even though they hate me, even though they're *scared* of me. And still... Mac—

Hunt's the best chance the crew have, the mech's canons and its blades will keep them safe more effectively than me slashing and burning through the battalion of red. That's what Hunt is telling me. Dude still isn't saying anything, and the pull... Well, that has a gravity all its own.

And so I keep walking. I concentrate on scanning the walls, on keeping my paws out of the little bit of viyusa patrolling these parts, keeping my eyes out for whatever it is the pull wants me to find.

There are gaps in the inner curve of the bulkhead, hatches open onto small cubicles made from the same off-white metal-stone covered in patterns. If these are meant to be crew quarters, I'm guessing the wohol didn't spend a lot of time in them or maybe small, tight spaces reminded them of home. Wherever that was.

Still... I've seen the beings who created *Aeotu*, the wohol, even if only in the kins' ancient training memories, and as frozen corpses in space. The wohol are bipedal aliens, a third again as tall as me – even with the extra few centimetres offered by my fug feet – with broad shoulders and a double set of arms, and the little cubicle I stick my head in looks okay for a human but squishy for one of them.

That these are crew quarters raises questions about their home planet. Why would beings who built such big ships, with their wide egg-shaped corridors, cram themselves into such small quarters? Or was *Aeotu* different?

I haven't seen another wohol ship, not on the inside. Maybe they're empty ovoid shells, just hull and engines and AI core, floating through space. Or maybe they're vast open plains, each deck a new environment, an estate where the wohol can roam at will, full of trees and fields of grass. And maybe I'm wasting my time thinking about useless things because scanning for I-know-not-what doesn't take much brain power, and if I don't think about useless things then I have to think about other things, like the viyusa, and the crew and Mac—

Useless thoughts are better.

I'm not sure if Dude would agree, and so what if the critter doesn't? It's not like he's my conscience, right? Not as if I need to answer to him for everything I do, and yet there's that place deep in my anima, where that thought doesn't ring true.

We've gone through a lot together, the fuzzbutt and I, so much in such a short amount of time and—

Here. My paws stop, sudden enough the rest of my body isn't ready for it. I stumble.

The corridor is still the same, carved off-white walls, openings where hatches have crumbled away or been left open. No bright flashing dots or screaming red signs, not even a hint of viyusa. I guess that's different; I must have lost the red nanites sometime while I was thinking useless shit, but it's not what dragged my paws to a stop.

No, that something is on the inner curve of the corridor, buried in the lines carved in the bulkhead. A whorl the size of my head pulses, the lines throbbing like veins or maybe a heart, but still, it's not that. No, it's the lines that curl off from it, trailing toward the deck, forming its own whorl, a spiral tight as a fist, sinking into a single point.

I'm on my knees, my forehead against the bulkhead, faceplate disappeared before I know it, sucked in by the pattern. Only Dude, the sharp sting of his teeth on my earlobe, breaks me out of it, stops me before I moosh my face closer, happily shredding skin, spilling blood to find the end point of that black hole.

Ekene's pull isn't helping. Whatever it is I need to do, it's through the spiral.

I touch it.

The deck falls away.

# CHAPTER SIX

What I want to know is who the fuck puts a trapdoor right where you have to stand to open it? And then I want to find said fuckwit and dump them in the sloshy, gooey shit crawling up my nose.

My faceshield reformed right bloody quick, but not quick enough that some of the goop covering my head, my shoulders, every fucking millimetre of me, didn't get in. It smells like mould, but something else too, something familiar that shivers up my nape and leaves shards of fear behind. I want to take another sniff, figure it out, but that'd just drive the shit deeper into my nasal passages and those icy little shards of fear warn me that wouldn't be wise.

Instead, I try to figure out where I am.

There's no light, no sensation – not after the initial stomach-hollowing drop and *plop* into whatever the fuck it is I'm floating in. Or sinking. I could be sinking.

I can't feel walls or a deck, hot or cold. Can't hear either, not the thrum of an engine or the throb of blood against my eardrums. Can't even feel Dude, save when I lift a hand to see if he's still there.

He is, hunched on my shoulder, back in his lump. Unmoving, not even the fuzz of his mental presence to keep me company. Today is obviously *not* his favourite day. Can't say I blame him, it's been pretty shitty for me too.

So, no sight, sound or sensation and the only smell I'm getting is the mouldy-fear smell of the goop in my nose. The HUD's not working either. Not so much as a flicker of power. The only thing working is Hunt. The mech is whirring along in the back of my brain, neither concerned nor anxious, emotionless as only an AI can be. Or at least, a human-built AI. Obviously the wohol did things differently, created a true artificial lifeform. One that doesn't just think but *feels*.

I never thought of it that way before and the shiver that clutches my spine rings with the memory of Ag, the madness in the sub-AI's holographic eyes.

A... vat? Tank? Room? Wherever I am it's not the place to be contemplating the existence of artificial life, of ships capable of deciding if I'm worthy to live or not. I should be more concerned with getting out, finding a pocket of oxygen and not suffocating, but the *pull* is weighing me down, holding legs and arms still when they should be swimming for the surface.

Is there a surface? Or has the trapdoor snapped shut, leaving just the ceiling? A thin film of oxygen between goo and metal-stone, enough to tease starved lungs with the suggestion of salvation before the goo pulls me back under?

Panic builds under Ekene's *pull*, churning in my gut, making my heart pound, my breath come harder. And still, the pull holds my arms at my sides, resists the urge to kick my feet. There's something I have to do here, a purpose for this trip into murks-ville; it'd be really nice if someone, namely Ekene, had thought to share that knowledge, but nothing comes from the thought-packet. Nothing save the need to be *here*.

A glow in the corner of my vision. I try to find it, but as soon as I focus in its general direction, the light becomes a ghost, or maybe a smudge, half there but mostly not. All I know is it's coming from my legs, or somewhere below them. I concentrate, think I see the thin lines of yellow wrapping around my calves and creeping over my knees. There's only one thing that could be; yellow and legs equals the slag lining the patterns in my armour.

The glow brightens until I can see it straight on, still kinda fuzzy at the edges, like the light is bleeding into the goo. And maybe it is, because as I watch, the light changes, becomes a nimbus, stretching into the goo in a way that's impossible for light, not a straight line fading at edges, but ballooning, getting brighter in the middle like there's something solid at its centre. The balloon grows, expanding outwards, less balloon and more hand, fingers short and stubby but lengthening.

As the fingers grow, the centre solidifies, grows veins. At first thin and then thicker and thicker still. It's hard to see, but soon enough I can't *not* see it. One moment they're filaments, the next they're thick as my thumb with more growing, taking to the goo like roots to soil. Really, *really* good soil. Super-fertilised.

The slag is going to be burned on the back of my retinas... if it doesn't fry my eyeballs first.

I have the use of my arms back, and my hands are plastered over my eyes, but even through flesh, blood and bone, through my faceshield and eyelids, the glow presses on my retinas, stains it red and lines it with the pulse of the blood in my veins. Dude had the right idea, hunkered down in his viyu shell. I could really use a little fug power myself. I imagine my armour curling over my head, scales forming over my faceplate, turning the transparent film of nanites opaque. So thick not even a sun could burn through, but the red glow doesn't dull, it intensifies.

*Hunt!*

The mech whirs, reaches back through the umbilicus and... Nothing.

*{{ Power drain, }}* it says.

Power drain, but what— The slag.

Fuck.

Should have thought of that.

It takes energy to make light, and the slag is doing its very best to out burn a star. I'm not sure, exactly, where the armour gets its power, I mean I'm ninety-nine percent sure it runs off me. It sure as hell has used me as a battery before, taking my body heat as fuel for the thrusters that formed out of the bone and armour of my back.

So, my guess is the slag is doing the same thing, taking the armour's power, *my* energy to fulfil Ekene's plan.

Ekene is really fucking up my day.

Don't get me wrong, I'm down with getting Ekene and the others out of their mounds, *more* than down with bringing all the pain and fear in my belly crashing down on Euiva. But this...

I guess I shouldn't be surprised, everyone is using someone else, I'm just not okay with them using me. If Ekene had asked I would have said yes, would have dived into this goo and lit myself on fire, but he *didn't* ask and this power is *mine*.

My body. My armour, and I didn't consent to this.

Did.

Not.

Consent!

The last is bottled fury, exploding outwards. The shockwave ripples through the goo, disrupting the light, and for a second my HUD flickers to life and armour moves, and then... The HUD dies, the armour stops moving and the light blazes yet again.

Fuck.

Determination isn't going to be enough.

Thought-packets like those Ekene shoved into my brain, made of knowledge and experience, are a telepathic ability. And even though I can read thoughts sent to me, that's all I can do. Digging Ekene's thought-packet out is beyond the realm of my talents, even if it hadn't already melded with my brain and wound itself though my psyche. I doubt even the Regan herself could do it. So there's no getting myself out of this by slipping into the eter and shucking Ekene's instructions like a bad dream.

No. To get out of this, I have to fight. Only problem... I'm fighting with myself.

Or maybe I just have to fight the slag.

I concentrate on it, the memory of it nestled in the patterns in my armour, how it stood out against the grey-green, made the whorls and swoops into something beautiful and delicate. The way it slithered up my ankle, wound around my calf. I imagine how it must have looked on my back, trailing down my arms, threaded through the thin stems curving over my face. I bet I would have made some of those fantasy knights Mac used to like so much, jealous.

And as I imagine it, I sweep my thoughts through it, *feeling* it, connecting. Hunt is there with me, reaching through the mental umbilicus that connects us. And there, a gentle fuzz, is Dude. Together we claim the slag and *pull*.

It's not the same as Ekene's *pull*, not an itch driving me toward a destination unknown. This is a reclaiming. This is us, taking back *my* body.

Warmth floods my skin, burning when the slag sinks through flesh, into veins and bones. Behind my hands, the sun-bright glare fades.

We *pull* harder. The glow lessens again—

The thought-packet pulls me back, the glare renews.

The musty scent of goo winds through my nasal passages, working its way down the back of my throat, metallic and familiar. For a moment the slag is forgotten and my hands are on my faceplate, scrambling to pull the shit out as it wraps around my tonsils and—

*{{ Wait, }}* says Hunt.

Under my skin, Dude takes control of my muscles.

The goo in my throat pulses. Around me the rest of it does the same, and my armour responds.

Or maybe it's Hunt responding through my armour. It's certainly not me, I'm too busy trying not to gag on the shit, too busy trying not to panic.

The goo, both inside and out, ripples. Warms. A presence, kaleidoscopic and huge, swims within it.

Aeotu.

The slag blazes in response, a tiny fish flashing its tail against the monster rising from the depths.

Alarm slams through me, not my own, not the *pull's* either. It rings with the dark olive of Ekene, the restlessness of the minds held together with the thread that makes him a Regan.

*Stop it,* Ekene says. The shadowy behemoth of Aeotu is bright in his thoughts, even as he presses a new command against my skull, this one thick with desperation.

It's the desperation that does it. Before Ekene's thought-packet was clear and clean, free of emotion, nothing for me to grab onto but this one... Wrap emotion like that around a thought-packet and send it to a kin, they'll recoil, maybe even slap you back into last millennium, but hand an empath the same thing and... Well, you get the idea.

I grab the new thought-packet in both hands and pull it apart, let the knowledge within unfold, a diorama spread before me. As if this packet is a key, the previous one unfolds too and I get it now, like *really* get it.

Where I am. What Ekene wants me to do. The whole plan. Laid bare before me.

It's pretty ingenious. Scary. Terrifying even, but ingenious. It'll probably work too.

Only problem is I'm seeing that little nugget of knowledge that had tried to wriggle its way out before, and now I'm not really sure I want the plan to work, not if it means doing *that.*

*It's our chance,* Ekene says. *It'll be just like when the Sistermind used you, except the other way round;* we'll *use them.*

The slag continues to blaze, branches spreading through the goo like roots spreading through soil.

The goo is viyu, or proto-viyu or something. I remember Grea telling me Aeotu produced it the way biologicals produced blood.

I'm in Aeotu's marrow and the slag... the slag is cancer spreading through it, infecting it. Changing it.

I should be jumping for joy, putting my psionic shoulder to the slag's wheel and throwing everything I had into helping it grow. Instead... Instead, I'm floating here, doing... Well, nothing. I can't even say that it's Hunt holding me back, or Dude. Not even the shadowy presence of Aeotu, although she's got something to do with it.

It's Mac. The memory of him in my arms, my blade puncturing his side. The look in his eyes...

Mac.

A shadow brushing my cheek, there and then gone.

Aeotu is all around me, the proto-viyu pulsing in time with the goo in my throat, matching my heart.

Sadness, the dark blue of grief dulls the slag's blaze.

In the back of my mind, Hunt falls silent and Dude's fuzz becomes soft, a blanket laid over my shoulder to comfort me.

The Ekene-mind reaches through it all, a dark olive lance oblivious to the emote dulling the world. It *pushes* a command before it, wrapped not in desperation, although that is there, barely contained within the shell of determination and command. *Stop Aeotu, Kuma.*

Stop Aeotu.

Kill Aeotu.

Kill Mac.

Kill him again.

Denial shivers through the goo, prismatic and dark. Half-awake, half... Dead?

No. Not dead. Almost dead.

I slip between the threads of reality, into the ora.

Aeotu waits for me. Tall, the colours of her being shifting under her skin, but slower than before and muted, her vibrancy being sucked away.

'You killed *Citlali*,' I say.

She does not respond.

'You *gave* me to the Sisters.'

Still no response, not even the twitch of an arm, just those colours shifting under her skin, but maybe... Maybe that was a response.

I try again, switching my attention from the featureless plane of her face to her torso. 'You gave me to them like I was a thing,' I say, pushing pain and accusation before me, staining the ora orange-red.

Blue and yellow and a hue I have no name for knot over her chest, where a human's heart would be. It's a gnarly, twisted thing that hurts to look at.

I tear my eyes away and it feels like tearing my *own* heart out, like plunging a sword through Mac's chest.

'You still did it,' I say, and even though I want to throw the words at her, to blame her, I can't. That knotted, gnarly thing is lodged in my chest, growing tendrils like the slag in Aeotu's viyu. A cancer spreading through my system.

*Sisters.* Her voice shivers through the ora, coming from everywhere and nowhere all at once. In the nothingness, bright lights appear. A constellation of suns linked one to the other with shimmering ropes. The Sistermind, ships just like Aeotu; artificial life bound up in metal-stone and propelled through the void by fusion generators powerful enough to destroy a moon. They're distant, cold, the space around them shivering with strange sounds, whispers felt by the prickle of hair on my nape.

Aeotu turns, or maybe I turn, or them, maybe the universe turns, distorts, enlarges, and there, hidden within the blaze of the closest star, is a point of red. A pinprick beside a leviathan, its light dull, its voice lost amidst the whispering. But familiar. The pinprick is restless, shifts and turns with sharp, uncoordinated jerks and shudders. It reaches out, thin strands of itself trying to escape the glow of the star, but held captive within its light.

Compulsion, a deep-seated need buried in the core of me, has me reaching back, zooming through the ora to—

Aeotu jerks me back. *No.* Fear stains her chest, the bright sickly yellow of it spilling up her throat, winding around each of her four arms. *That is Euiva.* She points to the brighter star.

Euiva. A snarl pulls back my lips. Euiva to whom Aeotu handed me like a piece of meat, whose plan it was to destroy my home. Euiva, who took my sister, *warped* her and then swallowed her up.

The red dot.

'Grea.' Her name is a breath in the ora, is my arms and legs, the very essence of me arrowing through the nothingness to touch my twin.

It reaches her and it's like the ora pauses, the entire universe standing absolutely still.

What comes back is not Grea.

It's a whip, lightning cracking back through the ora. Startled, angry—

Aeotu is in front of me, stumbles as she takes the lightning in my place.

It is gone as quick as it came, folded back into the star that is Euiva.

Why? Why did Euiva attack? Why did Aeotu step in front of me? Why, why, why?

Aeotu is on one knee, two hands held to the scorch mark on her chest while the other two are braced against the ground, head down, back of her neck exposed.

I'm standing over her and Hunt is in the back of my brain, calculating widths, reaction times, trajectories. It would be so easy to draw a sword, a nano-second to ignite the blade. I wouldn't even have to wait, it'd be molten by the time I lifted it over my head. Bring it down, a perfect thirty-three-degree arc, fifty-three millimetres per second, a hundred newtons of force and Aeotu's head would roll, bouncing across the ora. Would it dissipate? Turn to smoke like Mac, or would her corpse wither and shrink, flesh or whatever the Old Terra she was made of rotting away until only bones were left?

'Why?' My own voice shocks me, the hollow boom of it, all the questions tumbling out on that one word. Why did you protect me? Why shouldn't I kill you?

'Why?' I say again, stronger this time and kneel beside her, leaning to peer into that featureless face. 'You took us, ate my friends, destroyed my home. Grea is... ' I look but can no longer see the red pinprick within the star. I turn back. 'Whatever that is, she's there because of you. You started this.'

She lifts her head, and even though she has no face, no nose, no mouth, she captures me, holds me tight in a gaze without eyes. *No, you started this*, she says.

Black hits me; not the everything/nothing that pervades the ora but another darkness, a true darkness, one that sings with a million voices, songs of deep, cold places, of hate and death and pain. An ageless, endless myriad that sounds like kin underwater, for the single reason that centuries ago water-kin put it there. As sleek and sophisticated as the command Ekene pushed into my brain was, it is nothing compared to the precision and complexity of the thing nestled deep within Aeotu's mind.

I have never met a water-kin, there were none on *Citlali*; the lack of liquid water and the fear they inspired not just in humans but in their fellow kin made space inhospitable for them. They scare the shit out of me too.

'I'm not water-kin.'

*They are part of you.* The swirl of DNA fills the air, qwans perching on the nodules of genes, rucnarts stalking along the ladder between. *Your abilities are theirs.*

'No—' Because, really, they're not. Kin, no matter if they're water- or tree- or air, don't do empathy. It's as foreign to them as jetting through a vacuum is to me, or at least, as foreign as it *used* to be; Hunt and fug-thrusters notwithstanding.

But Aeotu isn't interested in that. Anger rises in her, born of pain and loneliness and fear. I recognise it, not because I can see the colours staining the ora, but because I *know* them, because they reside in my own chest, because they led me to kill my best friend. And now... Now as I stare into Aeotu's face, it's no longer featureless, no longer a flat plane. There are hollows for her eyes, the long narrow bump of a nose, the dip and curve of cheeks, the slash of lips, the rounded point of a chin.

Familiar, like looking in a mirror, because her face is *my* face. Not Grea's with her thicker lashes and the challenge flashing in her eyes, and not some strange amalgamation of slit-pupiled wohol and human, but *mine*. Right down to the slightly-too-prominent-to-be-a-girl bobble in my throat.

The only thing different are the colours coruscating under her skin.

I'm halfway across the ora before I know it, scrambling backward on hands and butt, denial an oil slick in my wake, but Aeotu keeps pace. Her face – my face – is in my face, inescapable. And still I try, scrambling across the endlessness of the ora, where time and distance mean nothing. As fast as I move, Aeotu stays with me, her face never far from mine.

I stop.

She stops. She's crouched over me, four arms caging my legs; leans closer, pushing the sticky black tide of the water-kins' poison before her. An offering or a threat?

*This,* she says, shaking that black tide. *This is you, this is why.*

She throws the blackness at me. I'm already braced, shields as tight as they'll go, as thick as I can make them and still it makes no difference. It could be the ora, Aeotu, or the fact that the tide is of the water-kin, has carried their species-crushing might through the centuries, unspoiled by time or distance. Whatever it is, I'm lost.

This is not like slipping into the Aer, the dream-world constructed by the kin. This is not meant to keep curious Jørgens out, not meant to shield and discourage. I can't twist and shake it off. No. The blackness is cruel and ruthless. Is the final act of an ancient war, an act of desperation by a species that knew it was outmatched. That turned its enemies' own minds against them, to make them not just destroy each other, but obliterate them from existence.

It is merciless.

I am swallowed, water like the void over my head, flooding down my throat, pushing through my pores, seeping into every bit of me, cold hard fingers seeking out my anima, burrowing into the skin between everything and what is me. If it gets in... Will I be Kuma anymore? Will it kill me?

No. I push it back, ripping and slashing, a snarl on my lips. No, I say again, turning the thought into a shield. Hard. Impenetrable. The fingers smack against it before sliding over the thin skin, over and under, seeking another way around.

The shield won't keep them at bay forever. I need to get out.

There's a glimmer overhead, a prick of light. I thrash toward it, hard strokes pulling me through the black. It is close. It is there, it is—

I burst through the surface, onto an off-white deck. *Aeotu*'s bulkheads curve overhead, soft shadows shifting over the off-white surface and beings – wohol – thundering past me. It's not like their size is a revelation, like I didn't *know* just how tall they were but this... Seeing them like this is different. Is a new way to appreciate the breadth of their shoulders, the weird play of muscles under their uniforms as their two sets of arms swing with each stride. The soft *thud* their paws make as they run, the grim set of their mouths, the alienness of their flat-nosed faces, the size of their hands. They could swallow my face with one of those hands, wrap their three fingers and one thumb around my head and pop it right off, the musculature in their forearms barely straining. Or else they'd just dig their short, blunt claws into the soft bits – eyes, ears, the dip at the base of my neck – and pierce my brain.

They're running, glancing over massive shoulders, pulling up others when they stumble, pushing hovers with the sick ahead of them. Fear. I can't see the sticky yellow staining the psionic plane but I recognise it, nonetheless. Even though I don't understand the speech that passes between them – sibilant sounds strange enough that I don't even know if what they're speaking are words. Whatever they are, there's a pitch to them, high and piercing, which reaches into my eardrums and leaves claw marks in its wake.

A new screech joins the cacophony and the wohol run faster.

I run with them, pounding down stairs – too-deep for human legs but perfect for wohol – join the stream of grey-uniformed aliens as they dash for the airlock, and then out, through the double doors.

I'm stopped at the outer airlock, slamming into an invisible barrier as the crew disappear down an umbilicus and into the soft glow of a sister ship.

*Natska*, Aeotu says from beside me. The giant ghost of another ship overlays the vision of the crew and umbilicus, the ovoid hull, the carvings, and the mournful cry of siblings parting.

*I tried to stop, but all I could do was warn.*

From within memory-Aeotu, the screech rises until is passes through human hearing. The crew run faster, their voices rising, strident, panicked. One stops, hauls another along behind it, pushing them into the tube, reaching back for another crew member even as *Natska*'s airlock *snaps* shut. Screeching. Running. Hands and bodies slamming against the sister ship's airlock, then—

The explosion of atmosphere slams into my back, would shove me into the void but for the invisible barrier. The wohol are not so lucky. Bodies tumble into the cold dark of space, the unforgiving nothingness of vacuum, sucked out by explosion decompression.

*Kill.* The command shivers through the memory, the water-kins' black tide wrapping sticky tendrils around memory-Aeotu's paws, winding through the patterns carved in her skin, much like the slag winds through mine. It wraps tighter. *Kill* it says again. And so she does.

# CHAPTER SEVEN

*I don't want to die.* The thought – mine? Aeotu's? – follows me back into the real, back into the goo.

I'm still floating, the slag is still blazing although not growing, not anymore. Viyu has formed around it, crystalline structures encasing the yellow branches, holding it back. It is fragile though, I can sense the cracks, the crazing. Just one good push, a burst of will and the slag would shatter it, eat it up and turn it to something different. Something new.

Dude vibrates on my shoulder, his attention on the slag, on the wrongness emanating from it, and the fuzz of his presence grates under my skin.

Aeotu is neither here nor in my head, but everywhere, a little bit of her here, a little bit there. And it was the echo of *her* thought I heard, her face with my features that I see in my mind's eye.

*Finish it.* That is Ekene's voice, his command beating against my brain.

*Don't want to die.* It is less speech than it is emotion, a wash of despair and anger, of hope and desperation.

No. And I don't know if I'm talking to Ekene or Aeotu or myself.

Power runs through the proto-viyu, strong pulses of light to rival the slag, lifting up from points in the deck – not so far below. I can see where I am now and the place is not as big as I thought, a couple of good kicks and I'm butting up against the top of the tank, running my hands over the surface, alert for the slightest bump or ridge of the hatch I came through.

*Finish it!*

No. And now I *am* talking to Ekene.

*Kuma!* Rage echoes through Ekene's voice, strong enough to ripple the goo, pulses from the crystalline slag, the trace-work wound around my own body.

No, I say again.

There's a ridge under my fingers, and I trace the outline of a hatch. A thought to Hunt, to Aeotu beyond it, and light rims the—

Pain. Knives slicing into calves and forearms, through flesh down to bone. The breath to scream is caught in my throat, stuck between the spasm of muscles and the desperate need to breathe. There is new light, the vicious yellow of the slag tracing the patterns in my armour, the pale white of the hatch outlined above, growing smaller and smaller as the slag pulls me down.

And pain. The knives becoming blowtorches, or perhaps Hunt's fug-blades turned molten, not content with merely slicing but burning and searing. The meaty stench of myself flooding my helmet. It takes my vision, stops my heart. Somewhere distant is Dude, the fuzz chasing the pain, flowing under my skin, trying to take over tendon and limb, and behind him there's Hunt, filling my head with numbers, scenarios, the power of a star at its heart but no way to help.

And there, a mirage floating in the goo, is Ekene, the hard set of his mouth, the dark line of his brow. Hands cluster on his shoulders, a dozen of them reaching out from the shimmer of the psionic plane, connected one to the other and then back to him, with a slim olive thread. Determination swallows his feet like an Old Terra genie, legs lost in the bronze fog of his power. No other emotion disturbs the bronze, not a hint of guilt or remorse, not the slightest waver of doubt.

*Finish it,* Ekene says again. *Feed the slag, let us take this ship and then we can take the rest. Do it, and we can rescue Grea and the others that the aliens have stolen.*

Grea? They can rescue Grea?

*Don't want to die.* Aeotu's words echo within my head, and in my memory her face becomes my face.

I don't want to die either, but I want my sister. I *need* my sister.

Aeotu, her forehead pressed to mine, lashes brushing my cheekbones, breath mingling with mine, void-dark eyes swallowing me.

For just a second, I see Mac in her gaze.

*I'm your sister,* she says and pushes power into my bones, a volcano to obliterate Ekene's knives.

I scream.

*I'm your sister,* she says again.

My bones are too narrow, my skin too small. The bands of slag tracing through the armour are shackles, my flesh rising in armour-covered mountains between them as the power fills me. They're going to slice me into Kuma-bits, going to fill the goo-tank with blood and guts and marrow, and the proto-viyu will feed, will take the pulverised bits of me and grow.

*Stop!* That is Ekene, but not just him. His voice echoes with the others piled behind him, eighty-four consciousnesses using his mouth, their bronze determination saturated with fear. *Kuma, stop! You'll kill yourself!*

I can't stop. It's not me. It's not me!

*They cannot take you,* Aeotu says and in her mind the Ekene-multitude is haloed in red. A target.

So you're killing me?

*Not killing. You are Brother.* She pushes more power through my bones. *Saving,* she says. *Saving us both.*

The armour explodes, and maybe I explode with it, pieces of myself shooting through the proto-fug along with the nanites flying from my body. There should be more pain, should be blood and fire, should be screaming. Instead, there's goo. And light. So much light. Enough to wipe out the slag. My bones are full of starlight, not a thin twinkle, millions of years old before it hits the back of your eyes, but the carbon-searing intensity of a supernova, the anima-obliterating heat of fusion, the reality-ripping strength of a black hole. My flesh is a thin layer of denial holding my insides in, stopping my guts from mingling with the viyu.

And then... *SHUUUCKKK.*

It snaps back. A rubber band slapping me in the face, except it's the fragments of the fug armour, the proto-viyu and slag mixed with it, slapping my entire body. A full-body *whomp*, and if I thought I was in pain before, with Aeotu treating my body like a power conduit, it's nothing to this, to *things* piercing my skin, my eyeballs, my hair, my tongue.

Dude! I reach for him, for Hunt for anything to pull me out, to stop the torture.

There is only pain.

It stops. The pain that is.

It stops and leaves me hanging in goo. It doesn't feel real, the absence of it I mean. Maybe I'm unconscious, slipped into the eter where nothing can touch me, or maybe I'm dead.

I don't feel dead. I feel tired, the kinda groggy tired where your mouth tastes like mouldy shit and your eyes burn when you open them. It's the kind of tired that comes from sleeping too long, where the only way to get out of it is to wake up and do something. Like kill a spaceship.

*I'm not going to die.*

'Aeotu.' The moment I open my mouth I remember the goo, about the lack of a faceplate between it and me, but proto-viyu doesn't rush in to choke me, doesn't coat my tongue with its familiar-mouldy taste. My eyes snap open.

There's nothing there. Well, not *nothing*. There's goo, although not the shit I remember, not exactly. I mean, it's still translucent and there's still crystallised slag threaded through it, but now... Now the slag looks different. It's spread through the tank in little bursts, stars winking in the ether, or maybe they're space stations, crystals formed up around them like tiny habitat rings. Each one is tethered in place, a thin vein of glowing yellow-green dropping from the bottom of it to the tank's floor, and on the floor... Well shit, that's kinda pretty.

*New viyu,* Aeotu says. *Stronger, different. Ours.*

A miniature nanite city sprawls below us, delicate spires of yellow-threaded green growing from the floor, thin at the top, nanometres wide, spilling down into intricately-worked bases. Filigree or lace or something, made out of slag and fug, or maybe slag-fug or whatever. It glows from within, the base of each delicate tower generating its own light, or maybe they're just sitting on the power nodes on the base of the tank. Wherever the power is coming from, the towers feed it out into the highways and bridges strung between them and neighbouring towers in gentle pulses. Some rapid, some slow. The towers at the centre, right under my feet, are the tallest.

*{{ Three-point-four-eight metres. }}*

Hunt!

It pulses in acknowledgement, sending warmth through my belly and in the next heartbeat my HUD flares to life. Numbers and diagrams spread before my eyes, tracing the flow of energy, measuring the distance between me and the tip of the tallest tower.

Three-point-seven millimetres— No, hang on. I move my feet and the tip of the tower moves with me. I move them a little more, and, okay so maybe it's a little more violent than it needs to be, but the tower follows every single twitch like it's attached... Because it is. Attached that is, with tiny filaments hooked around my toes, sliding up my paws, curling around the backward turn on my ankle.

I'm not going to panic. I'm not going to pan—

*Don't panic,* Ekene says. *It's almost done.*

Done? My heart's in my throat, pounding hard enough to give my airway serious cause for concern, and it takes me awhile to marshal my thoughts, to strip the lets-not-call-it-panic out and form the words in my head. I take a deep breath. Done what?

*Feeding*, says Aeotu, like that's something normal, like Aeotu's version of feeding doesn't involve chewing up bits of my friends and my home and—

*Kuma*. And I guess Ekene can kinda see where this was going, empath or not, 'cause he's got a mental hand on my shoulder, or should I say a clamp on my thoughts and he's pressing down hard. *It's okay.*

'Okay' comes with a packet of memories, images and emotions, not all of them his, but most. They're strange, because they're not physical memories, or images, not the kind of things you experience with skin and eyes, but with the mind. Interrupting them is the trick, prising out the fanciful stuff like fug eating my bones, to get to the truth. Or as truthful as anything can be when it's run through the filter of another's experience. These memories show Ekene and the ghosts of his multitude standing in the eter, me hanging in mid-air, slightly more visible than the ghosts, although not by much; Dude hunched on my shoulder, the umbilicus that connects me to Hunt disappearing through the threads of reality. And there, behind and *through* me, like I'm some kind of window, is another shape.

Tall and sleek, black skin under which a kaleidoscope roils, its face peering through mine.

Aeotu.

Memory-Ekene pauses, head turning slightly like he's listening to something. Has he heard Aeotu? But no, his lips are moving and the hands on his shoulders... the murmurs of the multitude at his back? 'What are you?' He/they say.

'Sissster.' The word comes out of my mouth, uses my voice, but it belongs to Aeotu.

'You are not Grea.' And apparently, it's not just me being used as a mouthpiece, except when the multitude does it, it echoes through Ekene's voice, a dozen voices, each speaking a different word. 'You're one of them, one of the aliens.' Accusation and the killing edge of fear spill from Ekene's feet.

'Yesss.' A pause, then, 'We don't want to die.'

'Then get out of our friend.'

'Friends do not kill friendsss.' There is something in those words, Aeotu referencing others more than just me, a dagger of knowledge thrown at Ekene.

Ekene doesn't move, but around him the air shifts, becomes hard, the bronze of determination forming spears in the eter. 'You're the one holding Kuma hostage.'

'No. He is Brother. Kill me, kill him.' Aeotu pauses and I wonder if she meant to make it sound like a threat, it doesn't feel that way, although the line between threat and warning is thin enough it's almost impossible to see. 'Kill you,' she adds softly. And okay, that *does* sound like a threat, except there's fear and loss and the dark black-pink of heartbreak in the eter, spilling from my feet.

Ekene's a Regan, which is pretty much the pinnacle of psionic power – telepath, empath, able to wind through the minds of other Jørgens and bind them together into a collective strong enough to take on the world, or at least that was what the original Regan did, the one the kin still have nightmares about. He should be able to pick up on the emotion, and maybe he would, except he's not the only one in the collective and the rest of them... Well, let's just say fear's really good at making you blind. And it makes your aim just as good.

The bronze spears fly through the eter, aiming for Aeotu's/my heart, their tips burning with all the rage and resentment of people held against their will, changed, eaten and left to rot under piles of alien fug.

A hasty wall, or maybe it's a fragment of the ora, takes one but the others— Oh shit. How did I survive *that*?

Dude. Dude is always the answer.

One moment Aeotu/me is about to become a pincushion, the next there's a giant, sleeked-out critter in front of me. Eight of the spears clunk into a chest covered in molten armour, the rest are flicked out of the air by his barbed tail.

Even as he growls – baring fangs that in the real can barely pierce skin but here could skewer a rucnart and still have room for a qwan – Aeotu/I strike.

And now *I'm* the one who's flying, punted into the next galaxy by Dude's rear paw. And, you know, it's not fair that *I'm* the one who's getting flung about and threatened with pincushion status, because I'm pretty sure that whatever happens on the eter, Aeotu is immune, safe in the ora. It's especially not fair when I wasn't actually *awake* during all this.

There's more growling, more spears and whips of ora-darkness flashing around the psionic plane, more me getting thrown hither and tither. No wonder my head aches. But in the end, Dude's got a paw on each combatant, has even managed to wrap his tail around Aeotu, buried in the ora – I think Hunt helped – and is pinning us to the ground, muzzle in our faces. There are no words, but then Dude doesn't need words, the message is pretty clear when he knocks our collective heads together and growls. He does it again.

There's no actual impact of bone on bone, no *thunk* as our skulls meet, instead... Imagine your brain is a water bubble, held in shape by surface tension, and then imagine someone smashes it against another water bubble, and yeah, you get the idea. We come apart and although we're mostly ourselves, we leave little bits of each other behind.

I come out of the memory.

Huh. I guess that's one way to do things.

*It was effective*, Ekene says. *Although we could have done with a little less head-knocking.*

Yeah. I rub my own head, feeling the phantom impact of our skulls meeting. It's hard to fight someone when a little bit of them is stuck in you.

I look down at the yellow-green city attached to my paw.

I'm not in love with this whole feeding thing though. The feeding is weird and freaky, brings back memories of body parts being carted through the void, of frozen heads and hands sticking out of rotting biogel. Makes me itch for a Franken-thrower.

*Not you.* That's Aeotu's voice.

What do you mean, not me?

Yellow flashes, the slag stars in their crystalline shells pulsing once and I get it. Not me, the slag. The city is eating the *slag*.

I study my hands. The yellow wound through the carvings over fingers and arms is... Not gone, but different. Greener.

*New*, says Aeotu. *Stronger. You will need.*

Need? For what?

There's no answer.

# CHAPTER EIGHT

I'm dumped back into the ship proper. Not the crew quarters, but somewhere else, somewhere they forgot to install lights. There's an impression in the back of my head of Aeotu supplying an answer. Her connection to me is stronger now, almost as strong as Hunt's, but not clear enough for the jumble of data and images to make sense. Which is strange, because the one time I communicated with Euiva, she had no trouble making herself understood. A worry for another time.

Wherever I am, it's dark and cold, even through my armour. A little concentration and that's fixed, the armour warming me from the inside out, a light shining from the shoulder not currently occupied by Dude. Who's back to being Dude-ish instead of a lump of fug. He's cuddled up close to my chin, tail hooked around my neck, barb embedded in my armour, and he's not happy. Not as *unhappy* as he was walking through the red sea of viyusa, but not fuzzing his little butt off either. It makes me nervous. Makes me worried. Turns the pit of my stomach into a churning ball of dread.

Dude's a rock, a warrior with tiny paws covered in golden fluff. Dude doesn't get scared, he leaps into the face of certain death and eats it. Dude comforts *me*, tells *me* to keep going, to push through. He doesn't huddle up against my chin, doesn't hide under layers of armour. Something's wrong, and yeah, I know *everything* is wrong at the moment – *Citlali* gone, Grea taken, Mum killing my friends – but this... What's worse than this?

I don't want to know, I really don't, but I've got the feeling that I'm going to find out, and real soon.

At least there isn't any viyusa down here.

That I can see.

There's a map on the HUD and faint green lines outlining what I assume is the space I'm in. The light on my shoulder isn't illuminating much, just a fuzzy circle of decking and the inwards curve of a bulkhead.

A pull at my brain, not Ekene's *pull*, not exactly. It's kinda like Aeotu and Ekene teamed up to plant new instructions while I was unconscious. Maybe they did, I don't know, Dude's not—

The impact throws me into the bulkhead, my head bashing into the metal-stone, something heavy slamming into my legs.

Pain explodes through my body, fires its way through my right paw, molten metal in my bones. I want to yell, but the breath has been squished out of my lungs and I'm trying to figure out how to unstick them long enough to scream.

Hunt is blaring in my head, Dude's claws are fully deployed and an emergency alarm is screeching in my ears, or maybe it's Aeotu in my head along with Hunt. Maybe it's all of the above. All I know is I can't breathe and my vision is grey and fuzzy and it's real hard to think, to remember—

Gold under my skin, pushing my ribs out, expanding my lungs. Air in. Hold it. Air out. Another breath and another.

The lights have faded from my eyes, and then pain... Holy Terra, it hurts, hurts worse than anything I've ever felt but at least now I can look down, can see... The giant fucking girder where my left knee used to be and there, on the deck, limp and bloody, viyu melting away from it, my foot. My human, fleshy foot, attached to a human fleshy ankle and a—

I throw up. Vomit splashing against my faceplate, bile and carrot bits hot against my cheeks, dripping down my chin, trickling down my neck, the rancid smell of it burning the inside of my nostrils, crawling into my brain— I vomit again. It's gross, but I can't help it, can't stop that image; mashed flesh, the red of muscle, the white of bone and the blood, all that blood pouring over pale gold skin, *my* skin. My leg. Gone. Gone—

Dude stops me before I heave again, golden fuzz freezing the flex of stomach muscles, the reflexive expulsion of even more grossness. More than that, he's pushing calm into my head, smothering the shock, the horror. It's almost enough, almost enough to make me forget the limb on the deck, but almost is all I need, all *Hunt* needs to push through and now I am we, and we can get out of this.

The girder that took the flesh's leg pulverised the knee, severing muscle and bone. Armour cauterised the blood vessels within nanoseconds, and the nanites that had covered the severed paw are reforming with the rest of us, climbing the bulkhead to re-join our armour. We are still pinned, but if we shift nanites to our chest, reinforcing the mass, and brace our functional leg against the bulkhead we can free ourselves.

We strain. And strain and strain. Every cell in our body, every nanite in our armour pushing against three-point-seven tons of metal-stone. Viyu is flowing from our remaining foot, our hands, our forearms, everywhere but our head, reforming on thigh and chest and shoulders. It occurs to the fleshiness that it might not be enough, that we may be stuck here, that we may bleed out and die—

The fleshiness is panicking, has forgotten that the wound is already cauterised, has yet to process the vacuum warning blazing across the HUD. It is still caught in the horror of its foot on the deck, using up oxygen, slowing us down. The fuzziness shuts it up, floods us with calm and warmth so that we may concentrate.

The girder will move. Seven-point-eight millimetres, that is all we need, the width of the unpulverised femur. The girder shifts.

Three-point-nine.

Another heave, viyu standing out in cords as we strain, the bulkhead buckling under the force.

Six-point-nine.

Nanites turn grey, become dust and flake away as they die.

Eight-point-zero-two.

We are free. Unbalanced on one leg we crumble to the deck armour flowing back over exposed skin, a little bit thinner than before as a new limb grows from the stump of the old.

We roll to our knees, hands on the deck, the bloody stump of our foot—

My foot. That is *my* foot, golden skin turning grey, the nails blue, frost forming on the tip of my big toe. Just lying there, the white mess of bone and meat unreal, it's a trick, an illusion—

We reassert control.

The hull is breached. Now that we are no longer trying to free ourselves or fight the flesh for control, that data can flood our senses. An impact to *Aeotu*'s stern, damage to the hull one deck below, near the engines, viyu already rushing to affect repairs. The girder that took our leg was a fragment of the superstructure. We are fortunate it was only a fragment, sheared from the giant ribs that support *Aeotu*'s frame, any larger and we would not have moved it – any larger, the mechanical part says, and we would not have been alive to need to.

Sirens wail in our ears, the bright strobe of emergency lights, the urgent pulse of *Aeotu* in our systems. We must go, *Aeotu* needs us.

*We need you, too.* The voice does not belong to us or a Sister. The fleshiness identifies it as human, Ekene, even as the foreign yellow viyu throbs in time with his words.

An image forms in our consciousness, of the hangar and the huddled forms of other beings, fleshed and furred and feathered, the shimmer of an emergency shield the only thing between them and the gaping hole in the hull.

We acknowledge.

The mech is already aware, but its attention is on the viyusa erupting through deck and ceiling, a wave of red vines whipping through the atmosphere, snapping and reaching. Fire shoots from the mech's first arms, viyusa screaming, but for every clump that turns to dust under the assault, there is another.

It can hold, the mech insists.

Vacuum is the biggest danger to us now; the lack of oxygen, the cold. We need more viyu, need more oxygen, need to get to the hangar and crew we left behind. Have to find the source of the hull breach, have to complete the new mission unfurling in our brain. Have to do many things, and quickly.

No time to think, only do.

The metal is prioritising, calculations based on need and proximity, completed in a nanosecond and—

*No, here.* Aeotu ringing in our head, a new map on the HUD.

We run, the HUD our only guide, outlining walls and hatches in the white of *Aeotu*'s schematics, obstacles in the bright green of our low-light sensors. Our stride is halting, pain shudders through the fleshiness with every step, the stump where our knee was burns, the memory of our other foot interfering with the function of the new.

The new limb is crude, a broad flat hook on the end of a curving blade of viyu, without the elegance or power of the paw. We stumble, the hook catching in a broken conduit, not retracting like we're used to, but it will do until we can replenish our reserves and have enough to rebuild our leg from the marrow out.

Another deck-rippling shudder throws us into a bulkhead. Pain bursts through our undamaged knee as we hit the deck, fire joining it from the injured knee as it follows. There is a wetness to the pain, the cool trickle of blood as cauterised arteries open. It is merely a microsecond, barely enough for the sensation to register under the agony lighting up the flesh's nervous system but—

The image of my foot is stuck behind my eyes, how it looked like it was waiting for me to pick it up and twist it into place. There'd be a click, the bone locking in, the flesh... Old Terra, was there flesh left? I hadn't looked at the end of the leg still attached, but the girder had been over my knee and the bit of me on the deck—

The sick catches me off guard, the hot rush of it up my throat the—

The flesh is becoming a problem, its processes stuck in—

Holy Terra, there's barely anything left! The thin bit of viyu replacing my leg is so long! Even if I went back and grabbed my foot, even if it could twist and click into place—

Darkness, not the dark of the corridor leavened by the green and white outlines on the HUD, but another kind takes us. The threads between what is real and what is possible parting, kaleidoscopic tendrils reaching through the umbilicus that connects us to the metal and wrapping around our bones, our muscles, reaching not for the metal or the fuzziness, but the flesh.

A tug, gentle at first, then insistent. Our fleshiness says no, clings to its pain, to the bloody memory of its limb. The tug comes again, harder, and we feel it spreading through the flesh, hijacking nerves and muscles, pushing the metal and the fuzz out even as it pulls the flesh in.

'No,' the flesh says again, breathing it even as its control of its mouth slips away.

*Yes, Brother.* Aeotu tugs a final time and the flesh slips between reality, into the endless black of the ora while the rest of us stays in the real. *We need you.*

We are gone.

# CHAPTER NINE

Chaos reigns. Or at least it looks like chaos. Lights and shapes flashing in the dark, things half-seen and then gone, mirages playing over mirages shattered by angry slashes of thought and intent, the shards slicing through the air.

None of it touches me. I'm safe within a rainbow bubble, colours twisting across the thin shell, constantly changing. First pink then red then yellow, then a shade of blue so dark it goes beyond black and into another dimension and if I chase it, press my hands to the bubble and *sink*, it's almost like that thin shield is a whole other universe, thoughts and emotions talking over and under and through each other. And if I follow that blue, ignoring all of the others, I can see—

Fire. My skin shudders, bows, my ribs taking the impact even as the grey-green flood of my immune system rushes to the wound, nanoscopic cells repairing stressed metal-stone, filling in cracks, shoring up bones. There's a puncture down in my gut, thin emergency shields holding atmosphere in place while more of those nanoscopic cells— as more viyu clears debris from the hatches, fixes power conduits blown in the surge of power that came with the strike. And still more viyu clusters around the intruder lodged in my belly, crawling over it in a thick grey-green tide, the newer, stronger yellow-green flowing through my systems, but not fast enough. The intruder is a long egg-shaped drone, I could stretch both arms and touch the pointed dome at each end. The dark matte-grey of its hull catches the glow of the emergency lights and throws it back in a pattern of stark shadows. Whorls and lines are carved into its surface. The thing is yelling into the dark, trying to transmit data through the buzz of interference playing under my skin.

Except for the colour, the thing reminds me of *Aeotu*'s hull, just longer and miniaturised. There's silver within the patterns carved on its hull. Sunk in them like the slag on my armour, but this stuff is moving, water flowing through rocky channels, or metal-stone as the case may be.

I scoot closer, even as alarms ring – other parts of me warning of danger, outlining the drone in blazing red, tracking rising levels of power and the movement of the silver blood across the drone's skin. And yet it's that movement that draws me in, that begs me to lay hands on the drone and feel the cool silk of the silver running over my hands, to let it trace the line of tendon and muscle in my arms.

My hands are out, hovering over the drone, and—

Viyu erupts from the deck. Not the new yellow-green stuff but the old, a vomit-coloured tide engulfing the drone, swamping the silver.

The silver blazes. Viyu screams, a shrill wail as it dies, patches of it turning black and drifting to the deck, other patches... The silver seeps through it, water rising to the surface of porous stone in little droplets, first one and then a dozen and then a hundred, until the grey-green is soaked in silver and... It's eating it; the silver is eating our viyu, growing, spreading outwards through our nanites, the tide of the enemy not just taking over the viyu but reaching further, infiltrating our defences.

*Stop it!*

Is that thought mine? It doesn't feel like me, it echoes in my head, a hundred different versions of me yelling the words. But the urgency, that is real, grabs me by the heart and I'm lunging at the drone, hands turning to claws and— Sinking through the silver, effective as a ghost.

No. No, I can do this! I have hands and fingers with bones, and fug-armour. I just... I just have to remember where I put them, where they are, where I left them... I just need to concentrate, to remember. The feel of the armour sliding over my arms, the prick of Dude's claws in my shoulder, the liquid heat of the fug-blades, the bone-deep cold as heat/energy is drawn from my body and into the blades. And... there, a pulse of acknowledgement, a familiar fuzz and... Okay, that's weird. I've found myself but... it's not here. How does that work?

A figure moves in the darkness, yellow-green, walking with a strange hobble-glide, like one of its legs is shorter than the other or... Wait a second. That's me. *I'm* the figure coming out of the darkness to investigate the enemy in my belly but how can that be when I'm standing right here?

I look down, at hands, arms, toes. Ten toes. Fleshy and see-through.

I'm not in my body.

I rip myself out of the blue, back into the endless black of the ora.

The colours, shifting and nameless, those are Aeotu. I think I knew that. Right? But... An image of myself, or my body, walking toward the drone appears out of the rainbow like I've summoned it.

*No. Sharing.* Aeotu is at my side, or at least one of her. There's another version of her, a mirage, standing on the other side of me, staring at a different piece of the darkness. *Easier for you this way,* she says.

'What do you mean, "easier"?' Slipping into the blue hadn't exactly been hard, I'd just—

*Watch,* she says.

I watch. I'm approaching the drone, the physical version of me. Why don't I remember this? Surely, I should remember this? Except it feels less like a memory and more like now.

*Not memory,* Aeotu says. *Now.*

Now? But how is that possible... Right. Stupid question.

It's Dude. I see him under my skin, flowing through bone and nerve. The real-me reaches for the drone.

The silver pulls back, retreating as slag-viyu gathers around not-my wrist and leaps from not-my fingers.

For a second it seems like the silver is holding its breath, except nanites don't breathe – don't have lungs unless they hijack mine – and then... and the—

There is no moment, no lapse between the breath and the action, no gathering of force, ripple of muscle, there is just the end. One nano-moment the silver is frozen, the next it is all over my/the mirage's face, all over its arms, its hands, in its mouth.

I can taste it, here in the ora. It's... strange. I can't describe it except as green and tingly, a forest growing on my tongue, full of the soil, stone and moss. There's a hint of musk, curling up the back of my throat and out through my nose, the warm smoke of a fire, of cold damp spaces and yeah, maybe even some shit, right on the back of my tongue. And maybe it's just the ora, because I can *see* the taste. I know that's weird but it doesn't change the fact that with every new sensation the image in front of me grows. First a stone and then a wall, rocky but not made of stone, uneven and cold. A shaggy carpet of a moss, so pale a green it might as well be white, spreads over the ground, spills around a fissure and comes for my paws. I'd shuffle out of the way except I'm already in it, and when I look up, I realise just how in it I am. There's a roof overhead, like a thin sheet of plasglas, glossy and clear but warped, the view of the stars above distorted and wavy.

There's no colour in this image, nothing beyond that pale hint of green, but the light... It moves, twists and turns, has the depth of an endless pond. I can see all the way to the bottom, layers upon layers of light and dark and—

This is a memory. An *alien* memory, truly alien. Not a training memory or a kin memory, not even a freaky Aeotu memory. Those I recognise, those jiggle and bounce against my psyche with an energy beyond that of my own brain, this memory...

It's static, an Old Terran painting hung in the emptiness of the ora. No thought, no feeling, not even a sense of the individual behind it. It's disturbing.

I push it aside and focus on the real me, the silver over every millimetre of me, on the lines of yellow-green blazing through it. The silver retreats, the yellow-green follows and now the tables have turned, the yellow swamping the drone, covering all of *its* millimetres and—

The yellow-green disappears, slips between the silver's nanites.

'What's happening?' My voice is loud.

*Watch*, Aeotu says.

I watch. And I watch. And I watch.

'Nothing's happening.'

*Watch*, she says.

I watc—

Where the silver leapt, first still and then everywhere, the slag creeps. Nanite-by-nanite, so slow I don't see it and then, when I do... It's a suggestion of colour at first, like that pale hint of green, almost too little to see. I'm not actually sure if I'm seeing it or just imagining and then, as I'm leaning closer, a thread of yellow pops to the surface and then another and another.

There's no screaming, at least none I can hear, I don't even know if they feel pain, not like I do, but they feel something, 'cause the silver shit is rearing back from the yellow shit, trying to split itself apart.

I'm really glad I'm not the silver shit, because in that moment, that very nanosecond, the slag strikes. Silver is yellow and yellow is... well, still yellow. Specks of silver rise to the top before being pushed under waves of slag. I know without asking that this is what would have happened in the proto-viyu tank, how Ekene planned to take over Aeotu. By eating her from the inside out.

And now... a new plan, or rather the new-old plan, version two or three or whatever-the-fuck-number we're up to, unfolding in the ora, Ekene and the whisper in the darkness.

We have the enemy drone, packed with slag-fug, its engines intact. If we can just push it out, tweak the navigation...

Perfect.

The mess of yellow retreats into the drone, flowing backward along the deck, leaving little pieces of itself behind. Those pieces sink through the deck, and if I turn my head and unfocus my eyes, I can see them merging with the veins of regular viyu underneath, can follow as it shoots back toward Aeotu's heart. But then I'd miss the fine threads breaking off from the mass retreating into the drone and curling over the mirage's hands, around its wrists. I'd miss the mirage putting its hands on the drone's casing, I'd miss its armour shifting, bulking up thighs and calf, miss the ripple of nanite muscles as not-me pushes the drone across the scarred deck inch by slow, grating inch.

Really, the compartment was already open to space, Aeotu should just turn off the gravity and—

The slap to the back of my head rocks me into my own body, into the real. Dude on my shoulder and under my skin, Hunt ticking away in my brain.

*Stupid*, follows me. It might be whispered in Aeotu's voice, but it sounds more like Grea, the way she'd roll her eyes, the shot of knowledge she'd pack into the thought.

Right, because turning gravity off with a switch would be convenient, especially when it's *your* body pushing shit out of a blast hole. I barely have time to feel the cold or register the burn in my thighs, the way my right leg doesn't feel right, feels short and stiff and *wrong*, before I'm pushing the drone back through the tear in the hull, push push push and then stop.

Movement. A bright spot of warmth flitting through from *Aeotu's* internal sensors.

My back straightens, my feet spin me around and—

Staring at me out of eyes the size of a fist, dark slit pupils slowly widening until they swallow the pale iris, is a wohol.

I freeze.

It freezes.

Both of us frozen, both of us staring at each like we've just seen a ghost. Or an alien.

It's tall. Really, really tall. Those memories I stole from h'Rawd don't do it justice, don't accurately communicate the breadth of its shoulders or the gravity-producing expanse of its chest. Its envirosuit doesn't make it better, the intense, light obliterating grey reminding me of a black hole.

My HUD is whirring and there's this feeling like worms crawling over my shoulders, dripping down my chest. I think, if I look down, I'll see my armour twisting, whorls and lines dancing across it.

Its gaze drops, and through the clear plas of the faceplate, furrows appear in the wide space between its eyes. It tilts its head, and the furrows deepen.

I feel like I should say something, but what's there to say? Hi, you invaded my homeworld before it was my homeworld and, hey, how about those water-kin? Or maybe, I hate you and your stinking Sister ships, roll over and die?

Its gaze snaps up, and I'm pretty sure those furrows between its brows are a frown. Kinda sure too that the way its wide, flat lips curl back, exposing blunt teeth and scary-sharp canines, is not a good sign.

The feeling is confirmed when it steps toward me.

It's not the walk of a being intent on peace. Neither is the short, blunt thing in one of its lower hands. The angry orange needle at the end pointed at me.

Right.

Hunt's got this one, is swinging my arms up, fiery blades sweeping through the alien's weapon, stepping into it and pushing it back with one fug/taloned foot, while I'm still figuring out what to do.

The wohol goes flying, its surprise colouring the air, widening its slim black irises until they appear to take over its face.

Hunt is still moving, propelling us forward in giant bounds. The wohol has yet to hit the bulkhead before when we're on it, blades high over our head, coming down—

There's no blood, the heat from the blades cauterises the wounds and sears the surrounding flesh. The solider is dead before it hits the ground. There's no last gasp, no words, no chance for it look at me and see its end. It's just gone. Not a flicker of anything in the eter, and in some way, that's even worse than if the solider had screamed.

Hunt lets go of my muscles. I'm not sure what to do. I'm all caught up in the blank stare, in the way the blades punctured its chest, in the slight pucker of its envirosuit around the knives, the way the material smokes. I stumble backward. The blades come out as easily as they went in, and I remember Mac. Remember him fading in my arms.

I thought I wanted to make things hurt – the fug, Aeotu, Euiva – and maybe I have and maybe I do, but this... Staring into those slit-pupil eyes is different. I want to throw up.

I never want to be the cause of death ever, ever again. Never. But a niggle in the back of my brain, a voice older than it has a right to be, wiser, tells me to get used to it.

There's a *SNNAPP* and what I thought was a bulkhead, isn't.

Another wohol stands in the open hatch. It stares at its dead... friend? I don't know, but it stares, pain saturating the air around it.

It looks up, eyes catching on my blades, on the patterns filling my chest. Sounds I don't understand spill from its wide, flat lips, the words low and sharp. I understand the anger though, the pistol in its upper hand aimed at my head.

The emote is instinctual, desperate almost, and rips out of me before I've really thought about it. It's messy and chaotic, a blast of fear and anger and wonder. All of it wrapped up in desperation.

It explodes against the wohol, splashing over its mind, staining the eter a rainbow of black and red and silver.

If I thought the first wohol had frozen at the sight of me, then I don't know how to describe this. They don't just freeze, they almost cease to exist, not just muscles and bones locked in place, but their very atoms.

Have I killed them? How can I kill? All I did was *emote*. Easy, simple. Not even a—

For every action there is an equal and opposite reaction. That quote floats to the front of my brain, kind rises out of the eter, like the sun over the horizon.

Whatever hold the emote has on the solider, shatters.

Rage. Movement. Violence. It explodes. One moment I'm standing in the middle of the corridor, wondering if I've killed it and then blades are shooting from my arms and only Dude and Hunt are keeping my alive. I've barely got time to blink before it's on me.

Where before anger over its friend's death had driven the solider, a desperate black rage has taken hold. It's the kind of emotion that powers fight or flight, that lends a new surge of a strength to muscles and turns the fire of fug blades amputating an arm into nothing.

Hunt is rushing through my muscles and Dude is under my skin, and I'm floating in the eter, staring not at the soldier's severed hand on the deck but at the horror unfolding before me. At the endless web of darkness burned into the soldier's brain, echoing with the crash of waves and the screams of kin.

It's the same sticky, deadly nothingness I found in Aeotu, but this is buried deeper, is wound up in its psionic DNA, like the need for oxygen is in mine. This isn't just part of the solider, it's a part of their species. A madness.

I've never encountered a psionic null before, never seen a mind so static, so... *flat*. There's no bounce, no tingle, nothing but pastel colours in the eter, dwarf stars in the midst of the everything. But the darkness, the darkness *lives* in a part of them, is sharp and hard and cold. It doesn't belong and yet it's embedded in their psyches like... like...

Dude hums, nudging my mind, sharing a thought, a memory, of cold, hard fingers reaching into his brain, slipping through the hole in his natural shields. White/black, commands implanted in the critter's anima.

Like critters. The darkness rides the wohol like the kin do the critters. Somehow, someway, in the minutes the water-kin wrapped around ancient Jøran to drive the alien invaders away, they did the work of generations. They made their command sphere part of a species.

How did the water-kin do that? *Why* did they do that? Is this why the kin don't do emotions? Because once, centuries ago, they planted so much fear, so much *hate* into another species they drove them mad? And why make them crazy, why not just make the wohol forget or run away? Why drive them to this?

Why drive Grea to this? The darkness is part of my twin. Part of me.

That thought rises out of the back of my mind, frightening, impossible, but true.

Is that why I killed Mac? This madness, this *infection*?

The solider is pounding at me, raining blows from above with thick, meaty fists and there is no more time to think. Hunt is holding it off, is ducking and weaving and slashing at it. There are new tears in its envirosuit, blackened slices in the flesh underneath, and then my fist is pressed up against its chest, and the smell of searing skin is crawling up my nose.

The solider slides off my blade, a dead weight hitting the deck.

A hand grabs me; not a fuzzy, wavy metaphorical or psionic one, but flesh and blood and fur, wrapping around my bicep and yanking me into shadows with enough strength to pull me off my paws— No, paw. Hard enough to yank me off my one remaining paw.

There's nothing to see in the darkness, just shadows on shadows and this... this *thing* isn't content with yanking me, now it's *dragging* me, uncaring that I'm scrambling to get my... my paw back under me, or that my motor control is all fucked up and I'm fumbling with the shit where my leg used to be. Nope, not caring. And I can say that with confidence because I can feel my captor's ambivalence like a wash of "fuck you" all the way down my shoulder and straight into my heart.

Fuck.

Clomp. Swoosh. Drag.

You.

And that, that cruel, callous ambivalence is all the water-kin's darkness needs. All the shock, all the horror, all the poor-little boy Kuma feelings are pushed under the black rage.

I put my good paw down, sink fug-claws into the deck. I stop. My captor doesn't.

My arm's just about yanked out of its socket. Once, twice, like the arsehole isn't quite sure, and then they're turning and Dude's under my skin, that fine golden web taking over for the failed connections between brain and new leg.

The third tug is harder, matches the nostril-curling snarl on the creature's face, a snarl that turns to shock as my fist slams into its gut.

I used my captor's last heave to lever myself up, shooting off the deck, armour thick around my knuckles and forearm, putting all my momentum and anger into the strike. Hunt is ticking away in the back of my brain, and Dude and I are moving in concert, pushing the arsehole's head down even as I bring my knee (the good one, with the foot still attached) up. There's a crunch, a yowl, and pain, pain, pain flowing through our hands from the creature's back, but we're not done, or maybe it's just me who's not done. Whatever the fuck, it doesn't matter, because we're still moving, pushing the arsehole backward, watching them stumble, arms wheeling as they try to get their balance.

Yeah. Fuck that. We shift our weight, and now it's the new foot... paw... hook... whatever flying through vacuum and my foot/paw/ hook passes through its neck.

The creature pauses, every molecule of its being freezing and for a second, it's like that moment of resistance never happened, and then my foot touches down and I'm spinning again. There's no pause, no question of movement, when my foot hits it square in the chest.

The thing's head topples from its neck. The body follows, knees folding first, torso flopping backward, arms splayed. There are four of them, the upper pair heavier in the shoulders, a little thicker around the bicep, the lower pair a little thinner, a little shorter maybe, or it could just be the way its sprawled across the deck, the angle of the emergency lights.

It's a wohol, one of the aliens that built Aeotu.

*Creator*, she says inside my head, grief in her voice. Loneliness. Despair. Anger. Each emotion a sharp point digging into my psyche, drawing blood.

Blood like the bright, bright red, frothing from the alien's neck, spilling over the deck like red soap suds.

I just killed someone.

An alien.

A wohol.

With my foot.

I'm not even sorry.

# CHAPTER TEN

There are screams coming from the hangar, the *phst stick* of weapons fire and hoarse yells. I'm running, but it's not fast enough.

Where is Hunt? Where are its cannons? The mech is whirring in the back of my brain but the connection is fuzzy, disjointed. I feel... lost, incomplete, like I'm missing something so much more important than a leg.

I keep running. Around the corner, paw digging into the deck, hook bouncing off it, sprinting down the wide, squashed egg-shape of a new corridor, open hatches and empty crew quarters flashing past on either side. White. White. White.

Red, so much red with silver twisting through it. Twisting and writhing, plunging through a giant hole in the deck. A shape comes out of the hole all flailing arms and terror with familiar eyes, hair I know as well as my own, a voice that used to sing me to sleep at night, made high and piercing with fear. Mum wrapped in the red-silver; a thick vine around her waist, more growing, catching legs and arms, pinning them to her body.

She sees me, tries to yell or speak or scream, but red covers her face before the air leaves her lungs.

'No!' I yell it for her, force my legs to move faster, feel the blades spring from my wrists, the pain and cold as armour shifts, thrusters forming on my back.

I leap. Cold digs deep into my bones even as the thrusters propel me forward.

One hundred eighty-one metres covered in a nanosecond and I'm coming down, teeth bared, blades hungry, nothing but rage feeding on the fear in my heart. The last thing Mum sees before the viyusa swallows her whole is her one and only son turned into a demon.

Viyusa dies with every swing of my blades, masses of red and silver flopping on the deck, yellow-green spreading from every cut, every slice. But for every strand, every fibre I kill, more replace it, so many and so fast that soon enough I'm wading through the stuff. Thin tendrils wind around my ankles, weigh down my arms, reach for my shoulders.

A vine around my thigh, reaching for my waist, a hard, muscle-ripping yank. I'm swallowed, viyusa all around me, sharp points pressing into my chest, seeking out the soft points between ribs and armour.

There are no soft points, but that doesn't stop the viyusa from trying, sending spears into my chest even as it yanks me down and down and down. I can't move, can't stab or slice. I try burning it, firing up my thrusters and— Pain, pain, pain! Armour ripped from my back, agony punching through my shoulder blades all the way out my chest, even as alarms soak my vision in red. Or maybe that's just the viyusa.

Where is the slag? The yellow-green that's meant to *eat* this shit? Why are Dude and I alone?

Fire exploding all around, viyusa turning to ash. Gravity grabbing hold of my middle and I'm falling, falling, falling. Thrusters gone, pain and the HUD still glazing my vision, but I gotta turn, gotta brace myself, gotta give the armour time to reinforce my legs, to adjust—

A hard surface, knees buckling, but no pain, no cracks as armour dies and flakes away. Nothing, just metal-stone under my palms, giant rucnart-sized fingers closing over me, caging me. Protecting me.

Hunt.

I see the crown of its giant featureless head in the gap between its fingers. Viyusa crawls around its legs, creeps up its knees and has sunk a giant spear through its other first arm. Energy spits around the point where its arm cannon used to be, and when I look, I see the same damage on the arm holding me aloft, feel the whine of broken conduits through my knees. Both lower arms are still free, and Hunt is swinging its giant blades with abandon.

And maybe, just maybe, Hunt's sword work is holding the viyusa off, but there's so much red everywhere, so many screams and calls for help. The red has Mum, does it have Dad or Onah or Mac—

Mac's dead and I killed him.

The thought is pain, the memory sinking into my chest is like my blade going through Mac. Agony, the kind that spurs you on.

Dude is a sleeked-out fug machine on my shoulder.

There's no time for pain or remorse or the fear gnawing at my insides. There's only that clear circle of deck, the flash of fangs, the screech of tree-kin, the *phst stick* of weapons and the encroaching viyusa.

I'm sliding down Hunt's arm, scrambling over its shoulder, down its chest, my movements more Dude's doing than my own. I'm halfway to the deck when I see it. The silver, blooming within the viyusa, first in the thick vines bursting through deck and ceiling, then more and more, fine threads creeping through the red, and then thick threads and then—

*Booooomm.*

The explosion rattles my marrow, loosens my grip on Hunt's knee, sends us plummeting to the floor. There is no hand to save us, no arm or leg or paw, just the deck, hard and unforgiving, or it would be except for the fine layer of not-so-dead nanites.

I am thankful for my faceplate, for not having a mouth full of half-dead viyusa as the opportunistic fug comes to life, races over my helmet and sucks power from my armour, giving my HUD more diagrams to flash in my face. And then, as I stagger to my feet, my attention not on the warnings, or the ice in my bones as my armour siphons heat for power, but on the silver forming a fine filigree cage around me, *then* I am grateful for the slag.

Yellow blazes in the carvings on my thighs and chest, and the revived viyusa screams. Dies. Falls to ash a second time.

I am free, and for as long as my body can meet the demands of my armour, before hypothermia sets in, I am untouchable. By viyusa at least. The silver shit taking over the red has other ideas, as do the giant, four-armed hulks striding through the valley of death carved in the viyusa.

The carbonised remains of viyusa stain the hangar entrance in a thick layer of soot that puffs around the aliens' knees. I wish I could hear Hunt, had its eyes and ears and sensors to count the menace stalking toward us. I don't know what the aliens consider a squad, but I bet there's a whole one here, upper hands holding rifles tight to their shoulders, lower ones holding blades and scanners. Or what look like scanners, matte-grey spheres with holos spread out above.

I can't see their faces, don't know if their lips are pulled back from their fangs or if they're pale with fear. I'm betting on fangs, and then I'm betting on terror, the exact same emotion I'm gathering up, dredging from the depths of my anima, from the kin and crew around me, and I'm throwing it, draining my bones of what little warmth remains to turn my emote into a tsunami.

It hits at the same time h'Rawd launches himself out of the sea of red, fangs and claws extended, ragged lines of blood and torn flesh marring his chest and face. But the aliens don't break, don't scream or cower or flee, don't freeze and then rage like the other one. They point their weapons, smooth, fluid, precise.

There are moments when I wish I was a telepath, when I want to be a Regan or a tree-kin to reach into a brain and *yank*, hard and fast, no mercy, no anaesthetic, just brute force. I'd pop the aliens psyches like ripe fruit, makes their brains leak out their ears, just so much insensible mush.

There are moments like that. This is one.

Time is molasses, the aliens with their weapons are a black hole and I'm on the event horizon, have the time to watch the longest of their three fingers find a groove in the barrel. Power forms like a thick lime-green glob at the end of the weapons and I can't move, am caught in the tidal wave of gravity as those globs become lances, picking up speed as they streak through the air.

H'Rawd doesn't see it. Or if he does, he doesn't care, or if he does care he thinks the sacrifice worth it. Whatever it is, the lances hit, direct shots burning holes in the tree-kin's chest, his legs, his face. Time restarts, the gravity well releasing me as h'Rawd slams into the middle of the alien squad, a ton of rage and claws ripping through the dark grey of their armour, shredding it like tissue.

Blood and snarls and another large shadow leaping out of the red, h'Lott joining the fray, the screech of air-kin, Onah's dark form hovering overhead. Dad, the alien weapon in his hands spitting that heavy lance of lime-green from its tip, grey-green armour plastered to his ribs, more of it crawling over his stomach, thin tendrils reaching for his collarbone.

And now me, blades extended, a whirling dervish of pain and fear. There are only eight aliens, but it might as well be a hundred. The silver shit is taking over the viyusa, the thin threads of it multiplying exponentially, until the red is gone and all that remains are gleaming tendrils forming spears and whips, fighting for the aliens.

They snap at h'Lott, pulling an alien out of the path of her jaws, forming a wall and then a cage. She yowls, high and piercing, rakes the stuff with claws and teeth, some dies, but there is more, always more.

H'Rawd is on the deck, trying to get his paws under him, to fight, to live. An alien points its weapon at him.

I scream, leap the distance between us—

A spear pierces my back, bright silver erupting from my stomach. I slash at it, watch the tip fall, the pain not yet registering, knowing it will come, and take the moment to reach around, to sink talons into the vine wriggling through my back and—

*Wait.* Ekene in my brain.

But I can't wait, h'Rawd...

H'Rawd is dead, eyes glazing over as I struggle on the end of the silver, half his skull gone, a smoking ruin of bone and gore. H'Lott is screaming, her yowl piercing my heart, even as it curdles my blood, and then h'Rawd's killer disappears under a storm of sand-coloured fur and enough rage to drown a city.

*Wait,* Ekene says again and nudges my grey matter, reminding me.

Oh. I study the new bit of silver growing out my abdomen, remember the drone, the way the alien nanites turned that sickly shade of yellow, and smile. As if my memory has seeped into my blood, the silver pauses, tries to retreat. I sink talons in and keep hold.

Weapons are aimed at me now, globules of power forming on their tips.

Yellow-green explodes out of the deck, wraps around the squad, clashes with the silver. There is darkness at its centre, a tall sleeked-out form with Mac's wide shoulders and Aeotu's kaleidoscope skin. And still more yellow-green is spilling out from me, the slag in my armour flowing from my fingertips, from the hole in my belly, racing through the silver.

This is no slow change, no subtle yellowing but a rush. I can *feel* the slag, feel it learning, feel its consciousness, and it's familiar, so very, very familiar...

*You feel us,* Ekene says, the other Jørgens in his voice.

The slag has no mercy, what was silver is now yellow and what was red dies. The aliens... The aliens will wish Ekene let them do the same.

I hit the deck, the silver spear through my stomach now yellow-green, threads of it spreading under my hands, patching the hole and... other things, I guess. Liver, intensives, kidneys perhaps? I don't want to think about it, don't want to imagine Ekene and the others spreading through my blood, being able to control my body like they've tried to control my brain. Not now, not in the face of... this.

I don't want to look but I can't turn away. The aliens' screams won't let me.

Their armour is crawling with slag.

One day, if there is another day after the endless nightmare that has become my life, I will wonder what happened to mercy, what switch got flipped in the heads of the people I once knew. I know what switch was flipped in my head, can't escape the mess of fear and grief and guilt in the deepest reaches of my anima, the hate that feeds on it or the sticky tendrils of the water-kin's darkness.

When the hate is gone, will this be all that is left? Ashes and screams, pain and fear? There's enough of both here to make another me, to build it from the marrow out then fill it up and animate it like some kind of Old Terran zombie, come to feed on the living.

As I drown in their screams, in their pain and fear I wonder...

What have the wohol done to us?

*Nothing*, Ekene whispers.

'Everything.' Grea, kneeling beside one of the aliens, her form shimmering in the air, more mirage than flesh. I'm not sure if it's just me seeing her or... No, everyone's attention is on the air beside the alien, shock and hope and fear and, in Dad's case, joy creasing their faces.

There's a smile on Grea's face, a quirk of the lips and a crinkle at the corner of her eyes that doesn't sit right. The way she watches the wohol writhe and scream with something akin to hunger is wrong, isn't the Grea I know.

'They built us, used us, abandoned and tortured us, and now... now they have come to kill us,' she says, and that's when I know. It might be my twin I'm looking at, but it's not her speaking, not even her behind her own eyes. It's Euiva, using Grea's image and voice.

In my head, that sense of wrongness clicks, gains a name. Madness. There is madness in Euiva, a frantic kind of anger twisting her insides, and beyond it... Beyond it is the darkness left by the water-kin, one bleeding into the other, feeding each other.

And this... this is... What the water-kin did all those centuries ago, the legacy they've left us. The madness, the hate, the endless cycle of death.

Euiva/Grea ripples, light shuddering through her body as she stands. 'Save us,' she says, and I know that she is not talking to me. She may be facing me, but her gaze bores through me, to the slag and Ekene floating in my bloodstream. 'Save us,' she repeats, and now she is looking at Onah, hovering above, and then at h'Lott. 'Save us, and we will save you.'

*You started this.* The memory of Aeotu's words, of her crouched over me, her face my face, hits me in the gut. You *started this.*

If she were here, Mum would roll her eyes and tell me that if we followed that logic, what we should really be blaming is the Big Bang because, after all, if there was no universe then our three species wouldn't be standing right here, right now, trying to kill each other, 'cause we wouldn't exist.

But Mum isn't here. The red took her, kicking and screaming, just like it has taken the rest of my family, my friends. Just like it's taken my life.

At some point, in some way, you just have to stand up and break the cycle.

I glare at Euiva, hiding behind my sister's image.

'Save us,' she says again.

'No,' I say, and shove her out.

# CHAPTER ELEVEN

H'Lott is still curled up beside h'Rawd's body, muzzle resting on his shoulders, her forepaws wrapped around his. She doesn't seem to mind the blood pooling under her belly, or the glob of brain stuck to her chin. I guess she doesn't feel them. The fog of grief saturating the air around her is a blue-black curtain heavy enough to cut out light.

I don't know what's worse, seeing her like that, her reddy-gold coat dulled as much by loss as dead viyusa, or hearing her. Not even my helmet can mute the sub-audible wail, a song of loss and heartache drilling through my chest and squeezing.

Half the little huddle of crew behind me don't hear it. The humanoid half. I know Mwat hears it, her ears are flattened, like burying them in her feathers will cut out the sound, and Onah's all hunched in on himself. I bet he'd stick his wingtips in his ears if he could. And Mac's dad...

I don't want to look at him, but my gaze keeps cutting across the deck like my eyeballs are laser guided. Doesn't matter if he's wading in dead viyusa up to his ankles, dragging wounded into the single lonely spot spared from the wreckage, or if he's huddled up with the others. I find him without thinking, without trying, short and dark and—

And returning my look.

I look away.

I don't want to know. Don't want to see. It's too late though. Has always been too late. H'Lott and Mac's dad don't have a duopoly on sadness, the cutting kind that leaves your guts hollow and your head heavy. The hangar is choked with it, the bitter blue-black so thick I could lay down and sleep on it, but I can block out the others' emotions.

His grief is like h'Lott's, piercing. It sinks into my brain without me even laying eyes on him, sidled on in there along with all the guilt and now... Mac is somewhere under all the dead nanites, maybe even under the slag writhing around the perimeter of the hangar. I haven't seen him, I just know he's there like a stone weighing down my gut – a sick, leaden feeling that only gets worse every time I seek out his dad.

Does his dad know I killed him? Did I even kill Mac? Does it matter?

Dude's clinging to my chest, I'm clinging to him too. It's a mutual clinging, except Dude's fuzzing his butt off, his warmth spreading through my chest, taking some of the tension off the strings tying me to the hole that opened the moment I stuck a sword in my best-maybe-more-than-a-friend.

The air shimmers.

Ekene hovers above the deck, almost real enough to touch, except for his feet. His feet disappear into fog, and I'd wonder how much of him was in my head and how much was actually *here*, in the real, visible not just to me and the kin, but to Dad and Jim and the rest of the crew. I'd wonder that, if Jim wasn't standing at Ekene's shoulder and Dad didn't look like he'd just swallowed a pill big enough to choke h'Rawd. Not that h'Rawd's got a throat to choke anymore, but whatever.

'So, Aino's plan worked.' There's pride in the way Jim says my mum's name, but it's the hope lighting his eyes that takes me aback. Makes me shiver as I remember slashed throats and the yellow geometric shit crawling over faces I knew as friend. Hope and pride don't feel real appropriate for the situation. 'The viral slag can kill the aliens.'

Yeah, it can kill aliens. At least something good came of all of *us* you killed, right? I want to spit the words in his face, or maybe just vomit, but a glance from Ekene and I keep my mouth shut. There are more important things to do. Things like rescue Mum and Grea and stop the wohol from shooting at us. Things like not dying.

'We control the slag,' Ekene says, and the words are in my ears, coming from the walls. 'Not you.'

Jim swipes a hand through Ekene, like a kid experimenting with a holo. 'Who said—'

'You did, when you killed us.' Ekene blinks and does... something. I sense the minds behind him reaching out, but only as the resentment colouring their thoughts.

It's like the whole world comes crashing down on Jim; the engineer just kinda crumples, knees buckling, white skin turning almost blue as the blood rushes out of his face. Grief and fear spill around him, an emotional pants-peeing adding another layer of colour to the mess already saturating the deck.

I could fix that, could scoop up all that emotion and put it in an endless, impenetrable box where it couldn't hurt anyone. I could save Jim from Ekene's vengeance, could explain to everyone that he and Aeotu have teamed up, that we had a plan and everything... or at least, just a tiny bit of everything, would be okay.

But I don't.

I leave Jim in his situation, feel a little good about it, maybe even stretch my mind out to soak in a little bit of Ekene's satisfaction. I wrap it over the guilt in my own chest, a buffer between me and the memory of my sword sinking into Mac's chest. It lasts until I catch Mac's dad looking at me, the pain in his gaze ripping away the comforting layer of Jim's despair.

He knows. He knows and... I don't think he blames me, I think...

*Thank you, Kuma.* Mac's dad's voice echoes in my head, warm, no judgement, no resentment, just that grief piercing my soul.

For what? I want to say, but the words are stuck in the bewilderment clogging up my brain, the confusion swirling in my chest.

But Mac's dad doesn't need the words, or maybe he just reaches in and plucks them out. Hard to tell with a telepath. *For ending my son's suffering.*

Mac hadn't been suffering, I mean, not anymore; not that I'd sensed. Mac'd been fighting, leaping about like one his favourite Terra damned superheroes, laying waste to viyusa and saving his family... saving Aeotu. Planting himself right in front of an alien AI and taking a sword to the chest. That hadn't been suffering, that hadn't been pain, that—

*That wasn't my son.*

There. A slap to the face, ringing my ears, saturating my vision with stars and beckoning forth a vision of Mac before Aeotu. Tall and broad, the dark bronze of his face dimpled as he smiled at me in those last golden moments of our lives before we knew of wohol and fug and terror.

That wasn't my son.

'Cause his son had gone into stasis/sleep and hadn't woken up, that's what he meant. Hadn't woken whole, how he used to be.

Which is shit; is the fear in Mum's eyes, the hate in Jim's, the hesitation in Dad's hug. It's not our bodies that make us who we are, it's the person – the being – underneath.

A telepath should know that.

*That* thought I plaster across my forehead, let sit in my eyes and shoot across the deck at Mac's dad. I see it hit in the way he flinches, the muscles in his face spasming as he turns away. And still, *still* understanding floods from him to me, gratitude an orange-pink knife to my heart.

'Fuck you,' I say.

Silence falls, cutting through Ekene and Dad and Jim, still curled up in that little ball on the deck. I didn't say it loud, not any louder than if Mac's dad were at my shoulder, instead of across three meters of deck.

*{{ Two-point-seven— }}*

Shut up Hunt, find Mac. My maybe-more-than-a-best-friend,

whose corpse was buried somewhere under all this carnage. The one who died saving the being who changed him. The one who deserves better than the shit-for-brains telepath across from me.

Everyone's looking at me, all the kin and all the humans. It's amazing how much disgust I can put into two words, how, even just thinking them feels like spitting. A putrid globule flying from my brain to land at their feet. And maybe it does, 'cause they all flinch, backing up so fast they stumble over their own feet. Even Ekene, in his incorporeal genie form, scoots away.

I look them in the eye, one after the other. First Dad, who stinks of grief and holds his left arm away from his side just in case it touches the fug holding his insides in, and then Mac's dad, and we all know what he's feeling. Mwat and Onah are next, and the things in their gazes, the bright orange-red of their upper eyes fixed on me, reach right in and twitch the dark sticky strings of ancient fear in my gut. They look away like I'm contagious.

And perhaps I am, and if I'm not, maybe I should be. Maybe if everyone felt what I do, saw what I saw, we wouldn't be in this fucked-up mess.

Only Ekene meets my gaze without fear or revulsion, and the things in his eyes... The girder that took my leg had more compassion.

All of them want something, all of them look at me and they don't see Kuma anymore. They see something that looks like the aliens that just killed their family and friends, except worse because I look like *them* too. Human. I'm reminded of that moment when Aeotu faced me and how much easier it would have been to feel compassion for her if only she were *more* alien, if only I hadn't seen myself in the way she stood, the shape of her head.

That's how they look at me, see what they could become and there's only fear in that realisation.

'Fuck you,' I say again, and this time I'm not just talking to Mac's dad. 'Fuck you *all.*' And then I turn on my heel and limp away.

✴

I leave them there, all clustered around each other, rebreathers and stolen weapons knocking into each other. Only Jim watches me leave, his eyes boring holes in the back of my neck, icy lasers seeking out my spinal cord.

Fuck Jim. Fuck Dad. Fuck the whole lot of them. Happy enough to huddle within the safety of Hunt's cannons and use my friends to save themselves.

Fire writhes in my belly from Mac's dad's words. Old Terra, the words themselves still ring, chasing themselves around and around my head. *Not my son.* With each lap, anger builds, makes the furnace in my gut burn hotter, darker.

Dude doesn't approve, and not of Mac's dad's words or the way the others look at me like some kind of freak, but of the anger. It's there in the fuzz vibrating from his paws, a hard not-quite-sad edge to the gold rippling through my system. Hunt though... Hunt doesn't care, it's calculating the distance between me and the platform at its back, and once I'm on it, it's jacking into the hangar's few functioning systems and lifting us through the air.

Which is good, at least one of us is paying attention.

Hunt's back opens, the space between the Kuma-sized protrusions of its thrusters parting, giant cords of metal-stone reaching out to wrap around waist and shoulders.

Hunt folds around me and it is like... Like hugging Grea, forehead to forehead, nose to nose, folding each other up in our arms and being *one* as our molecules slot together. And yet it is not Grea, the space where my twin should be yawns wide, empty. Cold. The dark tangle of resentment and anger is gone, melting in the face of that ice.

Dude chitters, fuzzy head butting up under my chin, leaving warmth behind. A reminder that I'm not alone.

I breathe deep, soak up the warmth, and wish there was room inside Hunt to hold the critter tight to my chest. 'I know, Dude, I know.'

New limbs tickle the back of my brain as Hunt becomes part of me, or I become part of Hunt. Not a full merging, not an "us", but enough to recognise Hunt's limbs, to feel the angry spark of damaged conduits, the ragged hole where the viyusa ripped its cannons out.

They are my arms, bigger, stronger, upper set of hands clenching in time with my fleshy ones. Conduits and nanites running under the metal-stone where tendons would be, the shape of blades just under my forearms. Attached to my ribs are the second set of arms, the input from them rippling up my back, forging new pathways in my brain. Moving them is strange, requires connections that slip and slide through my mind, impossible to master, but Dude is there, the golden fuzz of his presence playing under my skin, sharing what it's like to clamber through tunnels and over tables with six legs. And now there are secondary shoulder blades playing over my back like ghosts, new connections in my motor cortex, tendons and fissure connecting phantom muscles to my spine.

For a moment, I experience more than just a second set of arms, but fur over my cheeks and the slide of claws sheathed in my fingers.

*Careful.* The voice comes out of the darkness, deep and rich with familiarity and the memory of Mac. It disrupts the flow of golden fuzz down my throat.

Mac.

An acknowledgment from Hunt, the hangar lighting up on the HUD, shapes and fading heat signatures identified under the mountains of dead nannies.

*{{ Unable to locate. }}*

A bright spark of hope lighting my chest.

Mac?

A sad half-smile in the back of my mind and the sense of him is gone.

A memory? Wishful thinking? Or maybe, just maybe, Mac, real and whole and alive? But no, I saw him die, felt him fade in my arms. And surely, if Mac were alive, his shit-for-brains dad would sense him. Right?

There's no answer, no divine light or alien AI to offer absolution. Just guilt chilling my blood. Dude fuzzes, washing me with reassurance.

Hunt thrums in the back of my head. Waiting.

First arms, check. Second arms, double check.

Paws clench in time with my toes. Triple check.

Hunt?

*{{ All systems go. Releasing. }}*

The phantom sensation of cables disconnecting – *shnunk shnunk snick* – Hunt's heart spinning to full power, Dude bracing on my shoulder.

Adrenalin, born not of fear but excitement, racing in my veins. Anticipation.

*Thunk. Thunk. Thunk.*

The floor falls away.

We plunge into darkness lit by the yellow and green of the HUD, numbers racing, too fast for my human eyes to process, but it doesn't matter because the same numbers are in my head, bleeding through from Hunt.

Three-point-eight seconds and then... Space, the void stretched out around us. Stars upon stars twinkling in the black, the utter cold, the release of pressure, Aeotu getting smaller and smaller above us.

Three kilometres. Five. Ten.

Hunt's heart burns, power flowing outwards from its chest, the thrusters on its back firing in short bursts, just enough to spin us around.

At first there is only space, the vast ocean of distant stars, the shadow of asteroids and moons, outlined in white on the HUD. There is time to count them, like Old Terra sheep leaping through my dreams, and then there is the aura of the planet, a gas giant; diameter: fifty-two thousand kilometres; iron and carbon monoxide punctuated by bright flashes of lightning as the gases swirl around a dense metallic core. And then... and then...

Breath stuck in my throat, dread mixing with fascination as the reverse-thrusters fire and we finish turning. For a moment we hang there, two tiny bits of flesh wrapped in a giant four-armed living mechanicoid, and just breathe.

The graveyard hasn't changed in the last four days; it's still a cluster of dead and dying ships orbiting the grey gas giant. There is movement though, more than there was the last time we hung here, when I'd still dreamed of repairing *Citlali* and heading back to a planet I'd never called home.

Smaller vessels move among the broken hulls of the Sisters; Hunt picks one out and enhances it on the HUD. It's a mismatched collection of parts with viyusa filling in the gaps, or most of the gaps, there's a chunk of hull missing from its stern, enough to make out the glow of its generator and the turn of ribs. I shake the image off, and without it filling the HUD I can make out the trail of parts following in the vessel's wake.

It's not the only one. Little ships cluster around the larger derelict Sisters, the ones who are silent or mostly-silent, as well as the debris field where the space station once orbited.

It doesn't take a genius to figure out what they're doing, not when those little vessels disappear inside dead ships and come out towing pieces of superstructure.

It's like watching Old Terran vultures eat the dead but worse, because not all of the Sisters are actually dead. Energy readings play across Hunt's sensors, while wails play in my head. Some from the dying, most from those picking clean the bones of relatives to save themselves. The sound bites at me, rides in on the waves of emotion and strikes at my heart. I want to shut them out but I can't. There's a dread kind of fascination and a twisted sense of duty holding my mind open. I can't tell you why, only that I feel like I *have* to bear witness to the slow-moving horror playing out in the void. That someone has to record it and remember.

The piece of me that drove a psionic blade through my best friend, the bit driven by rage and hate, that bit wants to revel in the Sisters' pain, insists they deserve it. That they bought it on themselves. The rest of me, the parts connected to Hunt and Dude and Grea, the bit you might call a conscience, says that others transgressed on them first, that what the Sisters have done to me, to Ekene, to *Citlali* is nothing more than what I'm doing. Than what I've done. And that maybe, probably, what I'll do.

To survive.

There's more movement beyond the graveyard, a shape in the planet's outer atmosphere made out only by its energy signature, a little staticky as it passes first through Aeotu's sensors and then into Hunt's.

A blip on the HUD as energy spikes within the cloud. A ship rises from the atmosphere, grey and black fog parting over the hull, more of it being sucked into what looks like ramscoops, two giant ports in either side the ship's hull.

{{ *Reenu,* }} says Hunt. Details flood the back of my brain. Two hundred and five metres from bow to stern, another sixty-eight from starboard to port; eight decks, most of it cargo. Independent manufacturing facilities, proto-viyusa farm, one thousand three hundred and thirty-two repair bots—

I shut the flood down. I get it. *Reenu* is a repair ship, fitted with the sort of tech needed to fix her sisters, probably meant to follow them into battle or something.

In the back of my head, the remnants of Ekene's command sphere latch onto the image of *Reenu's* proto-viyusa farm and whisper: *There.*

I shake it away.

'She's harvesting the gases.' The words are out before I let them, swallowed up by the darkness the second they leave my lips.

{{ *Yes.* }}

'For fuel.'

There's a pause, a nanosecond as Hunt considers, reaches out to Aeotu and— {{ *Unknown,* }} it says.

Except that's a lie, not that Hunt's capable of lying. No, the lie leaks through Hunt and into me via the kaleidoscopic connection between the mech and Aeotu.

Dude is with me, lending me his strength as I reach as far back along that connection as I can. *Why?* I yell it, loud and hard and hope the echo makes it back to Aeotu.

Hunt's thrusters fire as I wait for an answer.

The HUD shifts, sensors no longer focused on the graveyard but the empty space above it.

A blip and suddenly the space isn't so empty.

There are more ships.

They look like the Sisters but they're not. For one, there are no holes in their hulls and two... Hunt's picking up power signatures, the kind that blaze like miniature stars.

{{ *Creator ships,* }} says Hunt.

Wohol ships.

In my head, the water-kins ancient sticky blackness unfolds.

There are two wohol ships orbiting the graveyard. A handful of smaller vessels spread around them – sleek, whole, no gaps or twisting parts in their hulls – patrolling the lines where the fence used to be. The images on the HUD carry the pattern of Aeotu's scanners, and how I know that, I can only put down to the connection with Hunt, because the mech doesn't say anything, and it's not like there's a "data courtesy of Aeotu" notice stamped in the corner.

There's so much debris where the fence once was, floating chunks of hull and superstructure, bright sparks of power lighting up the HUD like a mini galaxy. I'm pretty sure they weren't there the last time, by then we were busy doing other things, like blowing up power relays. And who's to say the debris isn't part of our doing, wasn't the scattered remnants of *Citlali*? The force of its destruction could have blown parts of it out here, or... My attention is pulled to the steady stream of parts floating from the wrecks to the other Sisters. The parts could have been carried.

Except that doesn't make sense, the composition is wrong, speaks of nanites and metal-stone, not the kind of materials Jørans used.

More data flows between us – numbers and equations, time stamps and recordings flashing through Hunt's processors, filtering through the umbilicus and playing out behind my eyes.

I shake my head, trying to dislodge the double image as the past overlays the now, but the images are stubborn and Dude's soft fuzz suggests that it might just be easier to watch. That maybe I *need* to watch. So I do.

A trio of smaller vessels shoot out of one of the wohol ships' bellies. The shuttles are bigger than the ones patrolling the graveyard now, but still tiny in comparison to their parent ship. Two aim for the hulking half-wrecks of Euiva and another Sister drifting beyond the old fence, while the last heads for where the power relay I destroyed used to be.

{{ *Repair pod,* }} Hunt says, not that the words are strictly necessary, not with the new connection. But still, they make the knowledge easier to swallow, like the different input paves the way for the rest of it to bloom in my mind.

The pod slows as it enters the debris field, and I sense the echo of its scanners, the moment when it slides up next to one of the few intact chunks of the old pylon. The chunk is small and round, the edges melted. Melted by us. That realisation hits me in the middle of the chest, makes the flash of concern from Aeotu – softened by the days in-between – and the sudden imperative make sense. A little. I guess.

What comes next isn't surprising.

The explosion obliterates *everything*, wohol repair pod and pylon wreckage. Sight and sensors obscured by a flash of radiation and light. When it clears, two-point-eight seconds later, the only thing left is more debris.

Can't have the enemy knowing about the Sisters' new weapon.

I want to know where the Sisters got explosives, did they make them? Scavenge them? If they'd had old bombs or torpedos lying around in their hulls, surely they'd have used them to free themselves?

And if they made them, where'd they get the explosive material?

The memory of *Reenu* rising through the gas giant's atmosphere, the repair ship sucking gas into its belly, comes to the forefront of my brain. All sorts of elements can be found in a gas giant's atmosphere, you'd just need the time and facilities to refine them.

Old, scavenged or made, the Sisters have more of the weapons. Two more explosions signal the deaths of the other wohol shuttles investigating the debris field that was once *Citlali* and the space station.

I expect more after that, a flood of small vessels from the wohol ships, or lasers or torpedos or something. But all there is, is nothing.

Silence.

Stillness.

I blink and the data is gone, the scene behind my eyes dissipating like smoke, leaving only the bright constellation of ships and debris on the HUD.

I can feel Aeotu vibrating through my connection with Hunt, her attention on the wohol ships hanging out of the reach of the gas giant's magnetic pull. There's wonder and awe, fear, hate and grief all mixed up in it, pulling at me. And yes, there's the water-kins' sticky black tendrils too, whispering kill, kill, kill.

But I don't care.

I'm not here for them.

I just want Grea, and Mum. And maybe, if I'm feeling generous, I'll find the others too.

'Where are they?' I say.

Hunt does not know and Aeotu does not respond.

I'm getting sick of that.

# CHAPTER TWELVE

There's one place I know to go.

It takes a few false starts, what with Ekene's command sphere pulling at my brain, wanting me to find *Reenu* and that ship's proto-viyusa farm. Hunt must have looked weird, stopping and starting as I fought the compulsion, thrusters spinning us one way and then the other.

I broke through it eventually, Dude a warm blanket under my skull.

*Euiva* floats on the edge of the graveyard, still a skeleton, all mech-width girders and patchy hull, but now she swarms with movement. Those small holey vessels stream in and out of her hull while what looks like *Citlali's* old workbots fix flat pieces of metal over her superstructure.

I would know her even without Aeotu's knowledge flowing through Hunt to me; I would know because in the eter, hidden deep within the endless darkness is a tiny spot of red.

*Euiva*, Aeotu whispers inside my skull.

*Grea*, I whisper, but not to Aeotu. I whisper it forward, shoot it into the darkness.

Is it my imagination, or does the red burn brighter in response?

The darkness moves, the unfinished hull with it. The activity on Hunt's sensors pauses, nanites and power fluctuating, shifting first one way and then another, before it explodes. Viyusa colours *Euiva's* superstructure red and a scan hits us in the chest. It's almost a physical weight pressing against my ribs, making Hunt's generator stutter. Even Dude flattens himself on my shoulder.

I can't breathe. The HUD goes dark.

The weight is gone as quickly as it came. I draw air on a ragged gasp as the HUD flickers back to the life, everything the same as before, except for the beacon pulsing in the midst of *Euiva*'s wreck.

I guess she knows we're coming.

Hunt's thrusters fire and we're hurtling toward the closest gaping hole.

Best not to disappoint her.

The place is a maze.

The workbots must be repairing *Euiva*'s hull first, because inside she's little more than a hollowed-out egg, the barest hint of a skeleton suggesting the shape of decks, the outline of rooms. There's not an intact bulkhead in sight, although Hunt's sensors suggest that changes closer to her core.

We drift through the superstructure, weaving between girders. Up, over, around, leaving no section of it unscanned.

You'd think the lack of bulkheads would make Grea easier to find, and it does, for a little bit, until we hit the first actual wall.

According to Hunt's map, we entered *Euiva* somewhere in the lower decks, where the spaces were large, built to accommodate vehicles and other bulky equipment. The superstructure in the outer areas was generous, the spaces between girders easy for Hunt to navigate, but as we travel deeper, things are getting tighter.

And now there are walls, if you can call them that.

The surface in front of us is a mismatched collection of metal in every shade of grey and brown, black patches scattered through it like bruises. Patterns are etched on most of the pieces, some matching, most not and looking at them hurts. It's like staring too long at a tangle of lines and swirls that you *know* have meaning, if only you could rearrange them.

It takes me awhile to realise that the patterns are the last words of dying ships, that *Euiva*'s wearing her sisters like a ragged cloak made out of skin. Or something.

I wonder if that patchwork of messages is full of tearful goodbyes or curses. I wonder what it's like to carry that around inside, all that hate and maybe some love, tattooed on your bones.

A flash of red breaks the grey-brown sameness. It looks like viyusa at first, until it winks at me. Once, twice, three times. There's a pause, another blink, faster than the first set.

'It's a code.'

Hunt agrees, pops the new scans front and centre on the HUD, even as its forward thrusters fire, taking us closer. There's something attached to *Euiva*'s inner bulkheads, a small sleek shape at odds with the egg-like Sisters and *Citlali*'s old workbots, but familiar enough that I know I've seen it before, that it was a smaller version of this, smashing through *Aeotu*'s hull, that took my leg.

A sick, angry sensation starts in the pit of my stomach.

Hunt's scanners are sinking through the thing's hull when the winking starts again. Three blinks, a pause. Two more.

'What are they saying?'

*{{ Unknown. }}*

"Help" probably, or "who goes there?" or "back the fuck off you creepy, huge mechanoid thing, before we blow your chest to atoms." That's what I'd be saying, at least. That or, you know, just firing. No point in giving myself any warning. But who knows right? Maybe wohol have their own mechs, or maybe their ship's toast and they can't see shit beyond their airlock. Maybe, maybe. Maybe.

There's a kind of heat map on the HUD now, as Hunt's sensors sink through the ship's hull. Two red splotches, bigger than a human, almost as big as a rucnart.

*{{ Creators, }}* Hunt whispers.

'Yeah, whatever.' As far as I'm concerned, all these dudes created was a big fucking mess that caught my family up and is repeatedly kicking us in the teeth.

I hate the wohol, hate them hard. Some of it leaks through from training memories, but the rest of it, the stuff that roils and boils, that is all mine. And the sticky black stuff, the underwater song of death... that's got no part of it at all. Has nothing to do with the power spiking in Hunt's heart, or the damage warnings overlaying the scan of the ship. Has got nothing to do with the frustration that fills my bones when I remember Hunt's cannons are dead, shredded by viyusa.

Nothing at all.

Nothing. At. All.

Hunt is still scanning, looking for a way past the mis-matched wall and into *Euiva*'s heart. But all I want to do, all I can think about is plunging my hands into the wohol ship and tearing it apart.

Dude is fuzzing away on my shoulder, and distantly I can feel him batting at the black sticky strings rising from that dark place in my anima. All I can hear is the pound of my heart, crashing against my chest. Kill. Hate. Kill.

Again and again and again.

Maybe it's my focus, or maybe I'm slipping into Hunt, or Hunt's slipping into me in that all-consuming merging of selves, taking over the mech's sensors, but I find the airlock first.

It's on the HUD, outlined in white, the ever-present diagrams and calculations shunted to either side. The airlock is on the wohol ship's port side, midway between stern and bow. It's big, at least by human standards, big enough to squeeze a workbug through but too small for Hunt, unless we get down on hands and knees...

{{ *No.* }} The negative echoes in my brain, along with other things, like the likely dimensions of the ship's corridors, the advisability of crawling through something to get to another space that may be even smaller.

Okay. So I guess it's just Dude and I doing this thing.

Dude is a small, anxious lump on my shoulder, curled in on himself, away from the sticky darkness.

It takes awhile, minutes for Hunt to align itself to the hatch. I'm not sure exactly what it's doing, but I sense the *CLUNK* as it melds with the airlock, the concentration as it sends a probe into the alien computer and then... I'm guided out of the mech, tendrils retracting from my arms and torso, leaving me in a strange half-light, staring at Hunt's back and the Kuma-sized cockpit rapidly disappearing behind shifting plates of metal-stone and fug.

My own fug has gone full commando, faceplate activated, and every millimetre of my skin covered in yellow-green. Even Dude is in full-armour mode, silent on my shoulder, only the barbed tip of his tail giving any indication that he's not a statue.

The outer hatch snaps closed, cutting me off from Hunt.

I turn around. Face the inner hatch.

Dude is back to fuzzing his butt off, gold washing out of him, trying to dislodge the sticky black shit crawling under my skin, beating with my heart. Trying. Trying and failing, but I don't mind.

I smile and let the fug blades slide from my arms.

Two bodies on the deck, too-red blood sprayed over the bulkheads, some of it on my faceplate, more of it running over the backs of my hands from when the fug blades retracted. Enough of it there to drip from my knuckles, a steady *plop plop plop* onto the pale grey floor.

Plop.

Plop.

Plop.

Hunt is spinning data through the back of my brain, although it's no longer the rush of a few moments ago. No longer adrenaline and fury making my heart race, the cold calculation of probabilities and tactics guiding my muscles, spinning me *here,* thrusting the fug blades *there.*

The throb of my pulse is loud, almost as loud as the rasp of my breath, although neither overpower the wail of the siren.

Dude is silent.

Dude hasn't moved since the inner airlock *snapped* open and I came face to chest with the first wohol. It had looked at me, brow ridges raised, slit pupils going wide – surprise as universal as fear, I guess – and I stabbed in through the chest.

No real idea where its heart was; if it was in its belly or its leg, or maybe wohol have two hearts, or three or some weird non-centralised cardio-vascular system that meant it would just keep going no matter where I stabbed.

So I carved up its torso, plunged both fug blades into the spot where a human's guts would be and pushed upwards. It was like tearing through brittle plasform, fabric and flesh curtains parting around the blades. The bone was a little tougher, but in the nanosecond it took me to reach what might have been ribs, I was on my toes and the tips of my blades exploded out of the alien's shoulders.

The blades retracted – *shhnick*, back into my arms – the wohol collapsed, still breathing, just for a few final seconds, and there was its crew mate, standing behind it.

It died a little slower. Had an energy weapon, smaller than the team that invaded the hangar and killed h'Rawd, but powerful enough to tear a hole in my armour in the second it took me to leap across the deck.

And now I'm standing here, panting, wondering what to do next. Plop. Plop.

I wait, but there's no third *plop*. I hadn't realised I'd been counting them until it doesn't come and I'm left hanging, waiting for the other shoe to drop. The blood's gone, sucked into my armour, nanites consuming carbohydrates and proteins, the burned-out hole on my chest partially filling in.

Unlike my rage. It's gone, burned away with the blood, leaving nothing behind. I should feel something, *Dude* thinks I should feel something, I can tell by the distance between us. It's not physical, he's still on my shoulder, but still, I don't sense him like I should, warm and comforting. He's as closed off to me now as he was walking through Aeotu's viyusa-filled corridors, except it's not the viyusa he's walled himself off from, it's me.

Me and the death at my paw/hook. At the hole in my middle and the sticky strings of darkness crawling out of it.

'Brother.' The voice comes out of the walls, low, sibilant, sounding more like the breeze than a word. And yet I know it, know it like I know my own. Like I know Grea's.

It's not Grea.

'Euiva.' My voice is crisp and clear, snaps the air. 'Give me my sister.'

'My sister.' There is a beat of silence, and I'm not quite sure what to make of that, if Euiva is just repeating my words back to me, and then... 'Little Sister.'

The way she says it, the possession in her tone, makes my guts go cold. 'You can't have her.'

'You can't take her, little Brother.'

A form flickers above the wohol corpses, slope-shouldered, tall and thin. Four arms, two legs, a flat-nosed face with Grea's eyes, Grea's mouth, Grea's hair and a constellation of shadows writhing under its skin.

Euiva, or rather her hologram, stares at me.

I've stepped back before the thought has fully formed, it's instinctual, like backing away from h'Lott with blood on her snout and her teeth in your face. Instinct wants me to take another, and another after that, until I'm tucked up safe in Hunt's chest. But no. I bare my teeth and plant my feet, sinking the fug-talons on my one remaining paw into the deck even as I build a wall in my head between my consciousness and the blazing star that is Euiva.

Dude comes alive on my shoulder, adds his strength to the shield.

In the back of my head, I sense Hunt's reactor spinning to full power.

Euiva smiles, pulling Grea's lips back over too-long incisors. 'Cute,' and that response is so Grea, right down to the inflection and the little curl of ridicule at the edge of her nose, that my heart stutters. And just like that, all my power, all that determination is gone.

'Grea?' My voice is small.

A shake of her/their head. 'But you can see her.' And Euiva turns away.

# CHAPTER THIRTEEN

Euiva leads me onwards, through the wohol scout ship – hatches *snapping* into the deck, another airlock opening and closing – into the patchwork of her inner self. I don't know what I expected, but I guess this is close enough.

*Euiva*'s insides are as holey as her outsides. Ice bites at the not-quite-healed hole in my chest armour, a fine frost digging into the bare patch of skin and sinking in its teeth. There's no atmosphere, no antigrav. I push out of the wohol airlock and my paw/hook are floating a hands-breadth above the deck.

It's shit. Takes a minute of wriggling about and arm waving before I've a hold on the nearest bulkhead and am pushing and pulling myself along.

The armour could give me thrusters, even starts reforming itself, adding little nodules to the back of my shoulders and ribs, pulling heat from my bones. I stop it. Just a thought, a firm "no" like I'm talking to the idiot me at the back of my brain, and the pull on my bones, the sense of things shifting over my skin stops.

A query from Hunt, a half-formed bundle of words, asks why?

I stare at Euiva's holographic back, trying not to see Grea in the way she holds her shoulders or sticks her chin out, like she's daring the world to get in her face.

Why? Because I don't trust Euiva. She's wearing my sister's face, and you can't tell me it's not deliberate, that she couldn't have used a million others, that she didn't mean to reach in and grab hold of my heart with that quirk of her nose.

Wherever she's leading me, I'm sure Grea is at the end of it, but I'm just as sure that whatever "it" is, is something I'm not going to like. Or want. Or do. And I'm just as sure that Euiva's not going to care.

The power and fug needed to give me thrusters? I'm going to need that. And soon, and I probably won't have enough to fight Euiva. There'll never be enough.

But I'll worry about that later.

*Euiva*'s inner decks, the ones right in the heart of her, are almost untouched. The bulkheads a pristine off-white, the carvings crisp, the deck smooth, light shining up from the floor, or maybe it's some kind of glowing moss or paint, because I can't find the source of it.

There's a map on my HUD, not of *Euiva* but of *Aeotu*, and if I hadn't had the inkling before, I have it now. The Sisters are twins, their layouts identical, right down to this little hatch hidden behind a bulkhead below *Euiva*'s core. If I could see through the deck, I'd be peering up *Euiva*'s skirt, right into the tangle of viyusa and power conduits that make up her brain. I wonder if *Euiva*'s core looks like *Aeotu*'s, a jungle of impossible colours like the kaleidoscope that plays under the AI's skin, or if *Euiva*'s core is as dark as her avatar.

This inner hatch isn't pristine like the other inner corridors but marked with the signs of battle. The bulkhead surrounding it is pitted and scratched, the off-white walls marked with soot and the ragged marks of claws. Someone tried to get in, with weapons first, and then their nails.

I hover my hand over the scratches, stretching my fingers and summoning fug-claws. The marks are too widely spaced to be human and there are only three of them, not the four there would be if Grea had made the marks.

That only leaves one possibility. Wohol were here, but how long ago? Moments? Hours? Centuries? And why?

The answer, like Grea, is behind the hatch.

It doesn't snap open like the rest. Not when I approach, not when I press my hand to the swirl carved in the wall beside it.

'Let me in,' I say.

Euiva doesn't respond, but I can see her swirling through the metal-stone, the thick shifting black of her presence in the weird overlay of eter and real, as much as the avatar by my side.

I turn to it, try not to see Grea in its slanted eyes or the furrow between its brows.

'You brought me here,' I say and there's no keeping the anger out of my voice, the sour thread of distrust. 'You said I could see her. Let me in.'

Still, the door doesn't move.

Hunt burns in my chest, and power ripples down my arms, blades springing from my wrists, yellow-green slag coating the edges. 'Let me in,' I say again.

Viyusa bleeds through the walls, red filling in the carvings.

On my shoulder, Dude snarls.

Viyusa creeps toward my toes, and on the HUD an alarm flashes silently in my vision as more of the red closes off the corridor behind.

And there, there is the trap, closing behind me like I knew it would. Somehow, seeing it makes me feel better.

In the space beyond the wohol scout ship, Hunt's generator spins, power pouring through its veins, pooling in the ports on its wrists, an echo of my own fug-blades. Its pushing calculations in my head, escape strategies and odds. They're all bad. Too much *Euiva* and too much viyusa between me and the mech, between Hunt and us jetting out of the ship into the relative safety of open space.

{{ *Retreat.* }}

No. Never. Grea is behind that hatch.

Dude's snarl deepens, and his tail whips around my head, the barb gleaming in the soft light.

I'm not sure if it's because of the viyusa or Grea that his claws sink into my shoulder, but still, I am not leaving.

Yellow-green slag drips down my blades.

I glare at Euiva, her avatar close enough to touch. 'I'll cut through the hatch, you know I will.'

A flicker, like a hesitation, but still no response. And that's strange, isn't it? Euiva has never been shy about laying out her plans and bossing me around. Was the one who used us like a tool. What was different now?

A thread of viyusa winds around my big toes. Yellow-green erupts from my skin, swallows it.

Euiva flinches, and for the first time I glimpse colour in the darkness of her face, a bright pop of yellow, there and then gone.

Fear, I literally just saw fear in Euiva's face. The realisation hits me in the chest, making my heart skip a beat, expelling air from my lungs. So, does that mean that the coruscating shadows I see now are another emotion? But what is that dark, that sticky... Even as I think it, the answer writhes in my anima, and gives me the key not just to Euiva's skin but what to do next.

Slag crawls over my hands, turns the tips of my fingers yellow even as the heat is drawn away from my bones, and my fug-claws become molten.

'Maybe you can kill me before I tear my way in, but you can't stop the slag, can you?'

Euiva's eyes are locked on my hands, and more yellow rolls over her cheekbones.

I smile, but there's no joy in my heart, only a dead, sticky sense of satisfaction and that dark ancient song rising from my anima.

I have her.

The hatch *SNAPS* into the deck.

I step through.

The space beyond is small, dim, the only light coming from a source somewhere above. If not for the tree-thing growing from the ceiling, I could walk across it in four large strides, maybe even squash h'Lott and Onah in here, shut the door and pray they never got out. The tree-thing though... It looks like an upside-down version of *Aeotu*'s core, and maybe it is. I look up, imagine *Euiva's* core above, a thick trunk of nanites pulsing in time with the ship's engines, a trillion shades of black shifting under its skin while viyusa crawls over the walls of the spherical chamber that houses it.

If the trunk was right above then this... This upside-down tree-thing would be its roots. Euiva's roots, plunging through the deck. The tips touch the floor and spread outwards, thin black runners seeking new dirt. Or whatever the fuck it is Euiva wants.

Grea's wrapped up in that shit. I know she is, right in my gut, even if I can't see her.

There isn't much space in the little room, but I suck my stomach in and scoot around the tree-thing, stepping over the runners. The blackness makes my skin crawl, and Dude... His growl vibrates in my bones.

I have to go right the way around, until the hatch is blocked from sight and Hunt is issuing warnings like oxygen. If Euiva turns on me now, I'm screwed, slag or no slag, but what's new, right?

My sister stares at me, and my heart stops.

*That* is Grea. She hangs from the ceiling, an Old Terra fly wrapped up in a cocoon of thick, pulsing vines. I wonder if I looked like that when Aeotu had me in the grow-field. I doubt it, just because I've seen the others under their mounds of fug.

There's no sight in her eyes, her pupils are dilated and her skin is a ghastly shade of grey, her lips blue. She looks dead, and yet the HUD picks up a faint pulse of blood, the smallest inhalation of air. As for the rest of Grea... There's nothing to see, just her face, peeking out at me from the cocoon, and I wonder, as much as I wonder anything else, if that glimpse of skin is for my benefit, another hook to reel me in.

It works.

I hesitate just a second before laying a hand on my sister's cheek. 'Grea?'

Nothing.

*Grea?* I say again, slipping half into the eter. *Are you there?*

A flicker, a ghost caressing my face, leaving a hint of cherry behind.

*Grea? I'm going to get you out, just hang on, I've—*

*No.* Euiva, face and voice shifting, power rippling under her midnight skin. For a second, I can't tell if the AI is in the eter with me or a hologram in the real, and then I feel her, sliding up against my brain. Cold, sticky, fear and hate moving under her skin like the currents of an ancient sea. *She is mine now.*

'Like shit she is.' And I don't care what Hunt is yelling, don't give a fuck that Dude's fug-claws are ripping into my shoulder, trying to hold me back. Grea is *my* sister, and no alien fucking ship is taking her from me.

Heat blazes through my arms, tendons turning to superconductors, slag blazing like a star as I sink fug-blades into Euiva's roots.

Viyusa explodes, turning the darkness to blood, vines wrapping around my arms, spearing my hands, my side, my feet. Pain is... everything. Is my lungs, my muscles, the blood in my veins, is every breath and every thought, and still...

There are alarms going off on my HUD, Hunt screaming in my head, Dude's golden fuzz winding through my bones, trying to take control, and still... Still I bear down, shoving the blades deeper into Euiva, seeking that one sweet spot. I don't even know if it exists, if there's a nerve or a heart buried in the mess of nanites that'll kill the ship, I just know that I'm not leaving Grea behind.

Never ever.

Not even if it kills me.

# CHAPTER FOURTEEN

I don't die. Dying would mean failure, would leave Grea in Euiva's clutches and there's no way I'm going to do that. Not ever.

It's hard though, the not-dying bit.

I'm not in the little chamber under Euiva's core anymore, Grea's not here and there's no black root thing piecing the ceiling. This place is bigger, big enough to kick a holoball around, maybe nab a pair of magboots and set up a little game of grav-ball, with the goalie on the ceiling. It'd be pretty cool, except for the cocoons plastered against the bulkheads, viyusa stringing us all together, like Aeotu's grow-field, except we're all upright and everything is red. It's so red that, after the initial smack to my eyeballs, it's monochromatic; I might as well be surrounded by grey fug or blue or green because the colour just kinda fades to nothing.

A whole heap of writhing nothingness.

Wrapped around my arms, my legs, everything but my face.

And Dude. The critter is the only spot of colour in the nothing-redness. He's perched atop the cocoon across from me, his armour more yellow than green, or maybe that's just the sea of viyusa bringing out the gold highlights.

It doesn't matter, he's sitting there, staring at me like I'm supposed to do something. Like I haven't been trying to do something for the past however-long-I've-been-here.

'You could help.'

He flicks his tail.

That's a no.

I squirm in my cocoon of redness. I don't hurt anymore, that's one thing on the bright side. No more stabbing pains, no more aches in my guts, no more big hole in my chest. Or at least, that's what I'm hoping and dreading in equal measure; that while Euiva has had me trussed up, the viyusa has been doing some repair work. The thought... the thought makes my non-aching guts shrivel, because it's more than just not hurting anymore, more than just not having a hole in my chest. It's what Euiva is fixing me with. Is she regrowing bone and tendon? Or are my ribs made out of fug?

I know the answer to that without seeing it, without Hunt or Aeotu or anyone telling me. It's been hours, maybe a day since I threw down with Euiva and lost. Not even the best regen tank can attach a working pinkie in that amount of time, let alone grow a rib cage, not even if it has the biological material on hand.

I look around at the sea of red, the cocoons – eighteen in all – lined up against the bulkheads. There ain't no biological material in here, none that I'd want anyway, and as much as Euiva seems intent on not killing me, I'm pretty sure she's not using whoever's hanging out with me for parts.

At least I know where the abducted crew are, some of them at least. I can't see faces, just paws sticking out the bottom of cocoons, the occasional twitch of a taloned hand, like they're dreaming. Old Terra, I hope they're dreaming, hope they're not awake under there, suffocating in viyusa.

I tried reaching out to them, hunted through the eter and dipped into the ora looking for any trace of them. When that didn't work, I yelled, screamed, sang and swore at the other cocoons. After that, I flooded the air with every emotion in me: anger, fear, desperation, all three of them at once.

Nothing. Just Dude, staring at me, like there's a clue I missed. And you know what? I probably did, I probably missed a whole bunch of clues, but him sitting there and flicking his tail like I ought to hurry up and remember, wasn't. Helping!

I yelled that at him, filled the red nothingness with my voice and frustration. If there'd been anyone but Dude and a whole bunch of insensible Jørgens there, they'd have choked. Literally, choked.

Hack hack, cough cough, lungs on the deck type shit.

I bet there are other grow chambers just like this one on the other Sisters. How many of us did they take? Are they all going to be like M—

My heart squeezes. Pain floods my system, but more awful than that is shame, a toxic green flood rushing through my veins.

Mac.

Was he actually alive? Was that hint of him, heard as I clambered into Hunt, real? Would it change anything if it was? I stabbed my best friend. A deep breath. Pushing the thoughts aside. They weren't helping.

Another breath, feeling lungs against muscle, ribs against skin. How much of that is me?

Dude is watching me, expectation heavy in the air between us.

'I'm *trying*.'

Try harder, his gaze says, piercing even behind his armour.

I wriggle, clench my hands, my jaw, my thighs, my toes and *push*. Nothing.

I slump in my restraints, panting.

Dude's barbed tail thumps against the cocoon, impatience in every strike.

I take another breath and—

'You should try asking.' The voice, low and mocking but happy too, whispers next to my ear.

I freeze, not looking, not doing anything but preying to every Old Terra god I know, and most I just made up, that it's not a trick.

'Grea?' I whisper it.

'Who else, fathead?'

The cocoon is gone and I'm on the deck – knees kissing metal-stone, hands out to stop my fall – still afraid to look, seeing only red and white, like muscle on bone.

'You gonna stay down there all cycle, baby brother, or are we going to do this thing?'

I'm still not looking, even though my gaze is travelling up, taking in the fug-paws peeking out the bottom of the opposite cocoon, travelling further, finding Dude.

'What are we doing?' I ask, afraid of the answer, but needing her voice.

I hear the eye roll, the hands going to her hips. 'You're not *actually* this stupid, are you?'

'I don't know.' My throat is dry, still afraid to take my eyes off Dude. It sounds so much like her, but what if it's not? And still... and still, I have to look, have to know. 'Am I?' I say and turn.

Grea raises a brow, perfectly arched and as black as her hair, a copy for the ones on my face. There's an almost-sneer on her lips, softened by the laugh in her eyes and that little tick at the corner of her nose. It's not the nose of her transformed, older self – half squished, like it's disappearing into her face – but the one from before Aeotu, another copy of mine.

Joy lifts my heart, taking my body with it. Arms are open and—

I stop.

I can see through her.

Grea's a hologram.

Every step echoes, *snick snick snick*, and even through the filters, the atmosphere smells like dust, enough that I keep expecting fine grey particles to puff around my feet. They don't, of course. The decks are so clean they'd shine if not for the nubble texture. I bet it feels like carpet, like if I got down on my belly and pressed my face against it, the deck would be soft, warm even.

'It's not,' Grea says. 'You get down on that deck and your cheek'll probably stick to it. Ambient temperature is minus five-point-seven degrees Celsius. Not much point making it warmer, what with just you poncing about, not when we need the power elsewhere. Besides, your armour is better at keeping you from freezing.'

I nod, not saying anything, like I've been doing for the past – I check with Hunt – thirteen minutes and twenty-eight seconds, since the nanosecond I realised Grea was a holo. It feels like eternity, like I'm back at the edge of that black hole, watching h'Rawd die. Except this time, I'm standing on the outside looking in, where every second drags into an hour.

I didn't even ask Grea about the other Jørgens hanging from the bulkheads, didn't even try to get them out of their cocoons. I was frozen, arms outstretched, shock holding me still. And honestly, why was I shocked? Why had I expected anything more from Euiva than exactly what she wanted to give? Why did I think she had a heart?

As I was frozen there, Grea hugged me; holographic arms wrapping around my back, light particles pressing into my cheek. I knew she squeezed, and squeezed hard, because I saw the muscles flex in her fug armour, but there was no warmth, none of the sweet scent of cherry blossoms in her hair.

The phantom hug lasted three long seconds, I know because Hunt counted, and then Grea leapt back, hands on my shoulders, excitement lighting up her face, and told me to follow her.

So I did, and now here I am.

I can still see right through her, literally pick out the carvings in the bulkhead, but somehow she *seems* solid, and it might be my imagination, but I swear I hear her feet *snick snicking* in time with mine.

And yeah, she's wearing fug armour, and while her face may be her old one, the armour isn't. It's as red as the cocoon room, and I guess it's no wonder I didn't notice her until she spoke, 'cause with her face-shield up, she blended right in, invisible. Out here though... She's unmissable, a fountain of blood gliding down *Euiva*'s pale grey corridors. I keep expecting to see bloody paw prints on the deck, or a smeared trail left in the wake of the viyusa tendrils flowing from her shoulders like a cape. A creepy, writhing cape with parts that occasionally reach out to flick my nose.

I'm really glad I don't have a cape, but not half as glad as I am that I don't have a thumb-width tendril reaching out the back of my armour and plunging into the back of my neck. Of course, maybe…

My hand's already on my nape, touching smooth armour wrapping up over my head and down over my shoulders. Not a tendril in reach.

There's not even a little smear of red. Dude checked, scampering over my body the moment the cocoon released me, a growl vibrating his tail. He left slag in his wake, shedding the stuff like dandruff, and I remembered how gold he looked against the viyusa.

When he was finished, there was slag back in the carvings, delicate trails of yellow whirling up my legs and across my chest, and I'd felt like me again. Or as much of me as was left.

My fug-talons make their own *snick snick* on the deck. I'm back to having eight of them, four on each paw. No more hook-leg. I guess, while she was repairing my insides, Euiva took care of my outsides too, although how she did it with grey-green fug instead of red is anyone's guess.

Grea glides ahead of me, the maybe-imagined-maybe-not sound of her paws snicking in counterpoint to mine.

I stop, and speak before that ghostly echo can fade. 'Where are we going?'

She looks over her shoulder. Smiles. 'It's a surprise.'

'I don't like surprises.'

'Since when?'

'Since now. Since Aeotu and Euiva and this.' I throw my arms open, gesturing to myself. 'Since you sucked me into a nest of viyusa and tortured me.'

She shakes her head. 'I didn't—'

'You did. You know you did.'

She stares at me, denial and grief and guilt spilling out of her in waves, grey and black and vomit green. And shit, I know how that feels and not just because of the emotion butting up against my feet, curling around my ankles with pleading fingers, begging for forgiveness. You wouldn't think denial could do that, but it can, I'm watching it, feeling it, holding its fingers back from my heart, because if I let it in... If I let it in, I'm going to follow her and I know that's a bad idea, even without Hunt whispering in the back of my brain, or Dude's talons sinking through my shoulder. I might as well just march on back to that grow chamber and join the others on the walls.

It's hard though, so hard. I want to forgive Grea for everything, not just because she's my sister but because if Mac was standing in my place...

I breathe. In. Out. How much of that flesh and bone is mine?

I breathe again, clench my fingers, unclench them and step deeper into the cloud of emotion around Grea.

'Take me to the root chamber, Grea, below Euiva's core.' I put hands on her shoulders, imagine that it's flesh and not light particles under my palms as I lean in close, so we're forehead to holographic forehead. 'Help me get you out of there.'

She steps back and frowns at me like I just asked if space was cold. 'What are you talking about? I'm not in the root chamber, I'm right here.'

I nod like that makes perfect sense, then ask, 'Where is *here*?'

Grea stops, and I might have just hit her by the way her head twitches. 'Umm... Not really the time for a philosophical discussion, baby brother.'

I get it then, the way she waits for doors to open, the way she hugged me. She doesn't realise she's not real, not fleshy.

'You're a hologram, Grea.'

Half of a laugh explodes from her mouth. 'Uh huh, so then I guess this doesn't hurt?' She punches, and her hand passes through my shoulder.

Her eyes are wide, mouth open, but the shock only lasts a second, and then she's scowling at her fist, at me. But no... She's looking *through* me and her lips... they're moving but no sound is coming out. And then she's gone. Just "poof" and no more Grea.

Silence echoes. Not even Euiva lurking at the back of my brain.

Shit. That can't be good.

The scream knocks me off my paws. It's coming from everywhere, comms, the eter even the Terra damned ora, an unrelenting wave of pain, anger and betrayal slicing up my insides, turning my brain to jelly, robbing my muscles of the ability to stand, my heart of the power to pump. I'm drowning, pushed under the tide of Grea's emotion, and I don't even think... don't even think—

Dude is a warm golden shield around my brain, lifting me out of the sea of Grea's *emote*. He can't lift me all the way out, can't sever that connection between Grea and me, he tries, a blazing mental knife coming down on the cord connecting us. But it's like cutting off my lungs, like trying to separate me from Hunt or my armour. It's not possible, not anymore, there's too much fug keeping me alive, patching up the holes and substituting bones.

*Grea...* I reach for her, thrusting hands for the surface, clawing endlessly upwards. *Grea*, and it's less a call than a whisper, strength gone like air, mental lungs starving for an emotion other than pain. *Grea*.

But there is nothing, only the crushing weight, and I can't keep it out anymore. It's in my mouth, down my throat and—

Gone.

I'm on the deck, faceplate pressed to the freezing deck, hands splayed either side of my face and all I can do is breathe. One lungful after another of glorious, musty-smelling oxygen, the faint tang of the recycler a delicious, metallic aftertaste at the back of my throat.

Dude's on the deck beside me, his sleeked-out head cuddled in close to mine. Somehow, even with his armour turning his usually puffed-out cheeks and pinkie-sized black nose into something sharp and dangerous, he's still adorable. It's his eyes, I can't see them under the armour but the huge black orbs are stamped on my brain. He nudges my hand. There's urgency and demand in the weight of his head against my thumb.

'Grea.'

I don't think Dude's urgency stems from Grea's abrupt silence, but mine does, and I'm pushing off the deck, barely waiting for Dude to scamper up my arm.

*Grea.* I push her name into the eter, seeing it wing away from me as the psionic plane overlays the real. There's no response, in fact... I concentrate, leaving my body behind as I slip further into the psionic, searching for something, anything that rings of my sister. There's nothing. The eter is still, silent as the grave, not so much as a hint of emotion staining the flat, endless white. *Grea!* I yell it this time, pulling power not just from the depths of me, but Dude and Hunt.

Hunt burns in the pit of my being, filling me with power, but Dude growls, rebuke thick in the wash of psionic strength that flows from him to me.

I ignore it. I need to find Grea, need to know what's wrong.

There, a trace of cherry slipping through the threads of the eter and the ora. I grab it, dive between the fabric of the psionic planes and—

Bounce back into the real world, my head ringing and cold seeping through my skull.

There's a metallic taste on the back on my tongue that has nothing to do with the air recycler and everything to do with Euiva.

An afterimage of the AI stares at me from the cold place on my temple, an imprint of the wall that kept me out of the ora, that kept me from Grea.

A growl, deep and rich and bloodcurdling rips from my chest, the sound amplified by the armour until it sounds like a hundred rucnarts promising blood. 'She's my sister, not yours!'

A vibration passes through the deck. It sounds like laughter.

'Euiva!'

Euiva. Euiva. Euiva.

'Let her go!'

Go. Go. No.

The scream is mine. Is frustration and rage, rusty orange and red swamping the white corridor, the smallest trace of hot, sticky fear curling around the edges.

I scream until there's no breath to keep screaming, and then I scream again. It's not as strong the second time, nor as long, and maybe, just maybe, there's more of that sticky yellow mixed in with the red, but it peters out before the rage in my chest is done. I take a breath for a third, drawing it deep into my lungs, even as the saner part of me, the tiny bit that keeps track of things like the need to piss, is telling me to get a grip. Telling me how stupid it is to be standing here fighting an alien ship.

Sane me is also knocking on the inside of my head, in time with the tiny paw patting my cheek, and it's pointing to the obvious. To the cord that connects me to Grea, the outline of it trailing through the eter and into the heart of *Euiva*.

A map.

I follow it.

# CHAPTER FIFTEEN

I think, perhaps, I mistook sane me for the remnants of Ekene's command sphere or else Euiva moved Grea.

This is not the tiny corridor with the hidden hatch in the bulkhead. This is the bigger corridor, the bigger hatch that leads to the smaller corridor that opens onto the command deck, and a little further down the smaller corridor... that's Euiva's brain; the core.

If I was in that core, instead of standing here like a dumbstruck idiot, I'd be standing over the root chamber. And if I were in the core... Fuck, it's a wonder I'm not already dead, or worse.

And yet, the thing that connects me to Grea pulses with our heartbeats, every throb shooting out of my heart and down that space, splashing not against the door leading to Euiva but the closer one. The command deck.

That's good, I guess.

My feet take me to the hatch – it *snaps* back – and every step brings back memories of the last time Grea and I were on an alien command deck. How the darkness wrapped around her, how she appeared out of it, viyusa curling over her shoulders, eyes alight with an Euiva-inspired fervour.

A deep breath, a prayer to those mostly made-up Old Terra gods, and I'm ready.

Or not.

Point one, the lights are on. Command is a soft twilight, spreading upwards from the deck, curving over bulkheads and the consoles. Everything is a pale grey, only the carvings on the walls breaking up the sameness, throwing intricate shadows as they shift. Unlike the ones in the main corridors, the patterns here don't stay still, and I'm having trouble picking out the individual meanings from the flood of translation Hunt is pumping into my brain.

As for the room itself, consoles are arranged in two concentric circles around a central space. There are no holos or screens, but I can imagine them, just like I can imagine the larger one that would take up the middle of the room, a space now occupied by my sister.

Not the hologram version of her. The *real* her. Older, taller, her face more than human with her squashed nose and pupils turning to slits. Viyusa moves at her feet, the tendrils in her cape undulating like a soft, red tide, the rest of her though... The rest of her is still, not even her chest moving, but I know she's breathing because her faceplate is gone and her breath is frosting the air.

'Grea?' I don't know what to say beyond her name. Joy and hope, trepidation and fear are competing for space in my chest. We've done this before, and it didn't go well for me.

She looks at me. She hasn't stopped looking at me, since before the hatch opened, but now she's *looking*, now she's *emoting* and... and...

I'm drowning again.

I'm on the deck, fighting for air through the desperation, the pain, the horror crawling down my throat. A breath, two, enough to shout, 'Stop!'

Gasping oxygen. 'Grea, stop!'

It stops.

The whistle of air into empty lungs is loud, but it's not mine.

'What've I done?' It's a whisper, full of all those things that were choking me a few seconds ago.

'It's... okay.' I'm getting to my feet, dragging in oxygen, chasing the starlight from my eyes with every movement. Hands on knees, breathe. Muscles bunching, pushing upward. Breathe. Shoulders back, look Grea in the eye. Breathe.

'It's okay,' I say again. 'We'll fix it.' And even as I say it, I know how absurd that is, how impossible. Nothing's going to reattach my leg, bring back Mac or *Citlali*. Nothing's going to erase the fear in Dad's eyes, the wobble in his hug.

And don't even get me started on the mess outside this hull. The Sisters, the wohol, Jørgens in cocoons on *Euiva*'s bulkheads, the sticky black of the water-kins' fear crawling through our brains and no way home, even if we had a home to go to.

We are fucked, well and truly fucked.

Grea's eyes are on mine and I feel her see right through me, to the lies inside, and she smiles.

I want it to be a star rising over a moon, light refracting through the atmosphere, catching in the rain and warming the rock. But it's not. Because she sees through me, and even if she didn't... Grea knows.

'We're past fixing it, fathead.'

On my shoulder, Dude hums, flexing his claws, and I say what he would say, if he could. 'We can stop it getting worse.'

She shifts, not much, just a little. 'How?'

Gold moves under my skin at the same time Ekene's command sphere raises my hand. Slag gathers in my palm, flowering with the opening of my fist.

'This.'

It's not as simple as throwing slag at shit. It never is. Euiva and the stand-off in the root chamber are proof enough of that. Slag hadn't done squat against her, maybe it hadn't been enough, but no, I know that isn't true because it was a filament that took over the drone in *Aeotu*'s hull.

There's something missing, something I'm not getting...

Dude chitters, his warmth moving under my skin, and I know what we need. I turn on my heel.

'Where are you going?' It's only been a second since I summoned slag to my hand, and Grea is still standing in the middle of the command deck, tendrils writhing around her feet.

'The grow chamber, we need to free the others and—'

'No.'

'What?'

Grea glides toward me, and it is so smooth, so graceful that I don't even think I see her legs move. 'You have to leave them there.'

I laugh, but it's not really a laugh, laughter implies humour and the only thing funny about this is me thinking Euiva was going to let go of my sister that easy.

I face up to her, hands down by my sides, slag gathering in both palms. 'They're crew, Grea. I'm not leaving them there.'

'If you don't, they'll die.' She leans in close, and with only millimetres between us the differences between us – us who had never been different – are stark. 'Same as Mac.'

That's a knife in the chest. Grea twists it, grabs the metaphorical handle, reaches in and pushes my own memories down the blade. Mac leaping in front of Aeotu. Mac impaled. Mac fading to nothing in the eter.

*I'm not dead.* A ghostly hand on my shoulder, fingers sinking through armour to squeeze the flesh. And for a heartbeat I almost believe it's him, tall and serious except for that twinkle in his eye.

Even though it hurts, I move in closer, going up on my toes until we're forehead to forehead. 'Why are you doing this?' And I'm not sure who I'm asking, Grea or the figment standing beside me, his hand on my shoulder.

'You're my brother. I'm saving you.'

The figment doesn't say anything, but I can feel him smiling like he's just waiting for me to connect the dots. If only I could see them.

I concentrate on Grea, her eyes, the almond-shaped pupils, neither slit nor round, searching for answers in the depths beyond the void-dark iris. 'What are you saving me from, Grea?'

Arms go around my waist, lifting me off my toes, while viyusa winds around my legs. 'From everything, from time.' She smiles, and it's in that moment, with joy shining behind her gaze, that I understand. 'We're going to live forever, remember?'

I remember. Curled up in the dark, just me and Grea, head to head, nose to nose, her whispering those words to me.

Like a bad echo, I remember Euiva promising the same, and as if that memory is an open gate, others flood after it. The Sisters linked in a golden web, Grea a tiny spark trapped in Euiva's glow; red cocoons lined up on the bulkhead; mounds of grey-green fug; Mac putting himself between Aeotu and my blade; the hopelessness in his eyes when he said not everyone is like me; and Aeotu using his voice, little more than a fleshy avatar.

'Yes.' Grea's too-long fingers are on my shoulders, overlaying Mac's ghostly hand, the points of her talons digging into my flesh. 'Like that,' she says, and I know she's seen my thoughts, has watched me connect the dots. 'But we'll be more than Mac and the others.'

'Because we're empaths,' I say. Because we can slip into the ora where the Sisters live.

'Yes, we'll be Sisters.'

I look at her, really look at her. Honestly, it would have been hard to turn away. Grea is lit from within, fervour blazes from her eyes – passion, belief. Joy. I see a future in the light of that miniature star, a perfect melding of ship and flesh, centuries spent roaming the galaxy, ageless and undying with Grea at my side. I would never be alone and I would be whole, whole in a way that only Grea and I can be.

It sounds perfect. Everything in me *wants* that, yearns for it hard enough to make my anima ache. *Yes* hovers on the tip on my tongue, but even as I lean forward, something in me says, 'No.'

Maybe it's Mac, the memory of him, maybe it's what's left of Ekene's command sphere. Maybe it's Dude, growling beside my ear. And maybe it's the other things I see in Grea's light, the zeal and the bloodlust.

I see war.

It burns under her skin, turning every molecule of her being into a bonfire, obliterating everything before it. Everything except the sticky darkness, thrumming with the sound of a billion ancient voices singing 'kill, kill. Kill.'

You *started this*. The memory of Aeotu rings in my head.

Grea's finger-spikes dig deeper into my armour, and for the first time I notice the veins of red radiating from them. 'We'll be Sisters,' she says again.

I jerk away, ignoring the pain as her fingers rip out, taking some of me with them, knowing it's just the first pain. What comes next is going to hurt more.

'I'm not a girl.' I step back. Yellow is filling in the holes Grea made, and I wish, I wish more than I've ever wished before, that it could reach inside and fill in the ones I'm about to make. 'And I'm not a Sister, and you're—' There's a lump in my throat, and Old Terra this hurts, but ghostly Mac is there, squeezing my arm, and I pull all those images of him and Dad and Mum and Onah and h'Rawd close, and I layer them up with Hunt and Dude and even Aeotu as she appeared to me on the ora, with my face and my voice.

I take all of those and I lay them side-by-side with Ekene and the mounds of fug, with the red cocoons in the grow chamber, and I use them to burn away the lump in my throat.

I take another step back.

Grea made her choice, and her choice took their choices from them.

I shake my head. 'You're—'

The words choke me and just *thinking* them hurts. But the woman before me, she's not my sister anymore. Not the one I remember, not the one I used to play toe wars with, or who raced cargo pallets through *Citlali's* freight tubes. *That* Grea wouldn't wrap crew mates in fug, wouldn't help Euiva steal Mum or destroy our home. That Grea died somewhere in the four years I spent in *Aeotu's* grow-field with Ekene and the others. A part of me dies with that realisation and another part... The other part straightens my shoulders.

'You're not—' I start again.

The words are cut off. I'm thrown against a console as the deck shudders. *Euiva* groans, not the AI but the ship itself, metal-stone superstructure and whatever-the-fuck makes up its walls crying out at the stresses rippling through its joints.

The big empty space in the centre of the room flares to life even as Hunt yells in the back of my brain.

*{{ Evacuate. Hostile forces breeching hull. }}*

Grea is lost in the ball of light, hidden behind schematics and broken holos of wohol in their light-sucking grey armour, heavy laser weapons and scanners held in their four hands. They stream through a hole in *Euiva*'s inner hull, the edges still glowing from whatever cutting tool they used to breach the bulkhead. I count the first six but stop as more flow through.

The holos shatter, turning to static around Grea's face. Her new face, the face of the woman in my sister's skin.

There is no joy there, but I can feel it in the atmosphere between us, a mad, sticky darkness twisting between her and Euiva, singing a song of death. *Kill. Kill. Kill.*

She is radiant with it.

'We have to stop them before they get to Euiva's core.' Grea pauses, looks at me but it's the AI I see behind her eyes, cold, calculating. 'Or the grow chamber.'

The grow chamber.

My heart freezes.

Mac's ghostly hand pierces through flesh to bone.

I run.

# CHAPTER SIXTEEN

One day, when I'm old and grey – if I ever make it that far – I'm going to have a hover chair and I'm never, ever going to run again. Maybe I won't even wait until I'm old, maybe I'll get one after all this is over and I'm… I'm doing… what? What comes after this? What's left?

I don't know, I only know I have to get to the grow chamber before the wohol do.

*Euiva*'s pristine inner hallways are behind me, and I pound through the ones that have seen some wear – scorch marks on the walls, pieces of bulkhead missing, exposing glowing conduits and metal-stone ribs. The only sounds are my feet pounding the deck and the air rushing into my lungs.

There is a map overlaying the corridor on my HUD and a small window in the upper left corner where I can watch the wohol advance, step-by-step.

Somewhere out in the wreckage of *Euiva*'s outer skeleton, Hunt is manoeuvring, scanning the shuttle that brought the wohol. It's big and boxy, with just two life signs left aboard. Which is something, I guess, not that it helps me much now.

The grow chamber is coming up, and if the indicators on the map are correct – and Euiva isn't fucking with me – so are the wohol.

I skid around the corner, fug shifting, reinforcing the armour on my chest, blades forming on my arms and—

The corridor is empty. I straighten.

That wasn't what I—

The laser bolt takes me in the chest, knocking me off my feet. I'm staring at the ceiling, wondering what the fuck, while a mirage shimmers the air and a fucking big wohol steps out it.

I want to swear, but all that comes out is a strangled grunt.

It's enough for the alien to point its ginormous gun at me and—

Red threaded through with yellow erupts from the deck, knocking the weapon sideways.

The lime-green bolt that would have killed me, hits the deck next to my ear, close enough to feel the burn.

Sibilant song-like yells, slag-threaded viyusa turning the wohol into a shish-kebab, other wohol erupting out of other mirages, more alien kebabs, more laser fire leaving black marks on *Euiva*'s insides.

And me, sprawled on the deck, still getting my breath back, Dude sitting on my chest, enjoying the show.

It's over a few heartbeats after it begins, one moment the corridor is a battlefield of nanites and laser-beams, the next it's a forest of corpses and almost-corpses, sighing with the death moans of the wohol squad. Most of them are still upright, held in place by the viyusa-slag, a few are slumped over, and there's one pinned to the ceiling, all six limbs hanging like a macabre umbrella.

I get to my feet.

There are eight wohol in the corridor. More than that came through the breech.

That should concern me almost as much as how fast this happened, but all I really have eyes for is the slag in the viyusa and behind the slag...

A form shimmers.

I slip into the eter.

Eighteen ghosts stand sentinel around a pulsing core of yellow, gazes cast down at the pale threads falling from their hands. Threads trail across the ground, feeding the conflagration at their centre.

I know those faces, or *knew* them as they used to be. Not all of the faces are whole – bits of flesh missing, bones... I'm not even going to guess. Others... other have *new* things on their face, growing out of their heads or shoulders or arms. Only Brennus looks the same, not just his face, but his body untouched by... by whatever this is. He's also the only one who acknowledges me.

'You can't be here,' he says.

I step forward. 'I came to—'

'Not you.' He looks behind me. 'Her.'

I turn.

Grea, at my back, close enough to kiss.

She smiles. 'Nice trick,' she says, gaze on the yellow flame. 'How'd you get that?'

Brennus's gaze flicks to me, or rather the spot on my shoulder where Dude sits. 'You delivered it yourself.'

Grea's gaze switching to Dude, her gaze boring through him. 'The critter?' Incredulity spills from her feet in a bright, sparkly swash of pale bronze. 'That thing?' she says again, although this time with a long spear-tipped finger pointed at him for emphasis.

A little part of me wants to object, to defend Dude, to get all offended by the derision dripping from her every pore. But the wiser, battle-weary part of me, the part that's wondering if I'll ever get old, quashes it.

Brennus is talking again. 'And in our flesh and bones and with every piece of *Citlali* you scavenged.' And as he says it, images flare over the yellow fire at their centre. Pieces of *Citlali's* hull pulled along in the wake of little repair bots, welded to *Euiva's* hull, small patches of geometric slag clinging to the nooks and crannies. Corpses towed along in trails of fug, fed into proto-viyu tanks, the slag embedded in their bones coming to life as the nanites begin to feed on skin and teeth and tendon.

All of that bright yellow, human-engineered poison sitting dormant, just waiting.

Waiting for me, with the neo-slag curled around my legs. A command key, a pattern to control the rest.

Dude chitters and there is rebuke in the sound.

Okay then, waiting for Dude.

For a second, nothing happens. Grea stands there, not a hologram or a psionic projection, but *her* whole and... changed. Different. And for the first time... for the first time she is alien to me, closed, thoughts moving under her skin that I can't follow. That I don't *want* to follow. Then—

A tsunami of red, not just rage but viyusa bursts out of the walls, the deck, from Grea. It's hard to tell if it's all in the real or in the eter, but it's all aimed at Brennus, at the eighteen with the slag spilling from their hands and—

The red stops, just halts like someone hit 'pause' on the great holo-drama that is the universe, and that someone isn't Grea, or Euiva, writhing under her skin. It's Brennus, it's the eighteen and the slag and even Ekene, the command still embedded in my psyche. It's all of that, but mostly it's the slag lighting up within the heavy strands of viyusa, thin filaments of yellow under its skin, pulsing, threatening to explode.

The universe holds its breath, me along with it.

There is no sound, no movement, there's just tension. Grea and Brennus stare each other down, vibrating the fabric of reality with the intensity in their gazes. I can't see it, can't even feel it, save for the knife-edged shiver racing over my skin – toes to temple and back again – but there's a silent battle taking place in the eter, a clash of wills between Grea/Euiva and the eight, with Brennus at their head.

I feel like I'm caught between two behemoths, a tiny, insignificant critter on the wall—

Dude grumbles.

—not-so-insignificant critter clinging to the wall, waiting to see what the two powers will do, hoping they don't crush me when they do it.

Standing here, in the corridor with freeze-framed viyusa and a psionic battle taking place probably isn't the best spot to be, but there aren't a lot of places to go and the wohol...

The wohol are just around the corner, the blunt, green-spitting ends of their weapons peeking around the curve, their grey-armoured forms almost lost in the chaos.

I don't think either Brennus or Grea have noticed them yet, and I don't move, don't speak, don't even whisper caution into the eter. Some primal part of me whispers that that would be a bad idea, and the last vestiges of Ekene's command sphere agree.

But still... those weapons...

The wohol move, the tension seeming to roll off them, and it takes me a second to realise that the aliens can't see the battle taking place in front of them, that they're blind to the eter.

For such large beings, they move with surprising grace, slipping around the corner, backs to the curved walls, carefully skirting the thick hunks of viyusa and their fellows still impaled on the ceiling.

There are three of them, two at the front, one trailing.

I thought there were more. Hunt?

A nudge from Hunt, and an image plays across my HUD, three heat signatures breaking off from the main group, the rest heading for *Euiva*'s core.

A change on the HUD, a bright warning highlighting the wohol at the back, the one trailing behind its fellows. Like the other two, it's armed, but unlike the other two, the weapon it's carrying is short and slim, carried in just one of its upper hands instead of two, while the other...

A ball of liquid silver, the surface rippling like it's alive.

I don't need Hunt or Dude or Euiva to tell me what that is, I remember it erupting from *Aeotu*'s hangar, eating viyusa like it was a tasty snack.

It's the wohol's version of fug, and they've got a great big ball of it.

There's no time for caution, at some point, the not-so-insignificant critter on the wall's gotta be a hero.

Dude agrees.

'Brennus!' I yell it, physically and mentally, projecting an image of that deadly silver sphere into the eter.

The rest happens in slow motion, the 'play' button hit but the universe is slow to catch up. The sphere launches into the air, the wohol fire, viyusa swamps the corridor, while in the eter more red impales Brennus, tearing at the eighteen and Grea/Euiva snarl in victory.

The snarl only lasts as long as it takes the silver shit to take hold. A second, maybe less.

And now there's screaming and panic, and silver-threaded viyusa smacking me into the bulkhead, and three big hulking wohol wading through it, firing their green bolts of death. A thick red shield cuts Grea off from the bombardment, but each pulse of the wohols' weapons turns another piece of it to dust, while the silver creeps through it, eating it, reaching for the real prize, for Grea.

Even though I don't understand her anymore, even though she's as alien to me as the wohol, she's still my sister, still my twin, and I can stand to see her hurt as much as I can tear my other leg off.

I struggle against the silver, unleashing blades, feeling the draw on my bones as they turn molten, but every move sends the silver climbing higher.

'Brennus,' I yell it again, except instead of the sphere, I throw an image of Grea. 'Help her!'

*Not yet.* He's at my side, hand on silver-red fug pinning me to the wall, then his fingers are sliding under the surface like he's reaching for something. Concentration lines his face.

'She's going to die!'

*So are you, and a lot quicker than Grea if we don't get this right.* Yellow takes over the silver-red, and I push against it, desperate to get to Grea, but Brennus – psionic projection Brennus, who only has form in the eter – holds me down. *Don't worry, Euiva's taking care of your sister.*

'But—'

*Don't worry,* he says again, and this time it's not just him but another behind him.

The girl holds down my other shoulder, her ghostly, psionic

fingers sinking through the silver, digging just like Brennus. I recognise her, even though there're new protrusions over her eyes and part of her face is missing – skin and muscle eaten away, leaving just white bone and teeth. Yellow is carved into her jaw, geometric patterns tattooed on the ragged remnants of her flesh, the same patterns that pulse over her hands, the same yellow that flows from the rest of the eighteen into the flame.

Into the slag.

The slag, the poison in Euiva's viyusa, which the silver shit just ate.

As if that thought, *my* thought, is the key, Brennus grins, victory lighting up the eter behind him, and yanks his hand out of my chest.

Slag erupts, a violent yellow wave shooting into the corridor. Another fountain gushes from my shoulder, and as it does the silver holding me shrinks, eaten, and I'm free, and I'm rushing at the nanites attacking Grea, at the wohol between me and it and—

The slag gets there first, the first wohol going down under its weight, the second firing at it, the third covering its fellow's back. I don't pay attention to it, don't pay attention to anything except the silver beating at Grea's wall, catching hold of tendrils flowing from her shoulders, creeping over her feet. Eating them.

I leap, fug blades blazing and—

Unlike with me, the slag doesn't erupt from Grea. It rises through the red, pressing against its skin, like the tattoo on the girl's face, and changes it, strengths it like it did the viyu.

In the microsecond I'm in the air, Grea explodes through the wohol's nanites, and where blades protrude from my wrists, long barbed tentacles pour from hers.

The first wohol, the one the slag swamped, screams as it dies, one of Grea's whips slicing through its chest.

I land in a crouch at her side, blades blazing, already turning to face the other two...

They're dead, impaled on viyusa-slag, just like the others.

Grea studies her hands, the new yellow patterns under the red, and her wonder spills about her like a delicate sparkly cloak before her gaze shifts, finds the last shreds of the wohol's silver turning yellow as the slag consumes it.

Euiva rises through Grea's skin.

On the eter, Brennus gasps, hands going to his throat, like something's choking him.

*You can kill us*, he says. *But the slag won't stop. It's in all of you, all the Sisters.*

A hiss of breath. Grea's face contorted in a snarl, and on the eter, Brennus starts to flicker.

It's my turn, and even through it's wrong, even though it hurts, it's the only thing I can do. I hit Grea.

My fist is a cannonball of grief, of loathing, of hate and fear and love, and it hits her in the side. Right in the soft, squishy spot under the ribs. Grey-green fug meets red, armour taking most of the physical impact, distributing it outwards, but it's enough to make Grea stumble, enough to break her/Euiva's concentration, and when it does...

The emote strikes, exploding through Grea's defences. Shock and pain – Grea's – widen the cracks and I'm there, blasting through, dredging up all the shit in my anima and pushing it in front of me, sharing it. Betrayal. Determination. Loss. Rage. Helplessness.

We're against the bulkhead, my hands on Grea's shoulders, her tendrils wrapped around my arms. Faceplates gone, forehead to forehead, our breath turning to frost on the air. We stare at each other, Grea and I, Euiva a shadow behind my sister's eyes but no longer in control.

In that moment, that breath, I share being in *Aeotu*'s proto-viyu tank, the city of lights at my feet, the melding of slag and fug making something new, something stronger. And then I share the memory of the probe in *Aeotu*'s belly, of the silver that spread from it, of the viyu-slag pushing it out. Eating it. I share the spear through my stomach, Ekene stopping me before I ripped it out, and the sense of him moving through the slag, controlling it. Controlling it so Aeotu and I and all the rest of the crew could live.

I hold tight to Grea and share all of that, and I keep sharing past the point where I feel her understanding, keep pushing to the darkness lurking on the other side. To the real power. The real danger. To Euiva.

There is resistance, her need to rid herself of the invader a wall between me and her, but I don't stop. I *can't* stop, and maybe part of that is the command sphere, driving me on, but I don't think so. Ekene's influence has faded the farther along this path I've gone, the more turns it's taken, the more decisions that were mine and now this... This is me, this is Mac, this is Aeotu and her desperate, *I don't want to die.*

This is all of us, human and kin and Sister, broken and beaten and remade because some four-armed, grey-armoured aliens got chased off of a planet by even more aliens. None of us want to die, but if Euiva can't get that through her thick, patchwork hull, that's what's gonna happen. So I am standing here, forehead to forehead with my sister, until that thought, that idea imprints itself on Euiva's core, even if I have to—

Grea's hand cups my jaw, and she smiles. 'Okay,' she says. 'Let's do this.'

# CHAPTER SEVENTEEN

Euiva was the one to come up with the plan and, as usual, it involves me doing stupid shit.

I have help this time, if you can call centuries-old deck plans and a load of freshly-brewed viyusa-slag, help. Grea is with me though, the bright cherry-red of her presence sitting behind my eyeballs. I would take comfort in it except...

*Euiva's as much a part of me as Hunt is of you,* Grea says. *Like Aeotu and Mac.*

'I killed Mac.' I say it before thinking, before the idea of *killing* Mac has time to take hold. I say it because... because...?

*Because you're going to kill me?* Laughter runs through her words, up and down like bubbles against my spine. *You'd sooner kill yourself.*

But I didn't, did I. I stabbed my best friend and it's a lump in my chest, a ball holding down my—

A ghostly hand on my shoulder, a kaleidoscopic orange and for a second, I see Mac, forgiveness mixed in with the sadness in his eyes, but his jaw determined, his brow serious. And somehow I know that, if he were here, if he could speak, he'd tell me to get my head out of my arse and do my fucking job. To sneak aboard one of the two wohol ships and deliver a payload of slag where it'll hurt the most.

Right in the heart of the vessel.

Right in the Core.

Where all the aliens are.

Because that's what's gotta be done, and I'm the dude with the fancy armour and the mech. And no one trusts Grea.

So now I'm in Hunt, and we're on the edge of the graveyard, playing like we're debris.

Hunt scans the large ovoid shapes – distant cousins of the Sisters, sleeker, meaner somehow with their pointed bows and the angled lines of their sterns, or maybe that's just Euiva, leaking through the growing connection with Grea.

Whatever it is, it seeps through Hunt's data stream, colouring the data filling the HUD, marking the alien ships in fierce, angry orange. The orange churns the acid in my gut until it burns in my veins, darkening my vision. Not even Dude is immune, the hate that rides me infects him too, crawls through the golden fuzz of his being in sticky strands of black.

A distant part of me whispers that this is wrong, that Grea's emotions, let alone Euiva's shouldn't affect me this way; and Hunt... Hunt is part of me, I remember being so enmeshed with it, with Dude, that the difference between us was little more than the composition of our molecules. Hunt does not have the capacity to feel, any more than I have the capacity to breathe vacuum, or Dude the ability to speak. No, this rage, this blackness is wrong, is—

Is kin, the fleshiness whispers, even as the rage takes hold.

We cycle energy, generator spinning faster before we remember our cannons are damaged. Errors ping off our consciousness from ruptured convertors and broken conduits, barely held together with strands of dying fug. We could swat a gnatt or a wohol, maybe even a tendril of fug, but a ship...? It doesn't matter, our entire being is a weapon. We spin our generator harder, feel the fusion hot and hard in our chest. There is an opening in the ship's hull, we track a patrol ship slipping out of it.

We will slip in there and once we are inside, within the protection of the hull—

*No.* A gentle hand in our psyche. A nudge flicking us apart.

I am Kuma once again and Holy Terra, that was scary. The sticky black still clings to the corners of my mind, beating against my brainstem. I can sense Hunt calculating the best way to destroy the wohol ship from within, but blowing myself up no longer seems like a reasonable option.

Dude agrees.

*Good.*

Grea?

She smiles, and I can't decide if she's there on my HUD or sitting behind my eyes, in the eter. *Eyes front, baby brother.*

The wohol ship sits over us, blotting out the stars. It looks like the Sisters, the same ovoid shape but larger, its hull sleek, the power thrumming under its skin more than anything I've seen from *Aeotu.*

Not that that is much of a comparison. I haven't seen *Aeotu* in her prime, or any other Sister, but still, it seems strange that with a millennium of technological advancement between them, the wohols' ships seem so... puny.

*That's because they are,* Grea says. *You should dive into their heads, little brother. The water-kin didn't just mess with the Sisters.*

'What'd they do?'

*What the kin always do; dig into your brain and neutralise the threat.* She cocks her head. *They did it good with the wohol. Euiva doesn't have much of their history in her databanks, but it looks like the water-kin scared them all the way back to their homeworld and straight into an apocalypse. Pity we don't have a whole tribe of the water-kin here, to do it again.*

I shudder, and not just because the thought of a dozen of the foot-high, lizard-like kin gives me the creeps, but because of the sticky darkness writhing in the pit of my belly and Aeotu's shared memory. Wohol crying out in alarm, stampeding across the umbilicus between ships, airlocks snapping closed and bodies sucked in space.

Some things are better left in the dark.

✳

It shouldn't be this easy to infiltrate an enemy stronghold. Even I know that, which makes the way Hunt slides into the launch tube and settles in the wohol shuttle bay disturbing. More than disturbing, downright creepy. There's got to be a catch, like maybe the whole thing is a hallucination or some kind of immersive holo-program and in reality, we're still tethered to *Euiva*'s superstructure, viyusa eating Hunt's hull. Or maybe it's already done that and the AI has me strung up in a cocoon next to Grea, together but forever apart.

Maybe. But the prick of Dude's fug-talons is too sharp to be a hallucination, the fuzz of his presence too comforting not to be real, and Hunt – strands of viyu squeezing around my middle, the temperature change as its hull splits, cold blasting against my back, and lowers me down to a smooth, pale grey deck – that is all-too real. Even the taste of the air – a strange tang on the back of my tongue – and the giddy rush of it as it hits my lungs... That is too strange, too detailed.

I stagger, light-headed and heavy-boned, the neutral whites and greys of the wohol's ship suddenly too bright, the hush of its air-cyclers too loud and—

My faceplate slides into place, not just the delicate fug-work to support my HUD, but the full thing shielding me from the light. A breath and the nano-steel is back in my bones, the dizziness receding as quickly as it hit.

'What was that?'

*{{ Low oxygen atmosphere. Armour compensating. }}*

Right. That makes sense, aliens and all that. I guess I'm lucky that the gravity is only a fraction higher than Terran-standard and there's armour reinforcing my legs.

It's one thing to stand in *Aeotu* or *Euiva*'s corridors, to have to tilt my head to see the ceiling and feel out of proportion to my surroundings. It's another to be here, where the lights are dimmer and the prevalence of white and grey makes it seem like there's a film between me and the real world, muting the colour, softening the edges of walls, hatches and the wohol's sleek shuttles.

{{ *Not shuttles,* }} Hunt says and presses new information into the back of my brain. Engine capacity, ports, weapons systems—

I stagger, Dude growls, and the information flow stops.

Right. Not shuttles, small attack vessels. Fighters. Fun. There are at least a dozen of the things—

{{ *Sixteen.* }}

—Sixteen lined up in two neat rows. I don't want to think about tiny attack craft swarming out of the alien ship's belly. Not that I think you can call anything the size of Hunt tiny.

The slag wound around my arm pulses, reminding me why I'm here. I have to get to the ship's AI core. Let's just hope no one sees me.

I creep across the deck, aiming for the shadows under the fighters and—

A clatter, metal ringing on metal, has me swinging around.

The wohol is staring at me, its big eyes getting even bigger. Even from three metres away I can see its slit pupils expanding, swallowing the muddy brown of its iris.

It's standing under a fighter, its two upper arms buried in the belly of the machine, its lower ones busy with the tools on the cart hovering in front of it.

We've both forgotten to breathe.

It blinks, translucent vertical membranes closing over its eyes.

I blink.

Its chest expands, drawing in air, its throat working as its mouth opens and—

The wohol is gone, obliterated in a flash of light and heat, only carbon left behind in a black streak across the deck.

A faint whine behind me, high enough to barely be a sound and I don't bother to glance back as Hunt's arm cannon slots back under the plates on its forearm. I just nod. Just nod. There's nothing to say, not to Hunt at least, not that the mech would care, even if it could care, and Dude... He's fuzzing, spreading calm through my system, but it's distracted, secondary to the intense focus radiating from his paws.

I don't think the alien registered for him as more than an obstacle in our way.

Dude's talons digging into my shoulder bring me back to the task at hand and the map flashing on my HUD. I scurry across the deck, finding the shadows of the fighters and sticking to them like nano-glue, and not because I'm afraid of being seen. Or at least, not entirely. I just don't want another carbon smear on the deck.

It feels a little late to care about a wohol, a little wrong. They've killed h'Rawd, taken my leg, and rained destruction down on me and mine. Plus, I've slaughtered a few of them, taken heads and lives with equal abandon, and yet...

Euiva's map leads me to a bare patch of wall, highlights a swirl carved into the pale grey. I touch it and the panel under my hand disappears, revealing what I can only guess is a maintenance crawl space. I'm in, scooting along in an awkward crouch, the panel snapping back into place a nanosecond after my heels clear the opening.

I've killed wohol without a blink and yet that lone alien, as shocked to see me I was them, haunts me. Maybe it's the way it blinked at me, how its thin-lipped mouth opened, its jaw dropping in an all-too-human expression. Maybe it was the way it was just standing there, doing its job, unaware of the fugged-up Jørgen idiot creeping about as if the big-arse alien mech wasn't going to give away that something was seriously wrong on this ship.

Yeah. Maybe it was that.

The maintenance crawl spits me out somewhere dark and the HUD switches to low-light mode, picking out crates and tubes in green. Like it did at the other end, the hatch snaps shut on my heels taking the light and my vision with it.

I concentrate, closing my eyes and imagining an orb forming on my chest, the same energy that powers my thrusters and lights my fug-blades, illuminating the space around me. There's the pull of heat from my bones and then a warm glow over my heart, and then there is light, not exactly flooding the area, but enough to make out the sharp edges of the cryo pods on the other side.

My claws *snick snick* on the deck. I press my hand to the lid of a goo-filled crate.

{{ *Eighteen-point-seven-four millimetres thick,* }} Hunt says, even as the numbers pop up on the HUD.

Holy shit, that's thick and why are there so many?

According to the map I'm in the bowels of the wohol ship, close to where its nanites are produced. All I should have to do is pop another hatch, stick my hand in and let the slag-fug do its work. But this... This is a problem.

This is less of an out-of-the-way utility access and more of a warehouse.

The data Euiva pushed into my system is worse than useless; it's just useful enough to land me in hot water, or right in the path of a trio of wohol, as the case may be.

Cryo'd wohol, but still... wohol. The three of them are hanging in stasis gel or whatever the hell they use, the front of their pods frosted over, silver nanites twisting around their paws, climbing over their hands and shoulders. The one in front of me, nanites are clustered around its sternum like a metallic bandage, and in the next pod... The nanite bandage is wrapped around the alien's shoulder and climbing up its neck covering what looks like claw marks.

I press my faceplate to the pod, even as the HUD tracks the wounds.

Fuck, they don't just *look* like claw marks, I think they *are* claw marks.

I push away and look around.

There are more pods, more bodies stacked all around me. The long, low boxes I thought were crates... Pods, not standing on their end but lying on their side and in them—

How the ever-loving fuck?

'Mum?' I bang on the frosted dome. 'Mum!' I yell it and push desperation and joy and wake-the-fuck-up emotions through the eter. Scream in her brain in the only way I can, with the biggest arse *emote* I can summon.

She doesn't answer, doesn't twitch or breathe or... Holy Terra. Holy Terra, what'd I do? What'd I do?

*{{ Nothing, }}* Hunt answers.

'It's Mum,' I say. 'I can't leave her here.'

*{{ Stay on mission. }}*

'But—'

*{{ Stay on mission, }}* Hunt says again, and floods my brain with scenarios. Me lugging Mum through the maintenance crawl, pushing and pulling her body through the tight space; carrying her over my shoulder with wohol on my heels, lances of energy firing from their weapons. Trying to stuff her into Hunt; oxygen running low as we jet through the void, fighters spilling from the wohol ship's belly, their weapons hitting Hunt's shoulders, its legs, taking out its thrusters. Over it all are percentages, eight-three, sixty-four, ninety.

Okay, so getting Mum out is a bad idea, means we all end up splattered against a bulkhead or turned into carbon, but still...

I dig fug-claws into the top of the pod—

A noise, a soft *huff*, jerks my attention upwards... And straight into h'Lott's yellow gaze.

The rucnart is stuffed in another pod, legs folded underneath her body, head twisted around until her muzzle rests on her knee. It doesn't just look awkward, it looks painful. She blinks at me, slow and deliberate, one slow movement of her upper eyelids and then of her lower ones. Her lip curls, half-command and half-fear spilling out of her.

My claws leave rents in Mum's pod, and then I'm across the deck and digging them into h'Lott's. Yellow-green flows over my wrists, winding around my fingers, turning the centimetre-long spear points on the end to six-inch knives cutting through the clear dome like it's butter. The yellow-green slag doesn't stop there though. Even as cold spills out of the dome, the slag is racing across the plasglas-like substance, seeking out the nanites embedded in its surface.

Hunt's in the slag, directing it even as I rip into the dome, and I hope it's sending it to whatever sub-system or AI that monitors the lifesystems or this is going to end just like Hunt predicted, except a whole lot faster.

Orange blazes, the plasglas shifts under my hands, forming a mess of swirls just like on the bulkheads, and I'm pretty sure that's bad, especially since I've barely sliced half-way down the front of the pod and have pretty much no idea how I'm going to get h'Lott out. And yeah, it's belatedly occurred to me that tearing into a stasis unit was a bad idea, that maybe it would have been a little more efficient, not to mention safer, to try and figure out its controls, but I'm here now, and the alarms are going and—

The alarms cut out. There's a *clunk* and a second later the pod splits open.

The cold that was freezing my fingers washes over my knees and I stumble backward as h'Lott tumbles out.

And all of sudden I'm not seeing h'Lott's orange and golden splots, but another rucnart spilling out of different stasis pod, pale blue stasis gel dripping through the grated deck, coughing and spluttering as she hacked fug-eaten lungs onto the floor. P'Ender overlays h'Lott in my vision, but this time, instead of standing there, I'm on my knees in the fug, lifting the rucnart's muzzle out of the muck and—

—Getting the tips of my fug-claws bitten off for the trouble.

H'Lott's lurching to her feet, fear-born rage pushing her upright, pulling a snarl from her throat. There's blood on her breath, the musky fish-scent of the wohol, and more blood clumped in her fur.

She's coming at me, eyes clear but her mind clouded. I don't even think about it, I grab her muzzle, fug-enhanced muscles holding it closed, and dive into her brain.

Dude's there with me, and together we push calm, swamping the frantic need to rend and tear clouding h'Lott's mind. And I wonder if it was actually me she saw in those slow blinks within the pod, or if it was just her fears. It feels like an hour, but is only seconds before she stops struggling.

She blinks, and for a moment we're stuck somewhere between the eter and the real, memories and thoughts flowing between us. I see *Aeotu*'s hangar, giant cables falling from Hunt's back, the mech disappearing through the deck. Yells and fear from the crew left behind. A flurry of frantic activity, every able-bodied person picking up weapons, holo-genie Ekene in the middle. Silver erupts through the holes in every surface, yellow follows but so do wohol in their faceless grey armour.

I see the viyusa catching h'Lott mid-leap, feel it wrap around every limb, know the moment she lost sight, then gravity, the cold bite of the void.

At the same time I witness h'Lott's memories, the tree-kin sees Grea hanging from the ceiling; the frozen moment when the wohol maintenance worker caught sight of me, and the scorch mark it left behind; sees my mum in the pod behind us.

Ekene hovers in the space between us, the memory of him and the slag almost as real as if he was actually here. Euiva follows, flowing from the same space, and the plan unfolds. How I'm to take the slag and infect the wohol ships. Save us. How together we're going to escape.

H'Lott latches onto that, tugs on the memory and I let it all go, the darkness behind the AI's eyes, the way she said "escape", the images that stained the air when she said it. The sticky darkness of the swatai at her core, the answering darkness in my own.

H'Lott jerks back, and our connection snaps.

She stares at me, her red upper eyes digging into my anima, before she snorts and shakes head to shoulders. *Water-kin,* she says. *I know their touch, ancient as it is. We can use it.*

I don't ask what for, somewhere in the exchange of memory we agreed on what came next. The wohol wouldn't know what hit them.

'How?'

I never want to see a rucnart grin again. Her muzzle wrinkles, and all I see are white teeth and red gums.

Dude shudders.

# CHAPTER EIGHTEEN

The wohol ship might look like *Aeotu* from the outside, might even obey the same layout of circular corridors with intersecting spokes, but somehow those familiarities make the differences worse. Is it because there are living beings on this ship?

Or is it because the wohol don't move in my brain? They have no presence, none of the bounce and jiggle of Jørgens or the restless stalk of kin, not even my parents' warm fuzz. Just... nothing. They leave streaks behind them, coloured shimmers like mental handprints, little bits of impatience and concentration scattered over the deck and clinging to the bulkheads like dandruff, but it's weirdly silent in my head.

It's the grave-like silence of *Citlali* as I ran around trying to save her from the fug, but worse because while I may not hear the wohol mentally, my ears aren't having the same issue.

*Swoosh.*

The sounds follow me and even though the HUD is clear of life, with not so much as a critter within the eighteen-metre bubble of its sensors, I can't help but feel that a predator is creeping up on me. I wish h'Lott was here, wish I had her claws and teeth, her ferocious intelligence, but I don't. Getting me through the ship's corridors is going to be hard enough, there's no way to hide a literal ton of rucnart too.

Still, I can't help but long for her presence, for that comforting bit of home in the midst of alienness.

Or maybe I've lost my capacity to judge alienness, that fug and the ora and waking to find I have paws, losing my leg, that all of it has burned the ability to ash.

The wohol ship's corridors are almost normal, the trump of heavy feet on the deck comforting, even the smell, like some kind of fish cake mixed with wet qwan and left to ferment under Ag deck's artificial sun is... Not normal, but not unexpected either.

Is that Aeotu's influence, her memories in the back of my brain? Or maybe it's just shock, or stress or the effects of trauma finally rearing their ugly heads. Whatever it is, it has me ducking through a hatch as something *swooshes* in the corridor ahead.

I wait, not breathing as the noise comes closer, the *swoosh* changing in tone as it draws near.

*Swoosh scrit.*

*Swoosh SCrit.*

*Swoosh SCRII—*

Silence as external audio shuts down – a warning light the HUD – but not before that sound reaches deep into my ear and pierces bone. And, oh shit, it *hurts*, not just my ears but my brain, my toes, my *insides*. Fuck, how can a sound do that? How do the wohol stand it?

I wait, heart beating hard, back flat to the bulkhead beside the door, concentrating on the thing moving on my HUD, praying it doesn't stop, doesn't pick up on residual heat signatures or air currents or my farts, or something. I'm praying even harder that *this* hatch, this *room* isn't the thing's destination, that I didn't just trap myself with the ear-shredding monstrosity.

And that's when I kind of look at the room itself and... Oh shit.

There's a head floating above a chest-high workbench, flat-nosed and big-eyed, staring at me, its slit pupils slowing widening.

It's an AI, the whole hovering over a bench bit and its faint shimmer of light give it away.

'Fuck.'

'Fuck,' it says, but the sound is strange, high-pitched and fluid, a song instead of a profanity. It opens its mouth again, and—

Whatever was making the *swoosh scrit* bursts through the hatch.

There's no warning, no *snap* of the door membrane retracting, just a tentacled *thing* exploding through the opening.

I throw myself on the deck, hitting the ground shoulder first, not taking my eyes off the silver cables slapping the wall where I was and now coming for me. On hands and butt, scampering backward, back slamming into the workbench. Crawling up it, eyes still on the thing. I'm pretty sure it's a machine, it's silver with a tail, or, I don't know, a really long neck sweeping over the deck like it's sniffing me out. Its legs are six long points and if it has a head, it's nothing I can recognise.

The lack of a head and eyes isn't slowing it down none, and fuck, but it's fast.

I summersault over the workbench, only aware of the AI as its light particles explode around me.

Fuck, fuck, fuck.

'Hunt, tell me this room has another exit.'

{{ *This room has another exit.* }} The HUD flashes, a square lighting up on the map.

Fuck, I hope it's right.

The machine-thing is over the workbench, flowing up and over it, disrupting the AI again. But just for a second, because no sooner has the hologram dissipated in a shower of cubes, that it's changed places to hover over the base of the machine-thing's neck. And, oh shit, if it wasn't creepy before, now it's fit to compete with the corpses haunting my nightmares.

There's no time to keep running backward. I spin, leaping and sliding over another bench, shoving something that might be a chair out of my way and lunge for the bit of wall outlined on the HUD, lunging for the swirl highlighted on the screen.

Slam into it, wait a heartbeat for the flash, the *snap* of an exit and—

Nothing.

I slap the swirl again, even as the HUD squeals and I dive sideways. Tentacles lash the space where my head was. Another is whistling through the air. I roll. The silver slaps against the deck.

Roll.

Slap.

Roll—

Stars, the constellation of Kuma making an appearance behind my eyes as I slam my head into something hard.

Dude under my skin, taking over as my ears ring and my vision blurs. I'm being moved, my feet under me, ducking and weaving, the motions spinning the constellation in my head. I'm blinking against it, fighting against the whirl trying to take my balance so I can take back my feet. One blink, then two. My teeth gritted, and I don't know if it's me willing it to stop, but suddenly the stars resolve and there's the hatch I came through, the corridor beyond it.

The AI-machine-thing is on my heels, a cable grazing the small of my back.

*Snnap.*

I slam into the space where the hatch was.

There's no time to think.

Knowledge flowing from Euiva – schematics and memories. The thing attacking me is a multipurpose repair and security bot, connected to the central AI. Hunt in my head, Dude in my muscles. I'm flipping backward, the machine-thing large, its front-leg spears aimed at my chest, then the ground is there and I'm meeting it with fug-reinforced hands, graceful and sure. And now I'm spinning, and lava is running down my arms, my bones going cold as blades slide from my forearms – *shnick shnick* – yellow-green slag gleaming on molten edges.

There's no flailing at the thing's legs; I bring my arms together, legs under me, and surge upwards, all my focus on the three centimetre spot on the thing's belly that pulses red on the HUD.

The tips of my blades piece the machine's shell. Silver blood gushes over my hands, down my arms, but I don't stop, not until my fists meet metal.

A flicker. The AI staring at me, holographic nose to faceplate.

I twist, imagining my swords are a drill, ripping through the thing's belly, following it up with a pulse of energy through its body, seeking the thing it calls a heart.

A shudder and then silence, from the machine, from my HUD, before Hunt screams in my ear. Ripping the blades out, throwing myself sideways, air exploding out my lungs as I hit the deck belly-first, and then I'm on my back as the thing crashes to the floor. Legs splayed, neck a limp noodle caught under its own body.

I breathe. In. Out. Do it again.

I'm on my paws and I'm getting out of here, but instead of heading out the hatch I came in, I'm vaulting over workbenches to the spot at the back of the room. This time, when I slam my hand against the whorl, the bulkhead parts and I'm diving into that maintenance crawlspace.

This is not the way I'm meant to be going, not even close, in fact... I think I'm heading backward.

That's what it feels like, even if Euiva's map doesn't agree. But then what would Euiva know? She's ancient, her design superseded a hundred times over, but still...

I keep going, sometimes crawling, sometimes shuffling through spaces built for beings larger than me. Even with armour padding my knees, my bones hurt from being on them for an hour straight. I must be on the other side of the ship by now, or close enough to it, even if the map is still telling me to crawl on.

What I wouldn't give for h'Lott right now, blood-thirsty snarl and all. Not that her sense of where we are would be any better than mine, not without a breeze or a tree or something, but at least she'd know if we were crawling around in circles. But h'Lott has her own mission, and if I'm lucky— No, if we're *both* lucky, it'll give us the edge we need to survive this.

I clump on, doggedly following the map. Dude is silent, as is Hunt. We're all just concentrating on finding the ship's core, dumping the slag and getting out.

There's an intersection, each branch of it looking just like all the others – squarer, cramped versions of the ship's squashed-egg corridors. Pale grey is still the dominant colour, but there're others here too, pulsing lines of red and green and blue – power conduits I guess – bright splashes of yellow that might just be there to look pretty, and silver. It might be another shade of grey, but the silver stands out even more than the brilliant pops of colour. It doesn't just gleam or sparkle, it's... I don't know. Alive I guess, in a way that nothing else on this ship is, not even the wohol.

It speaks to me, a whisper seen more than heard, like something in the corner of my eye. Maybe it's the shimmer on the edge of my vision, that space where ghosts reside, where images are only a quarter-seen and your imagination fills in the details. Makes you jump out of your skin or believe in Old Terra fairies.

My map is pulling me to the left, but that shimmer is beckoning me right, teasing me with promises of sugar plums and daydreams. I shouldn't follow it; even if *Euiva* is so far out of date she might as well be a fossil, but at least she's real. Right?

And still... The map screeches when I take the right tunnel, my heading trying to loop back onto itself, flashing and beeping. Even Hunt perks up, its query running down my spine. I shake the HUD and Hunt aside. I have to follow the shimmer, wherever it leads.

The determination has barely crossed my mind before the whisper stops, and I stop with it, right in the middle of the crawl space. No bulkhead in front of me, no intersection or panel, just a symbol on the deck, a complicated double whorl connected by curving lines, like a couple of donuts struck through with lightning.

I touch it.

Silver nanites bleed through the deck, filling in the carved hollows, finding other grooves, one to either side of the symbol, and shooting up the walls.

I follow it, up, up, up, twisting until I'm staring at the ceiling and the nanites spreading across it. The same symbol on the floor rises from the ceiling, and even as I touch it, I'm flashing back to *Aeotu* and falling into the proto-viyu tank, and fuck, I hope I'm not about to plunge into the same here.

The line of silver trailing up the walls glows bright-white. My breath is pent up in my throat, heart beating hard in my chest. Dude's claws are sunk into my shoulder and...

And...?

My lungs are burning. I let the air out in a rush, suck another in even as my heart slows and the adrenalin building in my veins is swept away. The light above dims to a gentle glow.

I let my breath out, feel my shoulders slump and relax the hand pressed against the ceiling—

Dude rushes up my arm, little fug body diving through the silver square.

He's gone before I can react, before the last soft thud of his paws leaves my skin.

Gone.

Through the silver.

I lunge after him.

This is the second time I've found myself in goo, except this goo feels more liquid, soft and floating. There's a current pulling me along, and wherever I am is a big tube, not as big as the maintenance crawl, barely big enough for me, arms tucked tight against my body, legs straight. There's no light in here, save the one on my shoulder. It's not much, not even enough to pierce a few centimetres of the thick gloom caused by the stream of nanites.

I haven't found Dude, but I assume he's somewhere up ahead and if I just hold on long enough, I'll catch up to him. After that... After that I'm going to act like a fucking armour-plated starfish and tear my way out of this fucking ship.

That's the plan, and I'm totally ignoring the not-so-little bit of me screaming that that's not going to work. But what the fuck does he know, right? I mean, I'm ninety-nine percent sure that I'm in a tube full of wohol nanites that'll skewer me through the heart the moment I rip into the wall, but I'm just as sure that whatever's at the end of this river/tunnel is just as bad. That little, quarter-seen whisper is telling me it's worse, telling me I don't want to be alive when I hit it.

Come on, Dude, where are you?

I need to go faster, need to catch up to him. A kick of my legs, ignoring the thud of my paws against the tunnel sides, the way the movement ripples up my body and scrapes my head against the roof. Ignore it all, everything but Dude.

Why the fuck did he dive in?

That little whisper, tickling the corners of my vision, colouring it yellow-green.

'Slag?' I don't realise I've spoken until the sound rattles in my ears, hollow and strange.

Another yellow-green pulse. Yes.

And you know what? That whisper feels a lot like Dude.

A wash of gold through my senses, a comforting fuzz. But how? Dude is Dude and the slag is… Holo-genie Ekene standing in the hangar, telling Jim that *he* controlled the slag. Dude sitting atop a red cocoon, a little yellow-gold statue. Tiny yellow filaments taking over silver nanites, filling it with the restless tide of Jørgen minds.

H'Lott's stasis pod, neo-slag spreading from my armour, Hunt directing it to the controls. It didn't come back. And now I'm remembering the way Hunt knew where to point me, the hidden hatch in the workroom, the way the mech just popped it open, like it had the keys.

And now I'm in a river of the stuff, so why isn't the slag infecting the nanites? Why—?

Dude, running up my arm, his little fug-self almost completely yellow, barely a hint of green to be seen.

A check of my own self, the HUD showing the viyu with the barest trace of slag. Dude took it all, but why? All I had to do was stick my arm in to let the slag infect the nanites. Why? Why'd he leave me behind?

{{ *Getting closer, for maximum infection.* }}

'Closer to what?'

The whisper, telling me I don't want to be alive when I find out.

'No.' My heart freezes, just a second before fear and adrenalin send it racing. 'Dude.'

I kick harder.

Hurry, the whisper says. Or maybe that's me, my heart pounding in my chest.

Kick. Scrape. Kick.

Hurry.

Kick.

Hurry. Hurry. Hurry.

A glow, burning through the gloom. Not mine, but coming from up ahead, lighting up the nanites in strings of silver, and is it my imagination or is the current stronger?

Hurry.

A splotch of darkness the size of my fist. The thin shadow of a barbed tail.

'Dude!'

Another massive kick. The constellation of Kuma going off as my head smashes against the ceiling, but I don't care. Dude is just there, and I'm reaching and—

His tail between my fingers, snapping tight as his little body continues forward. Jerks to a stop.

My legs shooting outwards, a shudder as my knees dig into the tunnel, another as my free hand joins them, my back a second later.

The glow up ahead is blinding, outlining Dude and making my eyes smart, even through my faceplate. It's hard to reel Dude in, jammed as I am in the tube with the force of the nanites pressing against me. It'd be easier if I wasn't bent in half, if I could dig my claws into the sides instead of just my knees. Dude's not helping either, straining against my hold like he *wants* to get smooshed or chopped or barbecued by whatever the whisper says is up there.

I pull him back – one centimetre, then two – ignoring the pain in my hand as his little barbed tail pierces my armour.

Against my back, the tide pushes harder.

'I'm not letting you go, buddy.' The strain of holding us in place, the burn of knees and muscle, the phantom pain from my amputated knee, riding through my voice.

{{ *Let go.* }} The voice is Hunt's but the impression behind it is more, is the whisper of slag and Dude smooshed together.

'No.' I pull him back another centimetre, feel the burn in the space between my shoulders. 'We're close enough, just dump the slag here.'

Sadness washes through the barb in my palm, a soft deep blue fuzz travelling through my fingers, shivering up my arm. It shines with determination, brilliant bronze tendrils sinking into my armour and slipping under my skin.

My heart stops, 'cause I know this sensation, know what comes next, and clamp down on the web flowing under my skin. It surges against my control, tries to batter its way through the wall I shove between it and control of my body.

Dude gets another centimetre closer, and I shove harder with my knees and back, envisaging spikes driving through the tube, wedging me in tighter, even as the current surges against my back. Harder than before. But I'm going to need my other arm soon, just another second and Dude'll be close enough to grab with my other hand.

One more centimetre.

The tide pushes harder, and there's a jerk that echoes all the way up my thigh and dislodges my left knee. Only for a moment, a millimetre lost, nothing more.

All I need is a second to pull Dude close to my chest—

The *snap* reverberates up my arm. The weight pulling at my

fingers is gone, the dark blob that is Dude shooting into the brightness.

'No!' I yell after it, lunge after his shadow.

Am jerked to a stop, knees and back embedded in the tube, outstretched hand clutching Dude's little tail, but no Dude. Dude is gone, disappeared into the light, but it's not too late, I can still—

The explosion takes me in the chest, a wave of force expelling the air from my lungs, the rush of nanites shattering my hold on the tube walls. Pain in my back as the anchors snap, tumbling me backward. My head impacting the wall, the constellation of Kuma going off behind my eyes before darkness devours the light.

# CHAPTER NINETEEN

I'm suspended in the tube, chest sore, shoulders smarting, hands and feet dragging against the walls.

Pain echoes through my palm, lances all the way up my arm to my heart. I close my hand around it, dig the little barb in deeper.

It's dark here. Silent. Peaceful. No engines humming in the background, no tide to push me around, no voices in my head. Just me, in the darkness.

I'm going to float here forever. By myself. Alone.

Until I rot.

Fine veins of yellow-green trace the walls. A few at first, casting the suggestion of light. A deep breath and I'd be kissing it.

It moves slowly, a winding throughfare building upon itself, growing thicker and brighter, branching into smaller thoroughfares as it goes until the wall is covered in slag. It moves inwards then, sending little towers into the space where I float. Those grow taller and thicker, casting even more light. They keep growing and I brace myself, both welcome and dread the pain that will come when the first tower pierces my chest.

I wait. And I wait.

A piercing tip touches my faceplate and... It stops.

A glowing point over my face, hovering just there. I reach to grab it, to shove it through my armour and—

I can't move my hand. Something's holding it down. I twist. Or try to.

I'm stuck. Held in place by glowing towers, ankles and legs and arms. All of them caught.

'No, let me go.'

There is no answer. Only silence.

Fine. If that's the way it wants to play it. I concentrate, visualise my armour becoming molten, remember the feeling of heat drawn from my bones.

New light shines in the darkness, coming not from some Dude-eating heart or the slag, but me. *I'm* burning, and I'm snarling in the face of the tower against my faceplate, knowing it can't see me but not caring.

Take that slag. Take that whispers. You can't stop me. No one can stop me.

Except perhaps the giant hand bursting through the tube, rucnart-sized fingers clamping around arms and legs, pulling me out.

'Hunt!'

I'm ripped out of the tube and thrown into chaos, literally *thrown*, shoulder hitting the deck and rolling, coming to my knees, fake paw braced to push me up. Pausing as the nightmare hits me.

Not my nightmare, not exactly, and Holy Terra, I *wish* it was in my head.

Wohol scream. At least, I think they're screaming. The sounds coming out of their mouths is high, a melody of fear and pain saturating the air. Yellow-green and silver cascades out of the hole in the ceiling, spilling over podium-like consoles, ripping through holograms, climbing the bulkheads. Spearing chests, legs, arms, heads.

A wohol comes at me, arms raised, its dark grey uniform torn, just like the white downy flesh underneath. Its upper set of arms are raised high over its head, its lower pair out to its side, sharp black talons extended, but all I can look at is its face. The madness in its eyes, the fear/rage ripping out of its throat, the blood on the sharp points of its teeth and the sticky blackness riding its brain, singing an ancient song of retribution.

Blood bursts over my face, a too-bright spray of red over my faceplate. Yellow-green and silver thrust from the wohol's chest, climb up its neck, wrap around its jaw.

I *think* the alien is dead before the slag starts eating it.

I'm on my paws and I'm running.

Another wohol gets in my way, leaping out of nowhere, those wicked talons raised, the same sticky fear in its eyes.

I don't think, I cut it down, my swords taking out its knees.

It falls.

I don't look back.

I kill more. Hunt keeps count, the number ticking away in the back of my brain, cataloguing not just the number, but the manner. Slashed knees, slashed throats, punctured lungs.

A database of death.

I wish it wouldn't, wish I could ignore it. But can't, no matter how hard I run. Every pound of my paws, every thud of my heart.

It's fear and death, ancient nightmares swarming along with the slag to take over the corridors. I feel h'Lott in the stickiness of the wohols' fear, recognise the sharp bite of her mind unlocking the water-kin in their memories. There are other minds swirling around me too, familiar traces of Ekene and Aeotu guiding the slag, even the red tide of Euiva.

What I don't feel is Dude or anything warm. There is only cold and death, is only the endless off-white corridors and aliens rushing past me.

I slide to a halt. All the aliens except the four standing in a line before me, matt-grey armour absorbing the light, turning them from aliens with recognisable eyes and mouths, to miniature Hunts, hulking and faceless. Three metres away, and they still tower over me, the top of their helmeted heads almost brushing the ceiling, the massive weapons in their lower arms swallowing the light. The water-kins' stickiness crawls over their heads, wraps around their shoulders and tugs at their feet, but it does not touch them. There is something between it and them, a slick, pearlescent film as foreign to me as the sounds spilling from their unseen lips.

{{ *Surrender,* }} Hunt translates. {{ *Or they will shoot.* }}

'What?'

{{ *They wish us to surrender.* }} A pause, and then a screen pops into the corner of my vision. On it is the hangar, another quartet of grey armoured wohol standing at Hunt's giant feet. {{ *They are attempting to breach my defences.* }}

'Can they do that?' The weapons in their arms don't look that powerful, but then I wouldn't have thought fug could destroy a ship.

{{ *Uncertain.* }} It pauses, just a microsecond, uncertainty travels down the umbilicus connecting us. {{ *I can eliminate them.* }}

Hunt says "eliminate" and all I see is a scorch mark on the deck.

There's no time to respond, no time even to ponder the microsecond of emotion. The trio blocking my way are making those harsh, sibilant sounds again. My HUD is split in three, one screen for the squad at Hunt's feet, another for me, and a blown-up view of the aliens three-fingered hands tightening on the barrel of their rifles.

The time for surrender is over.

Not that I was ever going to do that.

I leap, taking Hunt's uncertainty and sweeping it across the corridor like a blade. It connects, a murky grey crescent slicing through their knees and... and...

Oh shit.

I wanted a second, expected a moment of hesitation to carry me across the three metres of deck separating us before the wohol responded, needed it even. I don't get it. The wave off uncertainty slides off the strange film between them and the water-kins' influence, and what I get is a bolt of light to the chest.

There is pain, gripping my ribcage, squeezing my lungs, burning all the way down my sternum and seeking out my jaw. I'm on the deck, stumbling, desperate to keep my feet under me, to keep moving even as my armour screams and I scream along with it.

I don't know how I do it, Dude is not here to stop me from falling, and yet I'm in the midst of the squad, blades dropping from my forearms, slashing and stabbing in time with Hunt's prompts. It is not graceful, the movements do not flow like they did before, and there's no space left in my brain to slip into the eter and turn the aliens' minds against them, even if I could. Every part of me not focused on the pain, is focussed on not getting dead.

I've taken out three wohol before, three more shouldn't be a problem. Except it is.

An explosion in my back, another in the side of my head. Stars bursting behind my eyes, fire sweeping through my nerves, or maybe that is actual fire, turning my armour to a crisp. Maybe the fog clouding my vision is viyu dying and flaking away from my body.

And maybe this is all a dream and Dude is going to come back and save my arse.

Maybe. Maybe. Maybe.

But probably not.

A spear in my back. Real? Imagined? I don't know, all I know is that pain is making a new home in my spine, and all the other spikes, burns and agonies are joining it, ripping up and down nerve endings, making every muscle clench and taking my breath. The HUD is soaked in red and if Hunt had the programming to scream, I think it would. I think it would yell at me to get up, would flood the connection between us with fear and desperation, would shove all that emotion into my bones, inflating them from the inside out.

And maybe it does, maybe, as it makes scorch marks out of the squad at *its* feet, Hunt is reaching into me and twisting.

I don't want to die.

I'm on my knees, swinging my blades, catching a wohol behind the ankles, am scurrying over its body – stab, stab, stab – lunging for the gun falling from its nerveless fingers.

Hands closing over the grip, Hunt flowing through the umbilicus, telling me where to slot my fingers, how to fit my other hand into the groove in the weapon's barrel, to find the trigger.

It hums, a tiny vibration through my fingers, and light bursts out the other end.

One. Two. Three.

I imagine the wohol about to cleave my head from my shoulders staring at me, imagine they look just like the mechanic did – slit pupils swallow the iris, jaw slack. I imagine that even as I hit the deck, rolling to my back and shooting the solider coming up behind. Then I'm on my feet, stepping out the way as they fall to the deck, chests smoking ruins, and fire again.

One. Two. Three.

The hole in the first soldier's chest, matches their comrades.

There's no time to be sick, to mourn the loss of... Not life. The wohol would have killed me as surely as I did them.

For the first time, I am grateful for the sticky blackness. It slides from my anima and eats the guilt, the sorrow, leaving nothing behind.

I turn away, still clutching my stolen weapon, and jog down the corridor, away from the fresh heat signatures closing in on me from behind.

# CHAPTER TWENTY

I miss not eating. I think I even miss not feeling hungry. The growl of stomach acids, the way it burbles, like someone's blowing bubbles in my gut. I don't miss this part though, the body crunching spasms of whatever the fuck it was I just ate trying to bust its way out of my system. Old Terra, it hurts, although I guess pain is relative now. Before my leg, I'd have been making friends with the walls, or the floor, curled up real close like somehow the hard metal-stone could absorb the knives spearing my abdominal wall. Now... Well, now I might be hunched over like a shuttle bent my back in half, but I'm moving. One shaky paw in front of the other, over and again, doing my best to ignore the coppery taste of blood on the back of my tongue.

The fight with the grey-armoured wohol took more out of me than I thought, literally as well as figuratively, and the fight after that wasn't much better. My armour is patchy, bits turned grey and flaked off after each clash. It's retreating from my upper arms and thighs, leaving enough behind to support my fug claws, but not the blades.

I hug the pistol I wrested from the last wohol after my fug blades crumbled to dust.

Now, the remaining armour is concentrated around my torso and face, leaving my ears bare, allowing the wail of sirens to piece the drums.

The ship shudders. Somehow the barely-audible wail is worse

than the wholesale blare of *Aeotu*'s sirens. It might not drown out the gurgle of my stomach or the shuffle of my feet, but that fact just seems to make it that much better at shaving my eardrums down to nothing, a mini-grater tearing into my head. Not in a whimsical descriptive fashion either; there's actual *blood* trickling down the line of my jaw. At first, I thought it was sweat, but when I wiped it away, well, unless something seriously changed with my body chemistry, sweat ain't red.

I could really do with my helmet about now, a thought and I bet it would filter out the alarm, turn it into something that wasn't a knife.

I've had enough of knives.

Shuffle *snick*.

But it doesn't matter. It doesn't. I have to get to that storeroom, have to find Mum. There's not much time.

I'm concentrating so hard, it takes a second to recognise the snarl.

I stop, ice shivering up my spine, already imagining the talons wrapping around my neck.

Maybe it hasn't seen me. Maybe—

*Snick, snick, snick.*

Maybe not.

I spin, hand already on the gun attached under my ribs, armour moving to reinforce—

*Down!* The roar blasts through my brain; rage and fur and fangs.

I hit the deck, knees giving out before I have a chance to process the shadow leaping over my head, the short orange-red tail, the musty scent of fur.

A scream, the wet tearing sound of claws meeting flesh. Blood, a thick red spray across off-white bulkheads. The *phzit* and burnt ozone of a weapon followed by the stench of burned hair, the yowl of a tree-kin and then... and then...

A paw as big as my face, the short pale yellow fur dark with blood, a scrap of grey fabric caught between its toes.

I look up. H'Lott staring down her sharp muzzle, dark with the same blood that stains her toes, her breath hot and coppery, and all four of her eyes focused on me.

*Did you do it?* she says.

I nod, feeling old. Old as *Aeotu.* No. Older. The weight of those ancient swatai bearing down on my anima. I am so old I should be dust, scattered across the deck, blown away and forgotten.

H'Lott nods back, even as her ears dip, regret and disgust shining through her aura. But not disgust at me, no, this is different, is focussed elsewhere.

Everything should be focussed elsewhere, should be taken back to the hands that started us on this path, and if I had a time machine I would. Just wind us all back and lay this shit at their feet, make *them* clean this up. Except they left it to us. To me. To h'Lott. To Mac.

To Dude.

A nudge, h'Lott's nose under my chin, her forepaw around my waist, lifting me.

*Get on*, she says, an image of me on her back high in her mind.

I stare at her, at her back, the point of her shoulders taller than I am. I not quite sure how to process the image swimming in my brain, the action it implies. Part of me is missing and I'm not sure how to shuffle to my feet let alone climb all the way up there.

Another nudge, this one mechanical, and there's another presence in my bones, sliding through pathways used to something softer, fuzzier. It's cold and it hurts, but I let it take control of my muscles, let it lift me to my feet, stretching my hands out to grip h'Lott's neck and swing me onto her back. We're moving then, and that presence – Hunt, it's Hunt taking Dude's place – is clamping my knees against h'Lott's sides, is leaning me over her shoulders and holding on as she gallops through the ship's empty hallways.

*Mostly* empty.

There's a dark smudge ahead, the towering figure of a wohol, armour sucking in the light, the point of the weapon held in its upper hands spitting it out again.

H'Lott dodges, a sudden leap left and then right and then left again, her giant strides eating up the deck, her mind a spear taking the alien in the head.

The point of that spear breaks against the iridescent shield coating the alien's mind, but the haft makes it through.

It stumbles, knees going soft, lower arms stretching as if to brace itself.

I brace myself for the next leap, for the impact and the spray of blood as h'Lott rips the wohol's white throat out. It doesn't come. There is a leap, but not impact, no hot copper stench, no splatter of blood, just h'Lott stretching out, pounding down the corridor faster and faster, her lungs heaving, hearts pumping.

She didn't kill it. Why didn't she kill it?

Heat stirs in my gut, rips through the numbness and turns it to rage.

Sweet, hot, black and sticky rage.

My hands are claws, plunging into h'Lott's back, like if I can just grab her shoulders, I can turn her around, go back—

A scream, h'Lott's pain, her shock vibrating through my bones. She stumbles, forepaws going out from under her, hitting the deck.

I fly from her shoulders. Hunt is still there, curling my head into my chest, making me a ball, even as armour shifts from my front to my back. I hit the wall, lose some breath, but am rolling, back on my feet in moments, drawing more air. Not even a second from the fall to the recovery.

The tree-kin has barely stopped skidding across the deck, hasn't even got her paws under her.

I spin back the way we came, nanites shifting again, from back to hands and legs, reinforcing the muscles that will make me go faster, even as my HUD flicks to life and—

*{{ Danger. }}*

A dozen targets blazing red on the HUD, behind me, the way h'Lott was running.

I snarl.

Hunt is there, moving with me, filling the back of my head with trajectories and vectors, optimal angles of attack. We sprint down the corridor, skid around a corner.

The aliens are creeping down the hallway, two on one side, one on the other, their backs to the walls, the brows over their deep-set eyes furrowed, guns cradled in their upper arms. One of them, trailing behind the other, is holding a sphere of glowing light in their lower right hand, while the other two have smaller weapons in theirs. Concentration and not a little concern stain the eter around each.

It takes only a second for all of that to sink into my brain.

I'm two meters into the corridor before they see me, leaping high. They have time to twitch before I'm coming down again, claws slicing air and then flesh before the first one screams. Killing things shouldn't feel this good, the spray of blood shouldn't smell this sweet, their pain shouldn't be a balm, shouldn't soothe the agony deep, deep down in my anima.

But it does.

It does and I'm not going to regret it, not to going to second guess it even if a piece of me whispers it's wrong.

Fuck it. Fuck the wohol. Fuck h'Lott galloping up behind me, blood running down her forelegs, lips pulled back in a snarl. Fuck everything but the heady rush of adrenaline and the satisfaction of dragging my talons through flesh, of the aliens' screams.

There is a black tide rushing through me, boiling from the dark place in my heart, slipping up my spine. I whirl and slash, feel the hot burn of laser fire across my cheek, breathe in the stench of scorched flesh. There is pain, but the tide crashes over it, consumes it in a rush of anger, of hate, of the driving, inescapable need to kill.

Kill.

Kill.

Kill.

I scream and the voice is not mine, or not only mine. It is a million voices in one, the desperation of a species spilling from my throat, streaming from my arms, my legs. Two alien corpses lie behind me, and I spin, aching for the last— Only to see the wohol die between h'Lott's jaws.

Is it victory or rage that erupts from my mouth? The anger of a kill denied? It doesn't matter, there are more blips on my HUD, red triangles coming fast from behind, a whole swarm of them clogging up the corridor. *These* are mine. All mine. I'm off, forgetting h'Lott, focussed on the horde ahead, the thrill of carnage, the dance of death—

*Kuma.* The voice is familiar, rings between my ears, reminds me of boy with a square jaw and eyes the colour of an oxygen-rich sky. *Stop.*

No. Dude didn't stop, the wohol didn't, or Euiva or Grea. I was done stopping, was done listening, feeling, thinking. I was done with everything but the black tide and the whisper in the back of my skull.

Kill, it says, beating in time with my heart, rushing through my veins, driving my feet.

Kill.

There's another hatch ahead, still solid, still opaque. The aliens are behind it, close.

The darkness slides over my bones.

Kill.

*Kuma!*

No.

*Kuma!* No longer one voice but two, the boy and another, as familiar as the first, a kaleidoscope. They're reaching through my belly, riding the umbilicus that connects me to Hunt, invading, wrapping around muscles and tendons, trying to sink fingers into the black. *Stop!*

I stop. Not just slow and halt, but stop dead, all but vibrating as bones strain against muscles, the sudden interruption turning me into a tuning fork.

There's a scream in my throat; anger and bloodlust bottled up in my chest with no place to go. Trapped in my skin, the red triangles of my enemy getting closer and closer on the HUD. Just behind the hatch now.

Another symbol coming up behind me, blue and calming, except the emotions rolling off h'Lott are anything but calm. They echo my own, and I imagine, if I was in the grip of my own emotions, they would shiver across my skin with the same chilly menace, and make it crawl.

The hard, restless edge of another mind joins the two already in my bones, claws where the others are ribbons, commanding, taking over my brain with ruthless efficiency. H'Lott's breath is hot on my neck, her whiskers sharp pricks over my cheeks, her lower eyes black pits, the sharp glow of her orange upper gaze boring into mine.

*Obey.* It is less a thought than it is a command, digging through my grey matter, planting images of glass-eyed critters marching in perfect lines, scurrying about *Citlali's* hallways. Mindless. Obedient.

Inside, the black twists, is no longer just a sticky darkness but something deeper, stronger. Is the sensation of currents pushing against flippers, the pressure of deep oceans on my bones, the song of a million minds compressed into a single point. And it has a different message, an older one, deeper and more urgent. The black twists around the colours, and it's like the others can't see it, can't feel the ice, the purpose, but I can, and it is glorious.

*Obey*, h'Lott says again.

I am not obedient. I am not— "A. Critter!" It's more than a yell, more than an emote. The breath leaving my body has its own force, is a wall – physical and mental – slamming into h'Lott, into Mac/Aeotu, pushing them off their feet.

I can move.

My bones are my own.

H'Lott is on the deck, eyes dazed. She's shaking her head, muscles twitching spasmodically, like she can't quite get them to move.

Of Mac/Aeotu there's nothing, the afterimage of starlight perhaps.

The hatch shivers, energy running through its veins. The aliens are on the other side.

The white bulkhead flashes, is translucent and then it is gone, sunk into the deck with a *snap*. My prey is on the other side.

# CHAPTER TWENTY-ONE

There's not much left of me when I hear the whisper. I am red from head to paws, blood and ash staining flesh where armour and cloth have burned way. It's burned in a lot of places. Breathing is hard, even with the mask over my nose and mouth, the low-oxygen atmosphere making my bones heavy and clouding my eyes with starlight.

Hunt is trying to pump power through my veins, but with so little fug left to channel it, the glowing stream is barely enough to keep me on my feet.

No, what keeps me going now is the darkness, although that too is fading as the tide of wohol thins.

I guess that's why I hear the whisper.

Like before, when I followed it through the maintenance tubes, it caresses my cheek, pulling me from the corridor I'm stalking to another, smaller one.

I follow it.

There is a pull at the back of my brain. I'm standing at an intersection where a skinny corridor branches off the main ring, fighting with myself for precious seconds I don't have, not if I want to outrun the squad at my back.

According to my map, the hangar and Hunt are to the right, h'Lott and Mum too, toward the outer sections of the ship, but the pull, the same voice that whispered to me in the nanite tube wants me to go left. Deeper into the ship.

Pain still rides my nerves, echoes in my head and makes breathing an exercise in torture. I don't know how I'm still going, only that Hunt is doing something to the armour and that the armour is doing something to me, something like what was done to the trio of wohol, with the sliminess over their brains.

I clutch a gun, glance over my shoulder, wonder if it's the pound of armoured paws I hear or just my heart.

H'Lott will be waiting for me. If other wohol have the same film over their thoughts and she can't take over their minds, she'll need me too. And yet...

I can't ignore the whisper. What if it's Dude? What if he survived? I can't leave him.

I go left, toward the pull.

Shit gets weird, and I mean weirder than it already is.

I'm back somewhere near the ship's command centre, or where the command centre would be on *Aeotu* and *Euiva*, in the heart of the ship, and there are nanites *everywhere*. It's almost like crawling through *Citlali* where the fug was thickest; a jungle of vines and snapping tendrils, a fuzzy carpet of nanites covering all the places in between. Except the jungle is silver and the carpet is geometric, and yellow-green.

The edge of it crawls toward my paws, millimetre upon millimetre, slow enough I could almost convince myself it isn't happening. There are bodies in the jungle, ragged bits of white flesh and grey uniforms caught on spikes, things moving under mounds of yellow-green. And the whisper... It's everywhere, curling around my temples, invading my ears. Soft, warm, inviting – a kiss pressed to my cheek – and it wants me to step on that carpet, to follow it to the heart of the jungle.

Following the whisper further is a bad idea. A really bad idea.

But I do it.

No careful exploration, just plunge into the jungle. I'm a dozen strides in before I let myself think about it, a half dozen more before I give in to the urge to look over my shoulder. The untouched corridor is still there, pale-grey and perfect, the path back out clear, no vine curtains or walls of nanites. It should settle the adrenalin making my heart thump, should reassure the doubt squirming in my gut.

It doesn't. It makes it worse.

One day, I'm going to make better life choices. One day, when I'm not covered in alien nanites, following a whisper deeper into an alien ship where the crew wants to kill me.

One day.

Hopefully before I'm dead.

The yellow-green carpet sighs under my paws, tiny fragments breaking off with every step, catching between my toes and in the creases between claw and sheath. I don't stop it, don't bend down to pluck it out, not because it wouldn't do any good, but because the whisper says not to. It helps that it's just the slag, or what I hope is just slag, attaching itself to me. There's a familiarity about it, not only in the way it finds the grooves carved in the armour, but in the way it feels.

Silver tendrils writhe around me, some hanging from the ceiling, others growing from the deck. Some long enough to wrap around me, some thick enough to hold up the ceiling all on their own. It's a twisted version of *Citlali* where the fug doesn't want to eat me. It's eating the wohol crew instead.

The bodies trapped under the yellow-green mounds move, sibilant cries escaping as I pass. I don't stop, don't look. The whisper is getting stronger. I still can't make out what it's saying, if it's saying anything, but that slimy feeling is crawling down my back, even as the kiss on my cheek draws me forward.

Hunt is cataloguing everything, showing me the stream of alien crew scampering into the fighters, the two new squads of grey-clad soldiers gathered at its feet, unmindful of the marks that used to be their comrades. The mech is ignoring them, its attention on the fighters, the surge of power running through the ones closest to the hangar entry, the first to be occupied.

{{ *Weapons,* }} Hunt says, highlighting almost invisible protrusions in the fighter's sleek nose. It clocks more as the other fighters come online. {{ *Eighty-nine percent probability they will fire.* }}

I would have guessed a hundred percent but—

{{ *Structural weakness. Possibility for hull breach.* }}

Kill them first.

{{ *Not enough power.* }}

There is another possibility hovering on the edge of Hunt's processors, and even as I let it unfold in my brain, I know it's a bad one. *Hunt* knows it's a bad idea, has already calculated all the likely outcomes, the probabilities. It's why it hasn't done it yet, why it's waiting for me.

But it's either that or a billion smoking pieces of mechanicoid scattered across a wohol hangar.

{{ *Wohol powering weapons.* }} A vision of a wohol fighter, angry points of light forming on small protrusions either side of its nose.

There are no more mounds under my feet, no more cries or writhing wohol. Just a single hatch and a lone solider standing before it, weapon pointed at my chest and that slimy shimmer crawling over its head.

I reach back to Hunt. Do it.

I'll find another way out. I just have to get past this.

The whisper is behind that hatch, I know it, just like Hunt knows that I'm not getting past that solider, not without what comes next.

The explosion rocks the ship.

I leap before the first shudder knocks the solider off its feet. Nanites cascade over my body to form a single molten fug-blade.

It slides into the soldier's neck.

The solider dies.

I rip through the last of the hatch, force my way into the room and—

There it is.

*

The source of the whisper. It spills out of the pedestal in the middle of the room, a waterfall of yellow-green and silver oozing over the stark white deck. The room itself is spherical, the walls the same brilliant white as the deck, brighter than anything I've seen on this ship, bright enough to sear my eyeballs. I wonder what it would do to the wohol, with their love of dim spaces.

Now's not the time to wonder. This Core doesn't pulse like *Aeotu* or *Euiva*, doesn't have the same sense of being alive, and it's not just the lack of colour. The walls here move, have arteries pulsing with energy, snaking across the deck to feed the ball atop the podium. It's hard to tell what the ball once looked like under its coating of slag, but I guess it was the same sleek nothingness as the rest of the Core. Ordered and geometric where *Aeotu*'s core was a psychedelic jungle, full of life and creativity. Full of emotion.

The only emotion in here is in the slag and that slimy sense of... something. I still can't pinpoint it. Most of that is concentrated in the ripples of yellow-green within the silver. The slag is concentrated around the podium, leaving a couple of metres of clear space between the door and it.

I step deeper into the room.

The whisper, no longer a sound, caresses my cheek, its touch trailing down my jaw to rest under my chin and draw me forward.

I should resist, that tiny sane bit of myself – the one that's resolved to make better life choices – knows that nothing good can come of this, but my feet don't care, and this time I can't even blame Dude or the armour or Hunt or anybody but myself. One step, two. My toes are touching the slag before I know it, another step and I'm *in* the slag, the stuff sucking at my ankles, climbing my calves. Lifting my feet is hard, and I struggle to get closer to the podium, almost falling to my knees, but get there I do, and once I'm there...

...once I'm there...

Reaching out to the podium, hands passing through slag, cool and welcoming against my skin. Yellow-green breaking away from the silver to wind around my wrists and up my arms, a delicate filigree holding me in place. The slag is thicker than I thought, I'm up to my wrists in it before my fingers find the ball it's covering.

AI, the whisper says. Ship's brain.

Oh. Yeah, I guess that makes sense. And ewww, I have my hands wrapped around some being's brain. Not that it feels like a brain, or what I would call a brain. Instead of wet and squishy, the kernel is smooth and pulses with heat. With life, but not the kind of life I recognise, not chaotic and messy, bright with emotion and thought, this is... I don't know. Different in same way that Hunt is different, and Aeotu and the wohol, but more so.

Whatever it is, it's hidden behind a mental wall. I can see it but I can't touch it. It's alien in a way that's incomprehensible, which is saying something given the beings I've been conversing with lately.

A tiny bloom of pain under my chin, where the whisper had me, brings my attention back to the slag winding up my arms, except it's gone a little bit further than just my arms. It's wrapped around my shoulders and given I can't move my head, I'm guessing it's around my neck too. And is that a thin lacework of yellow-green I see crawling over my chin, and... Oh fuck, is that a *needle* aimed at my eye?

I jerk, try to pull my hands from the sphere but they're stuck as surely as my feet.

Oh fuck.

The needle looms large, but at least I have my faceplate, right? The armour will deflect—

It stabs, through my fug, straight into my eye and...

...and...

Time stops.

✳

I blink.

I went somewhere.

Take a breath.

Where'd I go?

I'm still in the wohol ship's Core, the slag lapping at my ankles, a lacework of yellow-green covering arms and shoulders, but I can move my head again.

One more blink.

There's nothing in my eye, no needles, no fragments of slag. No pain.

That's something. Right?

What the fuck just happened?

There's no answer save a gentle pulse from the kernel. It feels like... gratitude. Which is strange because before it didn't feel like anything at all.

I'm still up to my wrists in the slag coming out of the pedestal. I pull them out, half-expecting resistance, for the yellow-green bits winding around my armour to cut in deep and stop me. They don't, it's almost like they *want* me to go, sliding off my wrists, over the backs of my hands and leaving the tips of my fingers with a gentle caress.

A step back and the stuff around my ankles, more yellow-green now than silver, lets go just as easily. Another step, and another and another, and I'm standing in the hatch, feeling... I don't know. My chest is full, my heart aching like I'm losing something, like saying goodbye to an old friend, like a piece of myself is in the slag and I don't know what it is.

Warmth against my cheek, a gentle golden fuzz and... and...

'Dude?' I'm back across the deck, hands plunging into the slag, searching, even as the eter opens up around me.

Dude is there on the psionic plane. The fuzzbutt is perched atop the pedestal, tiny forepaws tucked in close to his body, the four hind ones lost in the explosion of his golden coat. I can just make out his ears, little triangles peeking out the top of his head. He *fuzzes* and the sound vibrates the air, warming my chest.

I have him cradled against my chest, tucked up under my chin. 'I thought I lost you, man.'

He *fuzzes* again and the sound is different, echoes in the eter like it's coming from all around me. Blue stains the air around him.

Sadness.

I hold him closer, burying my face in his fur and deny the deep navy creeping up my own legs, because I know. Even if I couldn't see the threads connecting him to the pedestal, thin lines of yellow-green and silver, I can feel it. His fuzz isn't the only thing that's bigger. It might be a fistful of critter I'm clutching to my chest, but out in the real... Out in the real, my fingers have found the centre of the slag and the thing under it isn't a ball of fur.

It's the same smooth sphere that was there before, except this time instead of the emotionless hum of power under my fingers, there's a golden fuzz, flooding up my arms to cuddle under my chin.

There are tears on my face.

I get it now, the whisper in the back of my brain. It wasn't the slag, not entirely, it was Dude talking to me *through* the slag, like Ekene aboard *Aeotu* or Grea on *Euiva*. The slag wasn't alive, was just nanoscopic bots looking for their next command. Technological critters, just smaller. And Dude – different, powerful, selfless – was the perfect carrier, and because he was a critter – engineered to take orders – the kin would have pegged him as the best choice to take over an enemy spaceship.

The thought of it squeezes a laugh from my chest. 'They're going to be surprised when they try to tell you what to do, Dude. You're a freaking spaceship now.' I sniff. 'All metal-stone and giant fucking engines. You'll tell *them* what to do.'

He *fuzzes* again, bright sparks of joy breaking up his blue aura. Agreement washes over my hands.

'I gotta go, buddy.' Another sniff as the almost-black navy miasma surges up my legs. 'I gotta go save Mum and all the others.' An image of Mum in that stasis pod, of Dad with viyusa sticking out of his side, all of it, everything I've been through, fills the eter. The miasma at my feet gains a hard edge and for a heartbeat, I hear the ancient song of the water-kin lapping at my knees.

Dude pushes it back. He pats my cheek.

I smile, it's wobbly, the corners of my mouth trying to turn down even as I force them up.

I put him back on the pedestal. Step back.

'Bye, Dude.'

# CHAPTER TWENTY-TWO

I don't have to cut through any more hatches. They open before I'm on them and snap shut almost before I'm through. The same happens in the corridors, except instead of hatches it's giant airlocks closing with enough force to send vibrations through the deck.

Dude is in everything, faint little touches of him in the bulkheads and rippling through the air itself. If I concentrate, I can see him in the slag flowing throughout the ship. His presence was stronger on the ship's inner rings, where flashes of gold and silver caught the corner of my eye, but out here, pounding toward the hangar where Hunt waits, he's nothing more than a ghost—

I'm blindsided. No warning, not so much as a blip on the HUD or a hint of fear, shock or anger, just a massive, grey-armoured weight crashing into my side.

I'm on the deck, ears ringing from the blow that made it through to my chin before my armour reacted. Two arms holding me down, another two smashing me in the face and chest, weight on my legs. Between star bursts, I see the faceless helmet of a warrior wohol, can make out the whorls carved into its armour, its buddies skidding to a stop behind it, weapons glowing bright with death.

Fuck.

The *emote* is big and bright and messy, bursting out of me without thought or plan. It's pain and shock, everything I'm feeling right this second, and it crashes against the soldier. The wohol pauses, just a second, the emote impacting before sliding off.

There is even less of me now than there was before, just the fancy lacework around hands and paws, the mask over my face allowing me to breathe. Hunt's in the back of my head, trying to push itself through the same conduits Dude once used, trying to take over muscle and bone, to coordinate defence, but it's not working. No matter how much of Hunt there is under my skin, it can't increase my strength, can't stop the blows raining on my face, can't dislodge the massive weight crushing my chest. Can't stop the bright, lime-green forming on the end of the soldier's gun.

And Dude... Dude is too far away, is still fighting with the remnants of the ship's AI, his presence barely even a whisper in these outer corridors. So close to the cargo bay, so close to Mum, to safety—

An orange and sand streak takes out the solider with the gun. Claws and teeth and rage filling the air, the hot stench of blood, and piercing, sibilant yells of the wohol.

The wohol on my chest jerks around, one of its four hands going for a blocky black thing attached to its chest armour, the other three still holding me down.

It's enough, *just* enough. The fug on my right hand forms talons, long wicked hooks, and even as the wohol glances back at me – the boxy thing in its free hand shifting, lengthening into a knife long enough to skewer my heart and still bury itself in the deck – I'm swinging for its throat.

Pain. Pain pain pain pain. Fire racing through my palm, down my arm, into my chest drawing a ragged scream from my throat. I have a moment to see the end of that wicked long knife protruding from the back of my hand, before it's pinned to the deck, and the wohol is leaning in close, helmet retracting, those slit-pupiled eyes staring into mine, flat lips drawn back in a snarl, it's short, too-sharp teeth bared in a gleaming row of fury.

A flash of green light. The wohol's eyes widen, just a little, white showing around the narrowed pupil, and then it's leaning into me, those teeth getting closer and closer—

It topples to the side, a heavy *thunk* on the deck. And there, in the off-white, squished-egg corridor is Mum, one of the wohol's big black weapons resting in her arms like a fucking cannon.

Worry and fear gather around her feet, tamped down by determination and focus. She doesn't smile at me. Behind her faceplate, her expression is hard, grim even, but relief rushes over her shoulders, a soft pink shroud.

She looks away, off down the corridor where the orange and sand streak went. 'Get it off him,' she says, and nods to the solider still pinning my legs. 'Quick, before more come.'

A snarl, not the high, sibilant sound off the wohol, but the blood curdling, fleshing-rending rumble of a tree-kin. Fuck, I never thought I'd be glad to hear that.

Head-sized paws grab hold of the corpse and tug. It flips onto the deck, freeing my legs but my hand—

Mum yanks the knife out, then, while I'm still gathering the breath to scream, she drags me to my feet and throws me against h'Lott.

It's walk or be dragged as Mum leads the way, the cannon held at her hips, her finger on the trigger. We're not going the right way though, the cargo hold is *behind* us but Mum's marching toward the outer rings, and I'm too busy coordinating my feet and hanging onto h'Lott to object.

Of the wohol, only stragglers remain, a few soldiers in their grey armour and others – crew, like the technician in the hangar. The soldiers stand or charge, pointing weapons at us, while the crew run. Or try to. Mum doesn't give them the chance. As soon as one of the aliens come into sight, she blasts them, the cannon spewing its deadly green light like a battering ram. Nothing survives.

When we get to the hangar, there's Hunt, carbon scoring like a negative sunburst at its giant feet, and a shuttle sitting on what's left of the deck. It's not much, the deck that is, and of the fighter craft that once stood there... There's a fucking great hole in the bulkhead, the metal-stone twisted inwards, and the carbon scorching there is...

If the marks at Hunt's feet were a sunburst, this is the big bang, or a torpedo. I'm betting on the torpedo, because beyond all that carbon scoring and twisted hull is the electric shimmer of a forcefield and the endless black depths of the void.

Someone blew a hole in the wohol ship and from the red nanites creeping over the still-glowing metal-stone, I don't need to guess who.

There are no words between Mum and h'Lott, but something must have happened because one moment the tree-kin is half-dragging me along in Mum's wake and then they're splitting up. H'Lott and I going for Hunt while Mum turns on her heel and runs back the way we came.

'What? Wait!' I stagger two steps from h'Lott, hand out, but Mum doesn't stop, and then the tree-kin has my arm in her teeth and I'm swinging back around—

*Others*, is all h'Lott says, packing in a bunch of memories – images and snatches of conversation fogging up my brain. The cargo hold. A cryo crate, thin filaments of yellow winding through the control panel. The crate opening at the tree-kin's paws, Onah spilling out. More crates opening, more crew joining the throng at h'Lott's back. The whole of them, crowded into a spaces between crates – flesh to fur to flesh – sharing not just the few rebreathers among them, but their psionic power, channelling it into Onah.

Onah perched between h'Lott's shoulders, his talons pricking her sides. All four eyes are open, his focus on one of the upright boxes, the ones with the injured wohol inside. He reaches for the wohol's mind. There is no subtlety and little finesse, Onah and the minds behind him punch right through the alien's mental walls, diving deep into its brain and— Darkness, the sticky black swamp of the water-kin rising to meet Onah's mental probe, an old vicious friend saying hello.

The memory cuts out.

I'm at Hunt's feet, h'Lott manoeuvring me around the back, holding me upright as fug tendrils wrap around my waist.

'No, the rest of the...' I'm about to say "crew" when Onah glides into the hangar, coming to rest on the wohol shuttle.

Mum's not far behind, the rest of the crew at her back.

Guess that answers that question.

H'Lott's gone, joining the rest as they pile into the shuttle, and my paws are a metre above the deck when Grea happens.

Just as I'm wondering how Mum thinks she's going to pilot alien tech, viyusa curls over the shuttle's nose. Hunt sees it first, alarms lighting up its system, but before I can yell, I'm not in the real anymore. I'm in the ora, forehead to forehead, nose to nose with Grea. The real Grea, the one whose face is a mirror of mine – small nose, stubborn chin, rounded pupils.

She smiles. 'We did it.'

'We did it,' I say back. Then... 'You can't have them,' and flash to Mum and h'Lott and the red winding around the shuttle.

'We're just getting them home.'

'No, you're not.' I grip her shoulders, fingers digging in. 'Tell Euiva to let them go.'

She shrugs, trying to dislodge my hands. A frown wrinkles the forehead pressed to mine. 'Let go, Kuma, you're hurting me.'

I hold tighter, imagining fug turning my fingertips to spikes, feeling them pierce Grea's skin like it was my own. She cries out, but I don't release her, because as much as I want my sister, as much as I want to *believe* in her, in this, I can't. I won't. Dude and h'Rawd and Mac, they died for the crew, gave every last thing they had. Now it's my turn. My turn to give up the very last thing *I* have.

Grea.

The old Grea. The one with her nose pressed to mine, who's snarling at me, calling me fathead and worse even as betrayal flickers in her eyes.

'Kuma, you don't know what you're doing.'

'Yeah, I do.' And I share it with her, the knowledge, the feed flowing from Hunt to me.

The viyusa curling around the shuttle stuttering its connection to

Grea and to Euiva through her, broken for just a second. And like most things fug related, a second is all that's needed. Silver bursts through the deck, little specks of yellow mixed in, wrapping around the red, eating it.

The last of the crew climbing aboard, unaware of the silent carnage taking place. The hatch closing with the sharp *snap* of metal-stone, ramp sucked into the vehicle's belly. And then more of that silver-yellow clinging to the hull, seeping through it... The vehicle hums and lifts off the deck, the last of the red clinging to the undercarriage turned to ash by the engines.

Grea's eyes still stare into mine, anger compressing her lips, but something about it is off, isn't... angry enough.

It roars through the hole in the bulkhead, forcefield shimmering as it passes through—

Victory, Euiva surging through Grea's skin.

Red leaping from the blast-mangled edges of the hole, spears aimed at the shuttle.

Hunt, second-arms held at the ready, already waiting, already anticipating. Generator spinning, power tripping down its arms, spitting from hastily repaired conduits. One shot, two, three. Viyusa obliterated with every bolt of light.

And then the shuttle is free, and Mum and h'Lott are free and all that's left is me and Euiva/Grea, staring at each other.

There are no words, just Hunt firing up its thrusters and spitting us into the void.

# CHAPTER TWENTY-THREE

We won and yet it doesn't feel like winning.

Only one wohol ship hangs above the graveyard, the other is gone, escaped with its evacuated crew and most of its hull intact.

Mum is safe, and h'Lott, their commandeered shuttle sits on the deck at Hunt's giant feet along with the remnants of dead nanites and wohol corpses. Of *Citlali's* crew there's nothing – human, Jørgen, kin. They're gone, not even a shimmer of Ekene with his genie legs.

It's just me and Hunt in this big ol' hangar. Alone. Waiting.

For what, I don't know. There doesn't seem to be much left worth waiting for. Not with Dude gone, without Grea, without Mac. There's no one knocking at our feet or in our heads, no one waiting for us. There's just… this. Nothingness. It feels…

*Like you're sulking?*

'Grea.'

She floats before me, before *us*, a holo standing eight meters above the deck, red dripping from her shoulders and curling around her feet.

'Is it you?'

'Yess,' and that is Aeotu, her deep not-quite-human voice echoing in Hunt's cockpit. 'And no,' she says. A blink, like someone flipping a filter and I see the shifting black of Euiva threaded through Grea's being.

Grea smiles and there is fire behind her eyes, a deadly fervour rising out of joy; death and war a mirage at her back. 'Shake it off, baby brother, we've just started. We need to hit the Eires Three outposts before the wohol realise we control one of their ships, and after that—'

'No.' I say it out loud and in the eter, hear the echo of it booming from Hunt and shake *Aeotu*'s corridors. I see Ekene and Onah flicker on the psionic plane, and through distant cameras funnelled back to me through *Aeotu* and Hunt, I see Dad and Mum lifting their heads.

Confusion clouds Grea's brow, but I see the anger – see Euiva – under it. 'Kuma—' she begins.

'No,' I say again. 'Fight your own war, we won't do it for you.'

And now Grea is gone, nothing more than a shadow under Euiva's skin as the AI melts through it.

'You belong to us.' *Us* sings with a multitude of voices, all the ships in the Sistermind gathered behind Euiva, ready to—

*No.* This time the voice is not mine. Aeotu is at my shoulder, a mirage overlaying a face that makes my heart squeeze and causes a tiny little bit of maybe-hope to light my chest.

'Mac.' I breathe his name.

She/he smiles, but their words are for Euiva. 'I will take them...' Their face wrinkles, like the next word is foreign. '...Home,' they say, distaste in the word, colouring the image of the blue-green world that comes with it.

On those distant cameras, hope lights Mum and Dad's faces.

Anger and conviction contort Euiva's and now it is her turn to say no, the denial pushed before the word in a shockwave of violence.

Warnings reverberate through *Aeotu*'s systems, ring in my ears, saturate Hunt's insides with orange and red, and I know, like I know that we'll die fighting, that Euiva is not going to let us go.

Viyusa floods the hangar, Mum and Dad yell, Ekene's mouth is a snarl. Viyu-slag runs through *Aeotu*'s veins, and somewhere, on the other side of Grea, deep in a red-lined room, I sense eighteen consciousnesses flicker to life.

It will not be enough, because even with all of our psionic might, with the slag working its way through our veins and the Sisters', we don't have any defence against the missiles lighting up at our stern.

'They'll take out the drives,' Aeotu/Mac says. 'I cannot stop them. I am sorry.'

An explosion. Another one, and another, and though each sends a ripple through *Aeotu*'s hull, there is no pain, no sirens, no damage.

On *Aeotu*'s sensors, the wohol ship's weapon ports flash red.

Dude. Dude is always the answer.

He shot the Sisters' missiles, blasted them right out of the void, leaving just the shockwaves to ripple *Aeotu*'s hull.

Rage— No, not rage, it's the black tide of the swatai's fury cresting her shoulders, rising over the AI's head and covering her in a shell of hate and death. Behind her, the other Sisters rise, the psionic might of the ancient ships showing itself for the first time.

I feel myself blanch, the blood draining from my head, hitting my feet and pooling there. Only the cockpit is keeping me upright. The Sisters are so.... big. They're not just the sky, they're the galaxy, they're suns, they're.... they're....

Coming for us, or rather, coming for Aeotu. Their intent rolls before them, bleeding through the ora, staining the eter and the real world alike. And even though *Aeotu*'s engines spin, even though she blazes – a giant in the midst of dwarfs – even though she is mostly whole, or at least more whole than the Sisters, not even *she* can defeat the constellation coming for her.

I know that, deep in my gut.

We need a miracle to survive what comes next.

It comes. Not from me and not from Dude. It comes from within the Sisters. From the red room with eighteen bodies inside, eighteen consciousnesses and a glittering yellow strand of slag.

And it comes from Ekene.

Ekene with his Regan gene, binding the minds of the fug-wrapped crew in *Aeotu*'s belly into a single, powerful whole. A bronze whisper reaches for me, a gentle tug on my mind, and I let it wrap me up, let it fold me into the multitude that is Ekene and the others.

It's like being Hunt-Dude-Kuma, sharing parts of myself with the others, sensing their thoughts like they're inside my own skin, and yet it's different too. I am myself, there is no metal or fuzziness or flesh, no blurring of identities. My arms are still my arms, but there is Ekene right beside me, understanding and knowledge flowing between us with no barriers, no words.

I know what he wants, I know what the *others* want, who agrees and who doesn't. Not that anyone actually disagrees, it's either this or the Sisters, after all.

I'd do it even if they *all* disagreed. That thought sends equal parts amusement and anger through the multitude.

With a twist and a flip, I part the threads of reality, and because I can do it, because I am one with the multitude, Ekene and the others do it with me.

Together, we stand in the ora. It spreads before us, endless and dark, only the Sisters lighting the void, and Aeotu. She is at our side, with her shifting, kaleidoscope skin and my face. Her hand wraps around mine, we *shift* again, and now we are more than a multitude bound with Ekene's bronze thread. We are a multitude wrapped in a shell of metal-stone and wires, with a fusion heart and *power* running through our veins. And this is familiar, this is Hunt-Dude-Kuma, a blurring of selves, and I'm the glue, the conductive fluid making it all happen.

Power gathers in our heart – the fire of *Aeotu*'s engines, the collective might of fifty-eight angry Jørgens, the fury of Mwat and Onah, h'Lott's mental teeth and claws, all of it. And within the star that is Euiva, the eighteen in their cocoons reach for us. They connect for a fraction of a second, just long enough to know our mind and share our plan, for their plan to resonate with us, images of slag and darkness shooting across the stars.

*Yes*, we say.

*Yes*, they echo.

Euiva swings about, her attention a molten razor aimed at our chest.

It does not touch us.

We strike first, following Aeotu deep into the Sisters' minds to pull out the darkness.

They say the Regan did this once, gathered all the minds in a city and fought back against impossible odds. Against the swatai themselves. They say she rooted a fear so deep in the water-kins' minds that it took them decades to recover. I wonder if she knew what the swatai had done to the Sisters, if she chose that defence consciously, or if it just came to her. It seems like a kind of justice, either way, doing to them what they had done to others. And now we're doing it again, or maybe redoing it?

Whatever it is, the swatai's darkness rises up and—

Grea, standing in our way. Darkness and Euiva wrapped around her and *through* her, until she is no more my sister than she is *a* Sister, a tiny version of the suns at her back.

Ekene and the others... they keep pulling, dig their multifaceted hands into the swamp to drag it out of the place it was buried all those centuries ago. One of those hands is mine, but the other... the other is standing in front of my twin, staring into those familiar eyes and wishing, wishing desperately, that things were different.

'They can be,' Grea says. There is no Euiva in her voice, there's just Grea, or as much of her as is left.

I shake my head, because even without the multitude whispering *no*, both Grea and I know that we're not going to change our minds. Not now, not ever.

Grea looks away, over my shoulder and I'm pretty sure she's peeling apart the Ekene-multitude, looking through all those ghostly hands. There's a sad kinda smile tugging at her lips and a far-off look in her eyes, like she's remembering. And maybe she is, and maybe—

She stabs me in the heart.

Literally. Stabs me. In. The. Heart.

There's yelling. The loud, golden *thrum* of something big and mean. Of Dude trying to come to our rescue. But he can't. No one can. No one save the eighteen in their red cocoons.

Us pulling the water-kins' sticky darkness out of the Sisters was a feint, a distraction so the eighteen could do their work. Right now, slag is erupting in *Euiva's* corridors, thick and fast and deadly, seeking out her core, gumming up her missile tubes and engines. More of it will be infecting the other Sisters, blowing out of those little nooks and crannies and corpses, digging deep into their marrow.

Whether or not the eighteen can take them over is a debate that came and went in the fraction of second we connected, a thought that flittered across the ora, mostly ignored, because winning was never the point.

Escaping was.

We've all made sacrifices – Mac, h'Rawd, Dude and now the eighteen. I thought mine was giving up Grea, but now…

My gaze goes down.

Darkness erupts from my chest, a giant fucking spear of shifting blacks. Grea's hand on the other end of it, gold filaments already wrapping around her fingers.

I can't feel my legs, can't feel my hands. I can feel *Aeotu's* engines though, the deep *thrum* as her fusion generator kicks in.

The ora is fading, the Ekene-multitude fracturing, slipping away as my brain closes down.

It's kinda funny really.

Reminds me of Mac.

Mac.

# CHAPTER TWENTY-FOUR

There's a place in the back of my head, a quiet, dark place. It's warm and comforting and feels like shock.

I've been here a lot lately, in those moments where shit happens and all I can do is stare while my brain decides how to respond. This time though... This time I don't want to respond. This time, I'm just going to stay here. This time I'm done.

I know I'm not dead because there's data tickling the back of my awareness; an irritating itch that makes me want to wake up and slap it. But I'm not. Because I'm done.

Dead and done. Hunt can deal with it.

Mum can deal with it.

Dad.

Fuck, even Mac's dad can get off his prejudiced arse and sort shit out.

It's their turn.

I'm just going to float here.

The itch *itches* a little harder.

Nope. Fuck off. I paid my dues. I *paid*, and paid hard. Paid with everything I had and then some. The bank of Kuma is officially broke.

Itch. Itch. *Itch.*

When I first woke up, groggy and confused as fuck, clutching at my chest and trying to drag out the spike, I listened. The itch is how I knew *Aeotu* was moving, that the graveyard and the Sisters and

Grea were far, far behind. That Dude, in his wohol ship-skin, was right there with us. It was how I knew where we were headed, how I knew the crew was safe, or, at least, those on *Aeotu*.

The others, the ones in the red-lined room... They covered our escape by staying behind. Not that we could have gotten them out, anyway. Not from within the graveyard.

There's sadness in that. Grief.

But I'm here, in my cocoon of shock and don't-give-a-fuckness, and nothing touches me anymore.

Nothing.

Rat-a-tat-tat.

Nope.

Rat-a-tat. *Tat.*

Nah-uh.

As much as the sound reminds me of Mac, I'm not falling for it. Mac's dead, dead on the end of my bla—

My blade.

I clutch my chest.

My blade, like the spike that ran through my own chest. And... Holy Terra, I'm not dead.

Not. Dead.

Hunt whirrs, is already scanning the mounds of dead fug, looking for that Mac-shaped mound underneath. The big, banged-up hangar lights up on the HUD, the stolen wohol shuttle outlined in blue, h'Rawd's body, the bodies of crew members, laid out in a neat line just *there* and Mac...

'And Mac?' I whisper.

Hunt has no answer. The human corpses don't match Mac's height, the breadth of his shoulders, let alone the black fug-armour covering his body. If it still did, if Aeotu hadn't taken it back after he... he died?

Rat-a-tat.

There's nothing at Hunt's feet, just deck and the scars from that last fight. Not even viyu.

So what's making the noise?

Movement beyond what's left of the hangar doors. A slice of black moving in the shadows. Hunt's entire face lights up, the blank, expressionless plane a torch to pierce the darkness.

And there, caught in Hunt's spotlight, a tall dark figure with shoulders that wouldn't fit through a cargo hatch.

My heart stops.

I forget to breathe.

Hunt though... Hunt's back is opening and its tendrils are wrapping around arms and legs. One moment I'm in the cockpit, the next I'm on the platform, nothing around me but air. The platform is lowering me to the ground, and if I could remember how to breathe, or you know, get my legs to work, I'd jump off that shit cause it's too fucking slow.

And all the time, all the time my brain in numb and my heart is frozen. I'm staring at that figure, at the way it strides across the deck. It doesn't have a face, just a smooth, dark shield where eyes and nose and mouth should be, but I know him. I know the way he walks, the long strides, the way he throws his shoulders back—

The platform hits the deck, and that gentle *thump*, vibrating up my ankles, over my knees, breaks me from my trace.

I'm walking, really quick. My heart restarts, and I'm not sure... Not sure...

Somehow, in those moments of not-suredness, I'm in the middle of the hangar standing in front of the figure. Looking up. Not so far as I used to, all those memories ago, but still... But still.

The faceplate shimmers, nanites shifting, changing, until it's just a thin sheen of energy rippling across Mac's face.

He smiles at me.

I think I might die.

'Hey, squirt.'

My chest collapses on itself.

I haven't cried since that first day, when I couldn't save p'Ender. Not about Grea, not about my leg, not about Dude, not even about

Mac... Mac, who's standing in front of me. Not a ghost or a mirage, or some freaky psionic projection, but Mac. Tall, solid. Real?

There are tears on my face, and it's like I can't remember how that's supposed to work. Like, water leaks from your eyes and there's this great big ball of pain, coming up from your gut, taking over your throat, making it hard to breathe, and just when you think you're going to suffocate—

Mac's arms around me, the soft green of shared pain, the pink of relief, the sour yellow of guilt flowing from him and wrapping around my legs. Real like the warmth under his armour, like the sharp ridges of the patterns carved in the fug and the chitter of the xin scrambling down his arm. Real. Really, really, real.

I cried for awhile, head buried in Mac's chest, arms at my sides, and when I stopped...When all that pain ended, I stayed there, tired, wrung out, not really sure what else I was supposed to do.

Was I supposed to do anything? Did I *need* to do anything?

*Aeotu* was safe. Mum and Dad and the rest of the crew were alive. Dude was... gone. And Mac... I'd shoved a sword through Mac's chest, held him as he... As he died. But he wasn't. Not dead. Not now. Now he was holding me, his emotions curling around us. Relief and sadness, happiness and guilt.

Guilt.

I took a breath, a deep hiccupping half-sob, a memory of the pain I'd just cried out on Mac's shoulder.

His very solid, very *undead* shoulder.

I step back.

He lets me go.

Mac looks at me, all dark eyes and square jaw and... There, right *there* in the space between blinks, I see it.

Determination to go along with the guilt. Righteousness or martyrdom, or some such shit like that.

'You're not dead,' I say.

He's silent.

'I killed you.'

Still no words.

A thought, nanites reshuffling, and then a sharp *tug* punch and a fug-blade springs to life.

'I put this through your chest,' I say. I point it at him, at the exact spot between his second and third ribs. 'Right here.'

Still, he doesn't say anything, just blinks at me.

'You *died,* Mac.' And now the blade is gone and I'm getting up in his space, lifting up on my toes so I can stare him in the eye. 'I *felt* you die.' And I let all that feeling out, drudge it up from the depths of my memory, from my anima, and let it roll out of me, the inky blue tide of guilt and grief another kind of sob.

It doesn't just roll up around our ankles, it swamps us, blots out the hangar and the lights, and I'm pretty sure that this one is strong enough for even a null like Mum to see.

Mac twitches, an uncomfortable jerk like he wants to get away from it but is forcing himself to stand. There's a change in his expression, the square, blunt jaw clenching and a pinch around his eyes. Discomfort, guilt, disgust, even fear.

And now it's my turn not to say anything, everything I need to say, everything I *could* say is in the emote. And it's pretty ugly. It's mine and even I don't want the smog to touch my skin, to get back inside me and eat my insides.

'You had to think I was dead,' he finally says. There's strain in his words, more on his face, and rather that look me in the eye, he's looking at the smog. 'And you had to think that *you* killed me.'

I...

The smog dies.

There's no words for what he just said. No thoughts, no emotions. Although, I guess shock is an emotion. A complete absence of anything, your entire being wiped clean as your brain resets, then a slow waking, new emotions replacing the old as you reboot.

'What?'

Mac's looking at me again, all pressed lips and stubborn jaw, like he's come to some kind of decision and— He grabs my head, those long, not-quite-human fingers wrapping around my skull, thumbs pressing into the faceplate above my temples. 'I'm sorry, Kuma, I had to do it. I *had* to, and this is why.'

Our faceplates *clunk* as he mashes his forehead to mine.

That's all the warning I get before thoughts flood my brain. Mac's thoughts, and in the back of his brain, intrinsically wound up in the dark orange of his mind, Aeotu as well.

It's the desperation that hits first, the all-too-familiar sense of time running out, of too many things to do and not enough hands to do them. Except that it's not mine, and in the centre of it is Mac, Aeotu wrapped around him. There are Sisters and slag and wohol, running around and through and between, all of them whispering the same dark refrain. Dead. Dead. Dead.

*We were going to die*, Mac says. *If not the wohol, then the slag, if not the slag then the Sisters.*

With each threat, the image of them slams into existence between us; the slope-shouldered wohol, the yellow geometry of the slag, the Graveyard and Euiva hunkered in the centre of all that death.

*If not the Sisters, then you*, Mac said.

The view changes, and now I'm in Mac's memory, watching as memory-me charges Aeotu. For a second, I do not recognise myself, or the hate on my face. My lips are pulled back, my eyes burn. In that instant, I could have been Grea – war and violence gathered around her – but instead of red fug tendrils trailing from my shoulders, it's the black swamp of the swatai's final command in ancient, fetid streamers.

*So I made you think you killed me.*

Memory-me leaps, fug-blades gleaming in the light of a thousand stars, and then pain. A hot lance of agony piercing my— Piercing Mac's chest. And then I'm back to me, my memories bleeding through Mac's retelling. Holding him as he...

'But you didn't die,' I say.

*No.*

*Almost.* And that is Aeotu, her shifting kaleidoscope pulsing under Mac's skin. But I ignore that, ignore her, because the important bit is that Mac's alive. Mac's *alive.*

Mac's alive and he made me think he was dead. Made me think *I* killed him.

There is an emotion for that, and I let it colour the ground at my feet, rise to my ankles. Anger, clean and red and cutting, cutting as the molten edge of Hunt's blades, deadly as the mech's lasers, vicious as the swatai's darkness, deep in my anima.

I let it rise, let Mac feel it, and then I cut it off. Roll it back inside and peel Mac's hands off my head.

Some things are better left unsaid. Some emotions are more powerful that way.

'Why?' I ask him.

Pain whitens his face, not the blade-through-the-chest kind mind you, but the I-did-something-really-shitty-and-now-I-have-to-stare-at-it kind. The guilt creeping around his feet is a violent yellow, but his shoulders don't crumple, his back doesn't slouch, and that fucking righteousness just tightens his jaw.

'Because you needed it.'

And fuck, if *that* isn't a punch to the gut. Just break off my fug blades and stab *me* in the chest.

Before I can speak, before I can even *choke,* Mac's speaking. 'We needed you, and you needed a reason to fight, Kuma. A reason to get in Hunt, to forget about Grea and do all the things you had to do, so we could survive.'

And now's he's got his hands on me again, on my shoulders, holding me up and I'm glad, because I'm pretty sure his words are going to make me keel over and die.

He's got his faceplate in close to mine again, and there's that earnestness, that deep-set belief in his own shit. 'Not just me, Kuma. Not just Aeotu, but our parents, Onah, h'Lott, *everyone* needed you to fight.'

I shake my head. 'No.' Because that is some fucked up shit. That is... 'No,' I say again. 'I wasn't the only one.'

Mac's turn to shake, except he's shaking me, just once like he's trying to dislodge something in my brain. 'Yes, you. Look at yourself Kuma.'

I don't need to look at myself, don't *want* to look at myself, all fugged out with paws for feet.

'You're the only one of us to successfully integrate the viyu, the first to talk to Aeotu, the only one with a freaking *mechanicoid*. Who else was going to stop the Sisters, let alone the wohol? Who?' He shakes me again. 'Grea?'

Grea, with war in her eyes and Euiva threaded through her anima.

'You—' I only get it half out before Mac laughs.

'Aeotu spent four years trying to make me into you, Kuma, and I still can't do half the things you can.' Mac's humour dies as suddenly as it came. 'It was you, squirt. All along, you were our hope.'

He lets go of me, steps back and closes down his face, wrapping all of his emotions – the determination, the guilt, the righteousness – back up inside, crossing his arms over his chest like a lock. 'We needed you to save us, so I gave you a reason to do so.' He says it like a judge handing down a sentence, or maybe a king offering up a quest. It was for the good of the country, so sorry you lost a leg and all.

I lost more than a leg. I lost Dude. I lost bits of myself, I did things, *felt* things that will stay with me forever. Most of that... Most of that I can live with, and maybe, just maybe, I could have lived with killing Mac, knowing that it was *my* anger, *my* rage, that took away my best friend. Maybe.

But this... Standing here, looking at Mac's closed face, at the hard bronze of the determination wrapped around his feet, a shield against the guilt peeking out underneath and knowing that he didn't just let me feel all that, he *wanted* me to.

There's no forgiveness for that.

None.

# CHAPTER TWENTY-FIVE

There's a hole in the pit of my being, a place as deep and dark as the void. It aches like the bones of my phantom leg, but she made her choice, like Brennus, like the others. Like Dude.

Dude left us a ship's year into the voyage back to Jørn. The only ones to mourn were me and Hunt, as much as the mech could mourn, which isn't much but I've been working on the AI. The fuzzbutt left a bit of himself behind though, a parting gift embedded in my armour, little flecks of bright gold caught up in the whorls carved into my chest.

I didn't notice them until he was gone. Maybe they were hibernating, or maybe they just took time to grow, but about a month after Dude's drive signature vanished from *Aeotu*'s sensors, the pimple formed on my shoulder. It was small and my armour was always changing then, always rearranging itself, and there were other things to worry about, other fights, other emergencies. Plus, it was Dude's dusty gold, and it was sitting where he always sat, cuddled up close to my neck.

So I didn't worry about it and Hunt didn't worry about it. Mac gave it a weird look, but then Aeotu passed behind his eyes and... And then one month passed and another, and soon enough there was a little yellow-gold critter sitting on my shoulder. Looking like Dude, smelling like Dude, fuzzing her butt off like Dude... Except she's not. Wrong gender, wrong species, wrong fucking molecular composition.

Banu's a xin, made of fug same as the critter-like construct that serves as Mac's link to his armour, but she's more than that too. A child of Dude – the new Dude, made of metal-stone and fusion generators, rather than the old fleshy one. And she's mine, and I'm hers, and while she's not Dude, every now and then I see a little bit of him in there, feel it in the way she snuggles under my chin and chitters in my ear. And it's enough to keep me moving forward, to remind me that I have a job to do. That *we* have a job to do.

We have to go home.

And now we're here.

Orbiting Jørn.

Home. My parents' home, Jim Engineer's home, Onah and h'Lott's home... but not mine, and not Mac's and not Ekene's.

Home. But not.

Jørn's star shines over the lip of the planet, the bright rays refracting through the thin layer of atmosphere and bouncing off the web-like hull of an orbital. Other shapes – the sleek ovoids of starships, the boxier harder lines of freight haulers – cluster around it, some forming thin lines to and from the surface, others scattered around the blue-green globe.

We journeyed for years to get here, through over a dozen solar systems, across fifty-eight parsecs. *Aeotu* dropped the FTL at the edge of the system and cruised us in close with the sub-light drives. She could have come in right on top of the planet, but no one wanted to give the homeworld that much of a fright.

We didn't need to imagine how that would go down, Mwat and Onah and Ekene tied us all up in mental pow-wow and we watched it play out. Lots of times, in lots of ways.

Big old alien ship just popping in out of nowhere, mass panic, water-kin getting their groove on. Hello, round two of that galactic fuck up.

So *Aeotu* parked our arses a couple of billion kilometres out and we sat there. It was days, then weeks and finally...

The outer hangar doors are opening for the last time, the final

Jøran shuttle slipping through the forcefield. Mum's on that shuttle, Dad at her side, and I wonder if they're looking forward to Jørn, or backward to me, the son and nightmare they're leaving behind. Both of us one and the same, bound to each other as inextricably as flesh to bones, or nanites as the case may be.

And I can't help the sad in my chest, the air bubble expanding like it's been doing all these last weeks as the Jørans came and talked and inspected. Human and kin wandering around the corridors and poking their fingers and noses and brains in every nook and cranny. Exploring, inspecting, acting like I couldn't see them taking notes on their data screens or snatching a sample of viyu, like I couldn't *feel* them and their curiosity mixed with fear.

But now they're gone and there's nothing to contain the sadness anymore, just me and Banu and—

Mac's hand on my shoulder, squeezing. 'You can still go with them, Kuma.'

I shrug his hand off and take a deep breath, locking the bubble of sad down, even as Banu *fuzzes*. It's not a comforting golden blanket like Dude's would have been, although there's some of that in there. No, Banu's *fuzz* doesn't soothe, it dances under my skin, a heady, anticipatory rush obliterating the sadness.

'No, I can't,' I say.

Because now that the job's over, we have a mission.

Jørn's not home for me. It's Mum's home, and Dad's and h'Lott's and Onah's, but it's not mine. My home is gone, blown to bits and welded to the hull of alien ships. My home is wrapped in strands of viyusa lightyears behind me. It's the pit in my being, the phantom ache in my anima, and no matter how hard I've tried, I can't leave it behind.

I stare at the planet, at that shining sphere of aqua and verdant green, ends capped with stark white and the middle a rich yellow-orange. Home, the end of the journey, the thing Onah and Dad and everyone else strove for, fought and died and sacrificed for. And yet it leaves a sour taste in my mouth, fills me not with comfort but a hollow dread. Maybe it's the darkness still swirling through my anima, through Aeotu herself, the sticky psionic swamp of the ancient water-kin filling me with the need to leave.

There was a moment when I tried to convince myself that the only thing preventing me from being happy, from joining my parents on that shuttle, was the mental debris left over from that ancient war and yet... And yet.

Mac at my back. 'She made her choice.'

Grea made her choice. A constant refrain. From my parents. From Mac. Even from Ekene. Grea made her choice, and now I'm making mine, have already made it actually. Made it before we first saw the glimmering ball of Jørn, before *Aeotu* entered the solar system, before Dude vanished, before we even left the graveyard.

There was never any other choice for me, although I tried to bury it, to ignore the tug at my heart and throw myself into fixing *Aeotu*, in Hunt, in the crew. I think Dude knew what I would do, even as I was denying it. That was why he left me Banu – eager and hungry – and not a copy of himself.

Anticipation rolls through the little xin, vibrates her fur and jives through her paws where they knead my shoulder. She *fuzzes* and it comes out as a purr, a small sound, almost inaudible unless she's pressed to my jaw.

'Kuma.' And there is Mac, tall and broad-shouldered, moving around the consoles and holoscreens of *Aeotu*'s command centre to look me in the eye. 'It's not worth it,' he says. 'Grea *made* her choice, just like all the others. Just like you.'

Frustration and not a little fear churn at his feet. We've had this discussion before, and if he thought I'd let him, he'd put his hands on my shoulders and shake. But I won't, and he doesn't.

On the screen behind Mac, Mum and Dad's shuttle enters Jørn's atmosphere, fire trailing in its wake, burning away their old life to make way for the new. And that fire is for me as well, burning my last ties to the crew, to the duty that Ekene and Mac laid in my being. Now it's time to do what *I* want.

What Aeotu wants, even if everyone else disagrees.

'Kuma,' Mac says, and there is as much warning in his tone as there is pleading. 'Please. Stay.'

I look him in the eye, not even stretching anymore. I've grown, gotten taller. Other things have changed too, more personal things, and some of that is genetics but most is a careful negotiation with my fug.

I'm not a boy anymore, and certainly not a boy with girl bits.

I'm a man.

A man with a mission.

The deck hums and, on the screens monitoring ship functions, dials hit red as *Aeotu*'s engines spin to life.

Mac blanches. He steps forward. 'Kuma—'

'I made my choice,' I say.

'*Sisster.*'

# FIND OUT WHAT HAPPENS NEXT!

Scan the QR code or follow the link below and sign up to Belinda's mailing list to find out what happens next in the Echo short story, *Brother*.

I love keeping in touch with my readers, it's the second-best thing about being a writer (writing being the first best). Every fortnight (or thereabouts), I send out a newsletter with details about upcoming offers, new releases and extra special projects.

If you sign up for the mailing you'll receive exclusive behind-the-scenes extras, such as:

- free short stories
- deleted and alternate scenes from The Echo
- previews of my upcoming books
- pancakes
- quizes
- and much, much more!

**Scan the QR code or visit the link below
to sign up and get your FREE short story!**
belindacrawford.com/brother

# DO YOU WANT MORE?

Take a journey through time and space back
to the Jøran homeworld, where it all began.

## THE HERO REBELLION 1

**The battle for human evolution begins now.**

Hero Regan is a freak; she hears voices, the kind only she can hear. Force medicated and isolated, her only solace is Fink, a six-hundred-kilogram, genetically engineered ruc-pard. They share lives, thoughts, triple-chocolate marshmallow ice-cream and the burning desire for freedom.

Their chance comes when Hero is allowed to attend an academy in Cumulus City, but in this super city nothing is as it seems. As Hero is drawn into an ancient conspiracy where two secret societies will stop at nothing to control human evolution, she must decide whether she's willing to risk the world for her freedom.

**Scan the QR code or visit the link below to get your copy.**
belindacrawford.com/hero

# ACKNOWLEDGMENTS

Books are a collection of lots of little things: words, thoughts, ideas, people and belief. That last one is important; belief (and sometimes sheer, stubborn determination) helps an author drive through the nagging doubts in her mind and put "the end" on a novel. It's not merely her own belief that makes it happen, it's her editor (thanks Amanda J Spedding), her friends (the incomparable Tracy M Joyce), her family (here's lookin' at you Mama Jen!) and her readers.

There are a number of very special readers who believed enough in this book to support it via Kickstarter *before* it was published. These people are my Kickstarter Heroes, and I want to send a very special thanks to them all.

Thank you Emma Morris, Beth Barany, Manuel Mendez, Jonathon Mast, Frog & Esther Jones, J. Leigh James, Mama Jen, Michael @mykesbytes Hricinak [Time Traveler], Meg Foster, Aliz Seraphim, Sci Fi Cadre, Andre Jones, Joanna Mazurkiewicz, Maureen Howe Henn, Jevin Kelley, Ken Cupples, Kelly Balding, Velera-Exi Studio, Treasure83, Annette Bennett, Janelle Drake, Thomas Schwarz, The Greener, Zannalov, Jaqcov, Hannetjie and Peter Prellwitz.

# ABOUT THE AUTHOR

Belinda Crawford is a science fiction author for readers who like their fiction action-packed, with diverse characters, butt-kicking heroines and complex worlds. The creator of The Hero Rebellion and the online serial *Demons & Battleskirts*, her philosophy is to buck convention and "follow the awesome". Which pretty much means doing the unexpected in the most interesting way possible.

As a certified crazy horse person, when she's not wrangling six-legged dynamos on the page, she's wrangling four-legged powder-kegs in the paddock. Belinda brings that same certified craziness to her writing, with unexpected twists and enough wacky ideas to keep readers guessing.

You can keep in touch with Belinda, or just pick her brains about sci-fi via her website, Facebook or by sending her an email (she loves email).

www.belindacrawford.com
belinda@belindacrawford.com

**Have news delivered straight to your inbox**
via her mailing list. Sign up at:
belindacrawford.com/newsletter

www.ingramcontent.com/pod-product-compliance
Lightning Source LLC
Chambersburg PA
CBHW020511120726
47904CB00003B/783